IRAN
101

By
Majid Babaie

Iran 101

ISBN number: 978-1-59712-273-3

Printed in the United States of America by
CB Publishing & Design
P.O. Box 560431
Charlotte, NC 28256
(704) 649-3585
www.cbpublishing-design.com

Table of Contents

www.Iran101-007.com

IRAN 101
"Perception or Reality"

You may be interested to know why I am writing a book about Iran. After all, I do not consider myself as the most educated person regarding the history of the nation, nor about the actual details of the politics inside the country.

As a matter of fact, I did not start writing this book about Iran, but it simply worked out that way. Most certainly, writing this book has helped me understand who I am, and it may help the reader obtain a better understanding of Iran and the Middle East; through one man's journey, his assumptions, perceptions, and the set of prejudices.

September 11th, 2001 had a huge impact on me, not only as the result of its immediate impact on all of us as a nation, but when trying to understand what really may have caused such an evil act against humanity, and what would be its ripple effect in decades to come. As an Iranian-American, who minded his own affairs as a business owner and a part-time university professor, I felt ashamed of such an atrocity. After I was able to clean the ice residue from my body, I started giving speeches at churches, rotary clubs, and some American political gatherings. I took a personal responsibility to engage people and share my knowledge and feelings. I felt this would help with the healing process.

Topics such as "East, West, Who Knows Best" and "Al-Qaeda versus Hezbollah" seemed to engage the audience rather well over a number of years. It was during one such setting that a very concerned lady in her early fifties approached me and asked me for the name of my book. She said her husband had looked everywhere and could not find it. After I assured her that I have not published any book, I quickly corrected myself, by saying "yet" at the end of my sentence.

After returning home that night, exhausted from a hard day at work and a three hour speech engagement in front of an audience of about forty, I started writing pointlessly. A month later, I found myself writing a political book that perhaps contained mostly the topics of my discussions. But I was not happy with any of my writings and topics, until one Saturday morning. While I was feeding our indoor cat and the two outdoor cats, I noticed while they were all cats, they behaved entirely differently. The indoor cat was a bit timid, very critical of the food being served, yet very gentle; while the two outside cats ate anything, and loved to get any amount of attention. Yet, they both maintained a safe distance from me. One could see that the environment had a great effect on their behavior.

As a Quality Engineer at one point in my life, I had to find the root cause of any problem, so I continuously had to ask "Why." However, as a University Professor, I always had to come up with the appropriate response. As we grow older, it seems to become harder to ask "Why?" and we start assuming and believing things that may not be correct. Sometimes there are too many assumptions, and many times incorrect information, deliberately or unknowingly offered by so-called experts. While there are more TV channels than ever before, more news analysts than one can imagine, we still seem to be lost in the world of spin.

Looking at the cats' behavior that day helped me set up this book to embody the following three areas; **a) what caused the socio-political environment to become what it was, b) its impact on one's behavior, and c) the net result of all those behaviors in forming the future environment.**

This book is based on my perceptions of reality, my understanding of the truth, and my judgments of right and wrong. It is not to teach you, convince you, or make you believe, but is simply a way of stimulating your mind so you question and ask "why?" We must not simply believe everything we read and watch on TV, or are told by our friends and neighbors. It requires hard work to search for the truth and to form an individual opinion about different matters. This is one reason why **there is a world of difference between reality and our perceptions.**

What is the color of pure milk? Our perception leads us to believe it is white, or is it? Reality is that the color of pure milk anywhere in the world is white; therefore our perception is the reality. What about our perceptions regarding the universe?

Over and over through science, for centuries, our perceptions were proven wrong, or simply reality was completely different from our perception. This is why we need to continuously ask "Why?"

One can argue that **giving respect is the answer to many questions in life**. To learn and gain knowledge, we must respect others and their opinions, whether we like them or not. This way the mind is allowed to examine many facets of a problem, to form the right opinion and hence our hearts would not be filled with pain at a later date.

While reading this book, try to learn and hold back judgment, for **change will only happen by the ability to give respect before demanding it**. Change in today's global community is the only constant, and the ability to change the way we look at things, is the only way to understand and solve monumental problems.

This book is an overview of the life of the author, to be offered as a learning tool to understand the environments that make a person. This book is a tasteful journey of a young man from birth up to the age of twenty-five. The book shows a man's broad understanding of cultural, social, philosophical and political values first formed in Iran and the later transformation of those principles in the United States. It covers the curiosities, emotions, struggles, evaluations, opportunities, and transformation of a person from the Middle East.

In the first two chapters, the Curious and Emotional Years, Majid captures the world of being and shows how the environment plays an important role in shaping him. In the third chapter, the Turbulent Years, Majid challenges and questions the environment that had defined him, and in the last two chapters, the Evaluation and Becoming Years, one can learn about what caused Majid's transformation into the world of Becoming.

Knowing yourself helps you understand others. Knowing others help you respect different values. Understanding different values break down any ignorance within, and challenge any outburst of arrogance. I therefore offer this book to **all those who have lost their lives in the history of the mankind due to the ignorance of those who had no courage to ask "Why?"**

Curious Years

Majid was born on January 17, 1961 in Mashhad, Iran. His forty-eight year old father Akbar was a bald skinny man with a relatively large nose and about five feet six inches tall. His thirty-five year old mother Ozra (Ezra) was only five feet two inches tall, skinny with long dark hair and brown eyes.

Why would one have a child at such an old age? After all Majid's oldest brother Ali was fourteen years old, followed by Mahmoud at age ten, and Ahmad at age seven. Why would the couple be having another child when they were not doing well financially? Logical? No, but **logic has no power against strong beliefs!**

The common belief at the time, in the town, and within the family, was to have another child to change their luck. I guess when you are poor, having three or four kids going to bed on empty stomachs does not make much difference, but it is worth taking a chance on having better luck. I presume that's why poor folks buy more lottery tickets than anyone else.

It was early in the morning, just before sunrise and the call for the prayer (Azan), when the lady in the white garment asked the sleepy old man to stop the carriage ride. She quickly got off the carriage, carrying a large bag. Before she had a chance to knock at the long wooden door, it slowly screeched open.

"Welcome, are you the midwife?" said Ali in excitement. Without responding to the question, Maryam rushed in and took the steps to the second floor as if she knew her way around the house. She barged into the room where Ozra was breathing very hard on a small bed with several white sheets surrounding her.

Grandma Zahra was already in the room holding Ozra's hand and helping her with breathing in and out. A big pot of hot water was sitting next to the bed with a few clean towels. Zahra had a big sigh of relief when she greeted Maryam. Without wasting any time, Maryam placed her bag on the bed. Nobody was paying any attention to the iced-up windows. It looked like a very cold January day, but the small heater was keeping the room somewhat warm.

Not long after Maryam's arrival, Zahra's voice, right at the sunrise, cracked the ice off the windows. "It is a boy!" she exclaimed proudly looking at the father standing in the doorway.

Akbar, as if it was all his doing, proudly looked at the sky, with his arms half raised, and with his fingers stretching toward the heaven above gave thanks to the God of the universe.

Before Akbar could bring his arms down, he heard from a far distance the call for prayer "Allah 'O' Akbar" which means "God is Great". He then thanked Maryam for delivering his son to the world, his world!

Akbar, with great joy in his face and tears dancing on his cheeks, held his son tight to his chest as if all his prayers were answered. Then he put his mouth to his son's ear and chanted a prayer, or perhaps some verses from the Koran, so his son would also be a man of God, and a good Muslim just like him.

Ozra, while relieved, seemed a bit disappointed. She had given birth to six boys, three of whom did not make it to age two, before the new arrival. She badly wanted to have a little girl. A few months before Majid's birth, she had made a collection of girl dresses, as Ozra informed Majid later. I guess **if you really want something badly enough, your desire will override any logic.**

Good thing that Majid did not realize the difference between a boy and a girl at that time, but he was surely teased by his brothers for a long time!

Majid from the first second, at the very first breath of life, had to bring about change. Even the name "Majid" meaning "absolute greatness", the adjective used for the Koran, the holy book of Muslims, was putting pressure on the newborn infant. Clueless, before gasping for air, and not even knowing all eyes were staring at him, Majid giggled in joy.

Majid could have cried for all the pains he had endured, but he smiled. He could have been angry with his mother for bringing him into the life of poverty, but he smiled. He could have been mad at having such an old father, but he smiled. He could have been upset for being treated like a toy by his older brothers, but he smiled. He smiled as if he knew, **life is not measured by the elements surrounding us, but what we hold dear within our hearts, and that is love!**

Although in poverty, Ozra and Akbar owned a large house, but why? Akbar for most of his life since age sixteen ran his father's business in Mashhad trading tea from India and wool from Russia. When Akbar at age twenty-seven married the sixteen-year-old Ozra, he purchased that house with the money he had saved during all those years. The house was not far from Ozra's parents', and was nicely furnished with her dowry after the marriage.

Akbar, after running the family business for almost thirty years and supporting his brothers' and sisters' education, asked his father for the ownership of part of the business. That did not go well with his father, and at age forty-five, he found himself starting from ground zero. After a year of learning how to make decorative bricks, he spent most of his savings into that business venture utilizing part of their house for that purpose.

By age forty-seven, Akbar's brick business was consuming the family and all their savings, and nobody could see a light at the end of the tunnel. That's when the family started talking about having another child, hoping that he would bring a new beginning in their lives.

Majid was about two years old when Akbar at age fifty decided to discontinue the decorative brick business for good. Knowing everyone moved to the capital city of Tehran in search of new jobs, he had little choice but to follow the pack. But having no place and no money, he borrowed money, left their home, and took his family to the city of Zahedan, where his brother resided.

After renting a small place for his family with the help of his well-to-do brother, he left for city of Tehran.

After a few months, Akbar was able to obtain a job as an accountant in a large cooking oil company. He only had six years of school education but had over thirty years of experience and knowledge in world trade. He was able to move his family to the city of Tehran when Majid was almost four years old.

Living in the capital city was not cheap, and what Akbar could earn could barely pay for one room on the third floor of an old house in Fozieh Square. He had to work long hours to make sure there was enough food for the family. Ozra after preparing dinner would wait until the family had enough food to eat before she had any. Some nights she went to bed having only eaten a small, hard and moldy piece of bread that she had saved for such nights like that.

At the location and at the time, there was no place to bathe in that house. People in most poor neighborhoods had to go to the public bathhouses to use the facilities to wash themselves. In most cases people had an opportunity to attend such places once or twice a month. Therefore, it was very important for the folks to clean themselves thoroughly. At a young age, little boys usually tagged along with their mothers rather than their fathers. So, Majid at age 5 was still attending such a setting at the women's bathhouse with Ozra. On one visit, one of the older ladies observed Majid, and with a red face exclaimed, "Next time, you might as well bring along his father too!" After Ozra was ridiculed by this lady and given curious glances by many others, the next time around Majid was sent with his father.

At the men's public bathhouses, a number of older men worked and were paid to rub the dead skin off people's body by using an abrasive material called "kisseh." That process was nothing but torture to a 5-year old child. This painful act was followed by pouring a large container of hot water on the person. Then there was the soaping of the body with a soft lengthy washcloth, followed by yet another container of hot water. Next one would use two "loangs," which were nothing but couple of soft long towels used in the drying process. Some of the older people even paid to get a good rubdown after drying.

Even though the family was poor, it did not stop the oldest son, Ali, at age eighteen, from being accepted by the prestigious Tehran University in the Mechanical Engineering program. However the family did not have the one-hundred fifty dollars to pay for the first year tuition. Akbar had to work extremely hard and step on his pride to borrow more money from his brother to make sure Ali attended college. Ali not only walked ten miles round trip to school and back, but he worked to help the family while maintaining an A1 rating with the highest grade-point average in his College of Engineering.

Majid was six years old when the family moved to a new apartment, which was perhaps a bit of an improvement. The two-bedroom apartment, on the second floor located on top of a neighborhood store seemed like a great change for the better. The couple and their four children seemed much happier. Ozra was extremely happy since they were within a mile of her older sister's house.

Majid started the first year of his education at the local elementary school that year and was able to spend some time playing with his cousins, Mehri and Hamid. Mehri, the girl, was a year older, while her brother Hamid was a couple of months younger than Majid.

Majid, having no toys of his own, looked forward to going over to his cousins' home to play on Fridays when the schools were closed. Hamid's oldest brother was in Germany and had a German wife. Hamid's brother would send them some of the nicest toys that Majid had ever seen and even though he enjoyed interacting with these amazing toys, he was somewhat envious.

One day on the way back home with his mom, Majid asked Ozra to buy him a toy, but Ozra refused since the money she had was for much more important things than a silly toy. Majid could not take "No" for an answer anymore. He ran away from his mother, and while crying, spread his body down in the middle of the street. **I guess that's why when the answer is always "No" many stop asking the question and find it easier to simply play dead!**

Luckily the street was not very wide, nor highly traveled. Ozra, with much embarrassment and pain in her face, ran to the street and yanked her son off the asphalt which had a temperature of over 100 degrees Fahrenheit. She spanked Majid lightly but she was torn apart inside. That night you could hear Ozra crying in pain, if you listened closely from the rooftop.

The next day, Majid's cousins came over with a balloon to play. Majid was very upset for all the things he could not have, and out of jealousy while playing, he pushed a small needle into

8

the balloon.   His cousins did not even have a chance to tell Majid that they had brought that balloon as a gift for him.   Majid on that day learned that, **"No matter how much pain you endure, you must learn and be patient, to never let the air out of your own balloon."**

Next week, Akbar had a surprise for Majid, a little solid plastic boy three inches tall with a clown hat on him.   Akbar did not spend any money on the toy; it was a gift from one of his co-workers who had heard the story.   Majid called his little toy companion "Jamshid" who in Persian legend was the fourth king of the world who could command all angels and demons.

Majid's parents put a lot of emphasis on education.   That was the ticket to a much better life.   That's why Majid was the top student right from the beginning.   While Ozra spent a lot of time teaching Majid and helping him with school homework, she did not spend much money, like many other parents, on nice book bags or colored pencils.   Majid always borrowed other students' colored pencils for drawing pictures and he always did an excellent job.

The family was not very religious but they did follow the Islamic rule of praying five times per day.   Unless severely sick the family also fasted during the month of Ramadan from sunrise to sunset.   Ozra never allowed any alcoholic beverages in the house as required by Islamic laws.   She also frequently attended the local mosque with her sister, more so on certain holy days.   On many occasions Ozra brought Majid with her, and as a result Jamshid tagged along.

At school every morning, right after the bell rung, all students lined up facing the Iranian flag. Majid seemed to always stand in front of the pack. All students made a simple prayer and gave their allegiance to the God, Country, and the King.

Majid's family never said anything good about the Shah. Ozra and her mother were upset with Shah's father for removing the women's veils decades earlier.   They believed that they would all go to hell for such disrespect to God's laws.   Father on the other hand was proud of all the rebuilding the Shah's father had done in the country but believed the Shah was brought to the power by the United States' American Central Intelligence Agency (CIA), so he had little respect for him.

Majid could not understand why you pray for a king that nobody respects at his house, and worst of all, why pray for him at school and not at the mosque. Majid like the rest of the family formed an opinion quickly about everything. He thought it must be the Shah's family that caused them to be so poor so that he could not have any toys and coloring pencils. **Angry people always find a way to blame others for their pain!**

After weeks of battling to pray or not to pray for the King, Majid stopped the praying and moved back in the line. Majid's brothers were always vocal about the Shah's wasteful spending of the country's wealth. Why was he buying old American Military fighter aircrafts with the oil revenue? Why was he not feeding all the hungry people in the country? Why were we pretending to be on the side of Arabs in the Arab-Israeli war and actually support Israel? And the answer was always that the Shah was an American puppet. **People in pain mostly focus on the unjust rather than the just, on what they do not possess rather than what they already have!**

The 1967 Arab-Israeli war seemed to have a major impact on people within the country. Considering that it was only 12 years after the Shah's return to power by a CIA military coup, people felt that the pro American Israeli government was a major threat in the region. Most of the Iranians also followed the challenges of Blacks in America at the time, and they did not feel comfortable with any of it. "Umrica" or "America" was considered by the majority of the people in Iran as an imperialist country, and that was probably the feeling in the region.

While it was unimaginable for the tiny nation of Israel to defeat three countries (Egypt, Syria, and Jordan) and increase its size by a factor of three in the 1967 one week war, that's not how it was seen in the region. People's perception in the region was that it was the United States and Iranian air force that helped Israel, defeat the three Arab countries. That **perception** did not sit well with the majority of the people in Iran who shared Islamic connections with their Arab brothers.

Majid at age seven was confused with all this information and the only thing he knew how to do well was to be angry. **All**

of us imitate the environment around us and Majid was just the same, a normal kid imitating his family's perception of a war. Perhaps, one could say, the environment in the Arab world and most of the region was bitter, but less so in Iran. That year, Majid had many questions for his three-inch tall friend Jamshid, but he was not very responsive, and that even made him more upset!

Majid continued growing up like any other normal kid in his society carrying his family scars and packages. It was on a cool September night, in 1969 when Akbar came home crying. Everyone ran to the door. Majid was in shock to see his fifty-six year old father in tears. "Did you lose your job?" Ozra asked in fear. "No" he responded and then he burst into tears to say "I lost my father". Majid did not have a close relationship with his eighty-six year old Grandfather since the family did not visit him often.

Until that night Majid had not felt death so close to him from actually anyone related to him and his bloodline. Ozra's father passed away when Majid was only three years old and he did not have any memory of him. That night Majid had a hard time falling sleep, as if there were some wild dreams waiting for him to close his eyes. Wild dream it was, for he dreamed of his Grandfather being laid inside a concrete casket full of light, even brighter than the sun. Outside the casket there were many small snakes crawling but they were all coming toward him.

When Majid woke up, he saw Ozra cleaning the sweat off his face and his brothers in black shirts sitting next to him. Majid was crying in fear and murmured the dream he had to his mom. Ozra immediately called on Akbar to wipe off his tears and come listen to Majid's dream. After Majid revealed the dream to his father, he smiled and kissed his son in joy. To Akbar it was only Majid who could have had that dream and no one else, for he was the deliverer!

Akbar at that moment was happy for his father; considering his father was a victim of two strokes and someone who suffered greatly toward the end of his life. Majid's dream indicated that he is now in heaven and God has forgiven all his sins. The snake was the indication of money, and lots of snakes crawling to you meant you will come into much money without having to work hard for it. **Dreams sometimes do come true!**

It was a couple months later when Ali had to spend a night at his aunt's house for fear of the Shah's secret police (SAVAK) raiding their house. That night Ali had his dinner and quickly disappeared into the night. Majid was very scared and hid in his favorite space in the kitchen. While praying to God for his brother's safety, Majid fell asleep in his tears, agony, and the fear of the unknown. It was that night that Majid's anger changed to hate for the Shah, even though no one even rang the bell to their two bedroom apartment! **Though anger is an emotion - if maintained, it can change to hate - with correct or any baseless perceptions.**

While Akbar did not much care for the Shah's regime, he had traveled to Russia (the Soviet Union at the time) and India and knew that Iran was better off. Akbar believed that while the Shah had some of the religious people in exile without reason, and held some of the University students at Evin's jails to their distress, the Shah was still providing much more freedom in the nation than communist Russia, and the hunger driven India with its exploding population.

Because he anticipated receiving some of his father's inheritance, Akbar seemed to become much happier and a lot more conservative. **Poor folks when they come to money, either waste it all, or become afraid of losing any!** Akbar had a lot of money earlier in his life with even a large house in Mashhad, and this time around, he valued every penny, or should I say every rial (seven rials equaled ten pennies at the time).

Afraid of losing any money to the government other than taxes, Akbar banned his family from any political discussion in front of him. He even asked Ozra to burn any political books stashed away around the house for fear of the unknown, or perhaps fear of losing any riches! However, Majid did manage to get a few new plastic toy trucks for five rials for his Grandfather's snake dream, and he could not understand why Ali was not just as happy.

Upset with the new ruling at the house, Ali took his anger out on Majid's homework. With a red pen, he marked a large "X" on all five pages of homework Majid had prepared for his class and asked him to redo it. After crying for ten minutes Majid took the law into his hand, barged out of the room and walked toward the little station where Ali kept all his books. "I will cross five pages of your book so you know how it feels," Majid shouted at the end of hallway.   It did not take Ali but three seconds to be there and teach Majid that he was messing with the wrong person. **When angry, it is always easier to pick on someone half your size.**

When Akbar arrived home that night at nine o'clock, he found Majid in tears, while redoing all his homework.   Majid did not hold anything back from all the injustice done to him.   Ali, fearful of any harsh consequence, was studying at the opposite corner of the same room, looking awfully pale.   Akbar without saying a word walked down the steps leaving the house. "Where are you going old man?" Ozra shouted.   Akbar replied, "To call on a police officer to put Ali in jail".   Ali once again had to leave home for the aunt's house at a late hour.   Majid was afraid of possible retaliation the following day.   After taking an hour-long relaxing walk, Akbar returned home and had his dinner without talking to anyone.   After that night, no one ever bothered Majid, and Majid never told on anyone.   **Before picking on someone weaker than you, it is always an intelligent practice to know, if someone with higher authority than you is protecting them.**

It was the second week of March 1970 and Majid was excited about the Persian New Year, or No-Ruz, a three thousand year-old celebration that was rooted in the Zoroastrian religion. The oldest record of No-Ruz was from the Hakha-mana-shian period over 2,500 years ago.   Most people in the West relate to one of their famous kings, King Cyrus the Great, whose name is repeated in the Bible.

The old No-Ruz celebration started five days prior to the actual new-year when Fourohars (Guardian Angels) came down to earth to visit their human counter parts.   Spring-cleaning was carried out to welcome them with a feast and celebration (very much like the Easter celebration around the same time frame). Bon fires would be set at night to welcome the Fourohars.   All this created a lot of excitement for the nine-year old Majid attending the third grade.

Majid was always rated #1 in his school grade with many Afarin (Great work) Cards being handed to him.   He even had received a "100 Afarin" Cards but was never given a gift.   Parents normally brought the gifts to school to be handed to their child for doing such a great job, but Majid never received one.   Majid was in the Arts class, the day before school closed for No-Ruz.   He was borrowing some colored pencils to finish his drawing when Mrs. Shokohi asked him to come to her desk.   Majid with his pale face staring at the floor, slowly walked toward her and apologized for bothering other children in borrowing their pencils, and assured her that would not happen in the new coming year. Mrs. Shokohi, to his surprise said, "But my son this is not why I called on you." Everyone in the class became awfully quiet, when she asked all the students to put their pencils down.   "I called to give you a 100 Afarin Card for your excellence at schoolwork and …"   Before Majid could wipe the tears of joy off his face, Mrs. Shokohi, for the first time ever, pulled a small wrapped box from her drawer and gave it to him.   "Do not open until No-Ruz" she said while she and the rest of the classmates clapped for him.

Majid always received new clothing and new shoes for No-Ruz and sometimes money from relatives visiting them during the five days of festivities.   That year Majid could not wait to open the wrapped gift, and Ozra seemed to be just as anxious.

While everyone was counting down the seconds to the new-year in front of the Haftsin table, Majid was not looking at the Seven Sins (Haftsin) on the table, or seven items starting with the sound of sin - but he was staring at his gift.

The mirror, gold fishes swimming in a bowl of water, the candles as the representative of fire, and even the Koran displayed on the table did not seem as exciting as that wrapped gift!

The second the old year unraveled, and the new-year began, Akbar started the year with a verse from the Koran. Then everyone had a freshly baked pastry, but not Majid. He had to open his gift. He could not wait any longer. There it was - twelve pencils in twelve different colors and Majid loved every one of them. His parents were very surprised as well, since they never purchased that gift to give to his teacher.   During all thirteen days of the new-year holiday celebration Majid drew pictures and sang songs. He actually was so happy that he started writing poems for his teacher. Mrs. Shokohi did not return to the school after No- Ruz after having her own first child, and Majid has never had a chance to thank her since, but he always had a special place for her in his heart.

Immediately after school ended that year, Majid and his parents traveled to Mashhad for a month and stayed at Zahra's house. The Saint Reza or "Imam Reza" shrine, the eighth Imam out of only twelve Shia Imams, was located in Mashhad. This is why many Shiites traveled there to give respect and get their prayers answered.

Qom and Mashhad were the two major Shia or "Shiite" holy cities.

Zahra's home was only a couple of miles away from the Imam Reza Haram (Shrine) and everyone could hear the call for prayer, called Azan. Majid's middle name, Reza, meant a lot to Akbar for he heard the Azan from Imam Reza Haram just a few seconds after Majid was born.

This is why Majid was always special to Akbar, and he believed Majid would bring about a positive change in his life.

While Majid was born in the holy city of Mashhad - the city of Qom, over five hundred miles away, contained the shrine of Saint Reza's sister Fatemeh or "Fatima". Mashhad was much larger and by many measures was considered a holier city than Qom, but Qom was a major Shia pilgrimage site, and most importantly the theological center of the country.

You may wonder what were Reza and Fatemeh doing in Iran, so far away from the base, pushing close to the Russian boundaries. You are absolutely correct, for most other major Shia Imams are buried in Najaf (Ali, first Imam), and Karbala (Hassan and Hossein, Ali's two sons, second and third Imams respectively). These sites are currently in modern day Iraq. To better understand how the two major sects of Islam, Sunni and Shia, were formed, one can follow the dispute between the two which began after Prophet Muhammad had died.

15

Prophet Mohammad was considered as the last of God's five major Prophets as Muslims believe (other four in order being Noah, Abraham, Moses, and Jesus).

The majority sect of Islam, Sunnis believe the rulers or caliphs started with Abu Bakr, then Umar and Uthman, followed by Ali who was assassinated during the prayer "Namaz or Salah". The minority sect of Islam, Shia on the other hand, believe Muhammad's Son-in-Law Ali should be the first Imam. After all, Shias believe Ali was the first one who converted to Islam, slept in Muhammad's bed while fearing the house could be attacked by unbelievers, and fought most of the wars along with Muhammad.

Ali's assassination at the time during the prayer created the major divide between the Sunnis and Shias. This was further aggravated by the death of Ali's two sons nineteen years later. That year Hassan was poisoned and Hussein was killed at the Battle of Karbala in 680. To this date Hussein's death is celebrated in the Ashura ceremony where young men beat their chest with hands in an orderly fashion, hit their backs with chains and even some use swords to crack their heads. This is done in memory of Hussein's unjust suffering over 1300 years ago.

Jaafar, the sixth Imam, lived longer than all other Imams and was very instrumental in the formation of many education centers used to teach, instruct, and train the faithful. He was able to stabilize and create an Islamic truce between the two sects. During the eighth century the **Caliph** Mamun while at a location in Russia close to the borders of Iran invited **Imam** Reza and later his sister Fatemeh to join him from Medina. Fatemeh before joining her brother and Mamun, became ill and died at Qom. Imam Reza on his way with Mamun to retake Baghdad from the political rivals died unexpectedly at Mashhad and was buried. Imam Reza's death to many Shias was blamed on Mamun and they felt he was poisoned.

The total population of Sunnis (over 80%) and Shias (below 20%) is about 1.2 billion people. Both sides celebrate the holy events, associated with and performed by Prophet Muhammad. However, Shias also celebrate the birth and death of the major Imams, in particular the return of the five-year old Imam Mahdi or Messiah. Sunnis do not believe that Mahdi had disappeared or ever existed. Some folks compare Shias and the structured 12 Imams to Catholicism and the 12 Apostles; others may compare Sunnis and the general usage of Imam as an Islamic scholar to the Baptist Preachers.

The very next day after their arrival; Akbar, Ozra, Majid, along with Zahra walked to the Imam Reza Haram. Like everyone else, they all had to take their shoes off, wash their hands and feet in a special ritual before entering the holy shrine. Men and women were always separated; however, Majid was still considered young enough to stay with his mother.

Clergy or Mullahs were everywhere, waiting for the arrival of new people entering the Haram. They were very good at identifying the locals, the poor, the rich, and the ones from a far distance. All it took was five rials for them to tell you all the stories of unfair bloodshed, how unfairly different Imams and holy Shias were killed and beheaded. Mullahs were very popular among the religious women who held their chador or veils over their body and most importantly their faces. As the Mullahs revealed painful stories from many centuries ago, you could hear the women cry as though someone had just beheaded their sons!

Majid and Jamshid were both confused and could not understand what was going on. The last time Majid was brought here he was only four and he could barely remember anything. Majid was trying to figure out if Shah had anything to do with Hussein's beheading, since he already disliked him. He had never seen his mom crying that hard; he could not understand why she gave his father's hard earned money to someone to make her cry so hard, and yet she would not buy a cheap toy for him. Majid kept staring at the Mullah to see if he was a relative or if he was someone his father knew. **It simply did not make any sense to give someone your hard earned money to make you cry!**

The 3.3 million square feet Haram and its seven Sahan (courtyards) were absolutely breathtaking to Majid. Mamun originally built Imam Reza Haram in 818 A.D. either out of compassion or fear. Haram was invaded a number of times and rebuilt prior to 1,600 A.D., yet the tall ceilings, architectural craftwork, and all those cuts inside were beyond Majid and Jamshid's imaginations!

Majid's daydreaming came to a painful stop when Ozra pinched him on the leg and pulled him closer to her. Children could easily get lost at that place both physically and emotionally. Majid could see his father in the far distance attached to the golden massive cage protecting the buried Imam from all the visitors. He saw his father crying with no reason, while slapping his bald head with the tip of his fingers. On that day, no matter how hard Majid tried, nothing made any sense to him!

The following day Majid was wandering with a stick in his hand outside the Zahra's house and not far from his parent's abandoned house, when an older lady gently patted him in the back. She was one of the neighbors and wanted to know if he was Majid. After he nodded yes with a smile, she stated that she was Maryam, the lady who delivered him nine years earlier. Then she showed him his old house at the end of the street and asked if they would ever come back. Majid had no response, and politely said he did not know.

Majid walked slowly and cautiously toward the end of street and knocked at the door, there was no answer. He then continued to follow the wall to the opposite side of the building, where there was a busier street with more traffic. He found another door and knocked on that. There was no answer but a small paper fell off the door, as if someone had earlier that day taped it to the door. After removing the note, Majid read it with a big puzzle on his face. The note was from some hotel that had the same name as him. It did not make much sense to him. He folded the paper and put it in his pocket and ran back home where his mom was calling for him.

It was about 1:30 p.m. and Akbar was taking an hour nap. Majid waited for his father to wake up and then served him a hot cup of tea. The cup was placed in the center of a saucer holding three sugar cubes. Sugar cubes were to be placed in his mouth one by one while drinking his hot cup of tea. In addition, below the surface of the saucer, Majid gave Akbar the folded piece of paper.

While drinking the tea, Akbar unfolded and read the paper. He seemed to be jovial, yet puzzled. It was a second request for the owner of that home to meet some representative of "Hotel Majid". Akbar quickly put his shirt and pants on and without

18

saying a word to anyone left the house. Majid was concerned, for he did not know why his father left without saying a word. Majid did not say anything about the note to his mom. Akbar returned home around 7:30 p.m. with some delicious pastries in his hand. Majid was confused but very happy, and his mouth was watering.

That night there was a lot of excitement at Zahra's home and a large feast was prepared the day after. Everyone seemed to be giving a lot of attention to Majid by pulling his cheeks and some patting him on the neck. Majid did not enjoy his cheeks being pulled by a bunch of older relatives but surely enjoyed all the attention. Majid kept hearing his name that night, or was it the Hotel's name?

For whatever odd reasons that morning, Akbar brought Majid home three of his favorite plastic trucks, 5 rials each. Majid was never treated that way before and he had to hit himself on the cheeks to realize he was not dreaming.

The following afternoon, two of his cousins Reza and Javad showed up to play. Majid generously and proudly, for the first time ever, offered his cousins some of his toys to play with. He was even generous enough to ask them if they wanted to keep two of the trucks. Majid had played in the dirt many times before, but that day, it was his day of glory in it. Jamshid even enjoyed the free ride on the back of the truck smashing into the dirt. **When you do not have much material goods in life, your life is not controlled by your possessions. It is only when we have more, it becomes harder to share with others.**

After the three days of jubilee, Ozra asked Majid if he knew what was going on. Majid innocently shook his head no. She gently pulled Majid into her arms and affectionately combed through his hair. Then she explained to Majid in the best way possible, that God's blessing had arrived. She told him that they took that trip to give thanks at Imam Reza's shrine for the inheritance they received from Akbar's father. However the note Majid delivered was ten times more important, for a major street was passing by their old abandoned house and now the hotel chain Majid was interested in that property.

She then kissed him gently with tears falling off her cheeks and thanking God. While holding her arms up as if she could see the heavens, she continued looking at her son "On this day, and all

19

his days, may my Lord, bless him the way his life has blessed us, through your might". Majid could sense his mother's elation and his tears started bouncing off Jamshid, as if both were crying in joy.

After that summer, Majid returned back to Tehran with his parents, and the family prepared to step forward to a much more elegant life-style. The week before the major move to the affluent neighborhood of Do-rahi-yoseff-abad, Majid was staring down from the second floor window. It looked rather odd; there were hundreds if not a thousand people in the street, all men in black, chanting "La-elahe-el-allah" which means "There Is No God, But One God." Many people were crying while pushing a casket over their heads and carrying it out as far as Majid could see.

All this was very scary to Majid. He asked his mom who was cooking in the small kitchen, "What is going on?" Ozra responded "One of the neighbors just passed away and people are carrying his casket from his house to the place of burial." "But all those people," Majid asked in confusion. Ozra responded, "He must have touched many lives in a good way." Majid shouted proudly "Mom, I will have millions carrying my casket when I die." Ozra responded "En-sha-allah" or "God Willing".

"En-sha-allah," like a few other expressions was very puzzling for Majid. He could not understand why something so good would not be - also God's will. Another one, **"Sabr Omad,"** was what people said right after a person sneezed. The direct translation is "patience is required" which in most cases resulted in postponement of whatever task was on hand. **"Ass-tagh-for-ellah"** was another one, which meant ask for forgiveness from God. That was normally used if a person had said something that would somehow offend God- like if someone said God's name in vain. At last, **"Allah-Omah-Salah-Mohammad-V-Alleh-Mohammad,"** which meant "Greetings to Mohammad (the Prophet) and all his family." This seemed to be chanted if some problem was just resolved or whenever a bus load of people went on a long trip. While all these expressions were intriguing to Majid, they seemed to be more popular among the poor and all those that did not have much wealth. When did these terms, with Arabic lingual roots, enter into the Farsi language spoken by the Iranians, and why? Were they just a tool to keep the poor and uneducated happy? Was it to give hope to the hopeless? Was it to keep them hoping, waiting, and praying while others needed distraction to take the last crumb from their tables? Majid and Jamshid were never able to answer such complex questions, perhaps you could!

As if Majid had delivered on his promise, the family that summer moved out of their shabby looking apartment, and relocated into a dream house which was beyond their imagination. Before turning in the keys to the apartment, the family formed a circle in one of the rooms, and gave praise to the God of the Universe.

Emotional Years

It was the summer of 1970, when the family moved to the magnificent dream house at the new location. Do-rahi-yoseff-abad or simply calling it Dora was a very well to do part of Tehran - perhaps you can compare it to Manhattan in New York City. Two hundred seventy thousand tomans or forty thousand dollars at that time (or well over three quarter of a million dollars today) was a lot of money to pay for a house.

Akbar, while very stingy, did not have a problem with purchasing that house in cash. Since the owner was on his way to the United States and relocating for good, he was willing to sell the house ten percent below market value. Purchasing a house was a long-term investment for Akbar. However, he always did "Este-khareh" before any major decision in his life, and the Este-khareh gave Akbar a positive sign to purchase that house.

If you do not know what "Este-khareh" is and what an important role it plays in people's life, you do not have a clue how Majid's life was changed as a result of it (be patient, you will find out later). Este-khareh is a ritual that can only be done by certain people that are considered holy and are accepted by God's grace, or at least that's what Majid was told.

Ali Akbar had a religious title of **Mirza**, but why did he have this title? Akbar never had any religious training, nor was he considered a religious man. The title Mirza did play an important role in his name. It meant his mother had a title of **Bibi,** meaning that she was fathered by a **Sayed**. With this Shia-based belief, Sayed was a title for only a man whose father was another Sayed which had nothing to do with the mother's side. Following this trend backward for a Sayed, it would go all the way back to the Prophet Mohammad himself (the first to gain the title of Sayed were his sons). Hence, a female child fathered by a Sayed was titled a **Bibi**, and the son to a Bibi was titled a Mirza, where the titles stopped. Since Prophet Mohammad had more than one wife, the likelihood of becoming a Sayed or a Mirza was largely increased.

To prepare to do the "Este-khareh," Akbar had to physically, mentally, and emotionally become in tune with God and his holy book, the Koran. It started with "**Vozo**," which is to cleanse with water the forehead, face, top of his feet, and both arms. Then it took at least an hour of reading the Koran in a very quiet location, followed by speed reading and chanting, while tears found their way to the holy book. Then and only then, it was time for the main event, or asking God for guidance, concerning a worrisome issue in a person's life.

Normally, a question regarding the point of concern was asked three times, and each time a response was obtained from the Koran. This was done by praying over the question, and then the holy book would be cracked open by the person. The top of each page in Koran indicated Good, Bad, or Average. There it was, - the response from God himself, - followed by a verse that would somehow relate to the question and the answer.

While some anointed people regularly did Este-khareh for the mostly poor or dispirited receiving some amount of cash or goods, Akbar never did. He only performed Este-khareh for his immediate relatives and never for any money, perhaps only ten times during his ninety-year life span!

The new house was not anything that Majid and Jamshid could have ever imagined in their wildest dreams. Their old apartment was even smaller than the basement. This house was only two years old and was built for an eye surgeon and his family. As a matter of fact, he had made two houses with the same exact design next to one another. An established engineer was occupying one of the two houses, and the doctor was occupying the second.

But it was not a dream; the two-floor modern designed home had a big basement and a huge yard with nine feet tall walls surrounding it. Majid was amazed with everything, even the doorbell. After people rang the bell, he would speak into a box asking who was at the door, and then without having to run 100 feet to the front main door to the house, with a simple click, all locks would become unlocked.

The first floor included a large master bedroom with a nice sized closet. Next to it was a modern bathroom with Persian and Western style toilets. Even the Persian toilet was not a rudimentary hole in the ground, but it was made of porcelain with nice features. To Majid, the Western style toilet looked like a bowl of water serving no purpose. Since there were so many

Americans in Iran at the time, all the upper class new homes had started placing those toilets in their houses.

Next to the bathroom was a good sized kitchen with a small pantry room, cabinets, stove, two sinks, one freezer, and a refrigerator. A large table with seating arrangement for eight people was on the opposite side. The kitchen was almost the size of a regular size kitchen and a dining room combined. It also had a door to the backyard which could have been used for an additional space to prepare food for over 100 guests at one time, or perhaps for exotic plants.

The reception room was definitely the biggest attraction of the first floor and probably the entire house. While on one side it was connected to the kitchen through a small dance floor and perhaps the space for a little bar, the opposite side was connected to the front of the building through all glass walls and seven full size blinds from the ceiling to the floor. It even had two glass doors opening to the front porch made of marble. There were a total of six doors and sliding doors to this room. The reception room occupied well over 1,800 square feet with three chandeliers hanging from the ten-foot high ceilings. The elliptical chandelier was shining over the eighteen-seat guest dinning table with twenty light bulbs, sparkling through the beautifully carved glass zircons. The other two chandeliers were a bit smaller and circular where they provided the light to the rest of the room. The furniture arrangement was to provide seating for well over thirty people.

The remaining area in the first floor was 600 square feet between the huge reception room, master bedroom and the walls to the next neighbor's house (since they were adjoining). This area that could have been easily added to the reception room by opening the two large sliding decorative glass doors was mainly used as a family room. This area did not have a ceiling, since on the neighboring side of the wall the marble stairs in a ninety-degree twist connected the first and second floor to one another.

The specially designed ceiling in the center of the house held two water-cooled air conditioners. There were twelve glass windows each three feet tall, high up on three sides of the ceiling. Those windows provided plenty of light during the daytime for the two floors. However, at night the six-foot twinkling chandelier right in the center of the majestically carved ceiling with six bright light bulbs provided the needed lumens to the reception area as well as the upper floor.

On the second floor, there were a total of five rooms, and a modern style bathroom with bathtub and western style toilet, plus a bonus small Persian toilet on the landing between the second floor and the flat-asphalt rooftop. While three of the rooms were relatively large, over 300 square feet each, one was about 200, and the smallest one about 100. All rooms were connected by a "U" shaped hallway, which overlooked the first floor, and with about a twelve foot distance to the bottom of the carved ceiling chandelier. Two of the side rooms had all glass walls with a large glass door opening through a six feet wide door to a marble porch right over the porch below it on first floor.

The rooftop was flat, lightly asphalted, so when it snowed, Akbar had to hire people to remove all that slush or even heavy snow rather quickly. They would shovel it off the roof and into the yard. During the summer season, the rooftop was really hot during the day, but, at night, many people right after sunset, would carry their doshaks (similar to a sleeping bag) to the rooftop and put them down to cool off. Later, they would go up and sleep in their doshaks and watch the stars.

The yard was another beautiful feature of the house. While the two four-feet-wide doors separated the inside of the house from the outside, they were the entrance to a three car parking area. The cars would be under a large open curved metal frame with grapevines grown all around it. Next to it was the 500 square foot flower garden. In the center, there was a six by four foot water pool with a fountain in the center and small goldfish swimming in it. It was surrounded with two 10-foot tall willow trees and three 12-foot tall pine trees, which were two-feet wide. The outside wall had honeysuckle growing all over it producing a heavenly smell, while within twelve feet of that, there was a 30-square foot rose garden. In the exterior of the yard, 40-feet on one side and 15-feet on the other, was a two-foot wide row of flowers, coming to a 90-degree angle. The flowers were of great variety, exotic colors, and lustrous shapes, teasing your eyes and challenging your sense of smell.

There were six steps up from the yard to the first floor and four steps down to the basement. The basement was over 700-

square feet. It held the central heating system to the house and all the controls between the gas-line distributed from the street to the house and beyond. It also had the location of the brand new washer and dryer, all in one.

The house was absolutely beautiful but Majid was having a hard time adjusting. He did not know how to embrace all the new changes. While he shared one of the rooms with his brother Ahmad, and he even had a studying desk, he did not have a sense of belonging. He did not know anyone in the new location and the neighborhood kids seemed too stuffy for him.

It seemed like Majid had traveled to a land of the unknown with a generational gap, a place where nobody cared about how anyone else lived their lives, but more about how others made a living. The immediate neighbors consisted of a well-to-do lawyer across the street, an established engineer to the left, and one of the Shah's ministers to the right. That did not match Majid's immediate family life style. Ozra was the only woman in the street wearing her chador while going shopping in the neighborhood store.

Was the family the odd ball in the neighborhood or was the neighborhood a mismatch for the rest of the nation? Was Majid the norm, or was the norm the spoiled kids that listened to the latest western music? The difference or lack of match was severe for Majid, yet he had to conform and get along. So, he pretended that he was in the right place!

A few weeks later the fourth grade classes started. School was just a block away from Majid's home, but the students seemed to have come from the moon. On the way to school, within one tenth of a mile, Majid passed a private Jewish School everyday, where the boys and girls dressed up in uniforms and attended the same school. He could not understand how the boys and girls could go to the same school without getting into trouble.

Majid was the new kid on the block at the new school. Nobody knew Majid and kids being kids, made fun of the new comer. Majid had to get himself established as a number one rated student at the new school to command respect. The very first time Majid was called to go to the teacher's desk to answer questions, Majid was prepared. He stood in front of the class facing all the students.

Teacher asked "What Is Art"? That was the topic of the chapter that was covered the day before. She expected Majid to mumble through and explain, but Majid took a big breath, and delivered the complete chapter from heart word by word without missing a single word. It took fifteen minutes, and when he was done everyone in the class, including the teacher clapped for at least ten seconds. That was never done before that day in the school. Majid was prepared and had memorized everything to that date in his books. Majid gained much respect and friendship that day, and gained the number one rating in the school once again. I guess, **when the things get tough, the tough deliver!**

Majid's parents for the first time ever had a birthday party for Majid's tenth birthday. Prior to that, Majid did not even know when his birthday was. People that do not have much money, did not value trivial events like a birthday, it was just another day. However now, the family had to show off their modernization and perhaps westernization.

Majid had three of his friends from school attending his birthday. There were a number of relatives and a few cousins that were Majid's age. All the adults stayed on the second floor, while Majid and his guests were in control of the huge reception room. This was all new territory for Majid; he simply did not know how to behave or even how to misbehave. Soon kids were running around the room and jumping up and down and making a lot of noise. Majid was warned a couple of times to keep it down, but how could he? **Why would a free bird return to the cage?**

Majid did receive a few toys that night, but none were as good as his old friend Jamshid. While the toys looked nice and somewhat expensive, there was no story behind them. The twelve coloring pencils from Mrs. Shokohi seemed to have colored Majid's mind far beyond the most beautiful colors on the wrapping papers on those gifts. **When people give someone a token of their love through the smallest of gifts, it by far trumps the most expensive gift wrapped in riches with no love!**

The next big event for his parents, which occurred a few months before Majid's fourth grade ended, was Hajj. For this, a Muslim is required to go on a Pilgrimage to Mecca, Saudi Arabia, once in a lifetime, if the individual has the means to do so, and both physically and mentally can undertake such a journey. With all God's blessings to Akbar and Ozra, this trip was a must for them. Hajj is a time when all the eligible Muslims, currently around three million, come from all around the world to Mecca at a same time.

A few days before the major trip for the parents, Majid heard a "Bah-Bah" sound in the yard. There it was - a sheep in the yard, roped next to the stairway. With blue eyes staring in Majid's eyes, he was asking for love and mercy, and most of all begging for some food. Majid had seen a lot of strange things, but this by far surpassed anything else. Was that a pet, where did it come from, what was the purpose? He never asked any questions and nobody cared to explain, or perhaps Akbar and Ozra chose not to say anything.

Two maids and their young son were hired during the one-month trip to Mecca, to cook and look after the family. They were mostly babysitting Majid, or as old as the maids were, Majid was keeping an eye on them, especially the husband, Asghar. He could not see from one of his eyes and had a stiff leg that could not bend. Majid was concerned about his health and felt really bad for him. During that month Majid fed the sheep for entertainment and grew really close to it. Jamshid was very jealous of Majid's best new friend in the house. Majid did not much care for the food that was prepared for him, so many times he asked for the maid's permission to make scrambled eggs.

That month went by very quickly with the exception of one accident. About three weeks into the so-called babysitting, when Majid came home from school, he found Asghar at the bottom steps with his face buried in blood. His wife and son were just cleaning the blood from the area in fear and calling the old man's name. Majid quickly ran to the neighbor's house and asked for help. Luckily, Asghar had only fallen from the second step down (due to his stiff leg) and his life was not endangered.

The day was full of excitement when the 58-year old Mirza **Hagi** Ali Akbar and the 45-year old **Hagieh** Ozra returned from Mecca. Hagi and Hagieh were the titles used to notify everyone that they had made the Hajj. That was not just the prestigious religious label, but also indicated they had the means and abilities to do so. The house was packed with mostly Ozra's family, as if there was a surprise birthday party.

When Akbar and Ozra, or should I say Hagi Akbar and Hagieh Ozra returned in a taxi and were dropped off at the door, everyone was ready.   Instead of saying "Happy ...," everyone chanted   "Allah-Omah-Salah-Mohammad-V-Alleh-Mohammad". Majid was too busy on the second floor playing with his cousins. When Majid heard his parents' voices, he rushed downstairs.   He was totally surprised, or should I say shocked, perhaps angered, and started crying furiously.   Those were not cries of joy to see his parents, but the tears of anger for seeing his best friend, Bah-Bah the sheep, fighting for his life in front of the door.   He was the victim of a four-thousand year old ritual, all the way back to the days of Prophet Abraham, the sacrifice in place of his son. Majid's heart was full of pain that day, and no matter how hard he tried, the tears found their way down his cheeks, once again proving the laws of gravity.

Majid could not understand why people follow rituals four-thousand years old, even to the cost of his best friend.   On that day, in that minute, the ten-year old Majid promised himself "**Not to follow any ritual that causes pain and suffering for the weak and helpless, no matter how old, no matter who says, and no matter who demands.**"

The depressed Majid sat in a corner and listened to all the great stories on how on the first day Akbar and Ozra wearing their white garments to show their brotherhood and sisterhood to all the other Muslims, went on a circular, counter-clockwise procession around the Ka'bah or the house Abraham and his son made to honor God.
They had to chant "Labbayka Allahumma Labbayk" which meant "Here I am at your service, O God, Here I am!" This was done to teach the pilgrims that the center of everything was God.

When Majid heard the story about how at the town of Mina the pilgrims had to throw seven pebbles at the Devil made of stone, it gave him an idea.   He went down to the yard, and threw seven pebbles at the sight where his friend Bah-Bah was beheaded.

He found the devil in ignorance much more dangerous than any stone in lieu of the devil in the weak minds.
Later that day, beggars were lined up behind the house to take the meat and every organ in the sheep's body; that was the custom. The worst part was that Majid was in charge of handing Bah-Bah's body to all those savages in the line. It was as if he was giving up different parts of his own body.

Jamshid felt bad for Majid but enjoyed having him back, since he received a lot more attention for the next few weeks by sleeping very close to Majid's heart. Majid since that day never looked into another sheep's eye. The family had a hard time understanding why Majid gave up red meat for three years, after that day. **We never can understand why people in pain act strange until we feel their pain**.

The month before Fourth grade was to end, Majid and other students were required to write a composition on "**What is better, Knowledge or Wealth?**" The popular answer was normally "knowledge", for it can never be stolen, but a thief can always take away your wealth. But Majid used this assignment as his first political foot print to express himself. For all those years of having no toys to play with, living in neighborhoods where people were struggling for some basic necessities and having seen his mother eating moldy bread, this was his best chance to let the rich kids know his mind. Here is briefly part of what he wrote:

What is better, Knowledge or Wealth?

I believe Wealth is by far better than knowledge. It is our wealth that has allowed us to have a beautiful school, has paid for the best teachers, and has provided us the nicest desks and all the things that poor children never have. It is our wealth that allows us good education, while those that are poor can not afford literacy, and at best they are left ignorant.

Knowledge by itself serves no purpose, for mountains under the sea are never seen. We have the knowledge of the poor, but have we done anything to stop the cycle of poverty? We know how to build bridges, schools, and even nice toys, but have we ever built anything for the poor and unfortunate?

A wealthy man will never give up his possessions for a college degree, for he knows, **wealth brings power and control, while knowledge can only deliver a better understanding of a subject matter**. **An educated person within a society, controlled by wealth, is just a pawn who feels like a king.** It does not take but a few moves to realize, everything including his knowledge is for sale. So, I kindly ask you...

> Why does a poor man need to write, if he has no paper?
> Why bother drawing, when there is no coloring pencil?
> **Why gain knowledge, if there is no wisdom to use it?**

This is why I prefer to be wealthy than just gaining knowledge in a blind society!

Majid's teacher did not expect such a composition from a ten year old kid. This was also the time that university campuses in Iran were involved with massive demonstrations against the Shah and his family despite all the crackdowns. This was reported on May 10, 1971 by the American Embassy in Iran to the White House. Majid's teacher did not want any part of a political writing, and conveniently chose to give a grade of "0" out of "20" to Majid.

The next day Majid's brother, Mahmoud was at his school complaining about the grade. "But there is no way a ten year old child can write such a composition" explained the teacher to the angry brother. "But Miss, we did not even know about this composition at home, never mind helping him" said Mahmoud. The teacher did not continue the conversation and in much pain placed a "2" in front of the "0" and made it a perfect score of "20". "I should have known better" she murmured bitterly.

A few weeks later Majid finished his fourth grade degree with the highest ranking, and started a summer from hell. Hell probably is an understatement for a ten year old kid and what he went through. The three months of the physical, mental and emotional roller coaster started by the simple statement from Soraya. She was one of Majid's cousins who planned to study and pass her sixth grade through the upcoming summer.

31

The school system in Iran was going through a major change. It was changing from six years of elementary and six years of high school to what we are accustomed to in the United States, that is, five years of elementary, three years of middle, and four years of high school.

All these changes to Ozra with her six years of elementary school education were nerve racking. Everything seemed to be changing for the older generation and they had no way of stopping it. **When the rate of change supersedes the rate of adjustability, people resist the change.** So Ozra decided Majid must pass the fifth and sixth grade during that summer. She preferred the old proven system over the new one, and she then convinced the rest of the family.

But how could Majid prepare for such an exam? Who would provide any classes to help such students? Ozra even had the answer for those problems. After all, she was not the only possessed mother doing such a crazy thing to her son; there were quite a few more.

Majid was given one week of summer vacation. This week was very much used to prepare him for the three months of nightmare. That summer, Majid's days started before even the roosters had an opportunity to clear their throats, right around 5:30 a.m.

"Brush your teeth and wash your face" every morning Ozra whispered in Majid's ears while gently rubbing his back to wake him up. Then there was the breakfast, mainly some bread resembling pita but thinner and wider with feta cheese, and most importantly the sweet hot tea which made his eyes pop wide open.

Majid then left home at 6:00 a.m. and walked for a mile through the dark, yet very safe streets of Tehran to catch a minibus to his destination. The seven mile trip with the frequent stops in the already congested streets of Tehran seemed like eternity. The four and half foot tall Majid was probably the youngest person on the minibus that early in the morning and he raised many people's curiosity.

These private classes began around 6:45 a.m. and continued until 1:45 p.m. Majid would then take the minibus back home and have his lunch around 2:30 in the afternoon. Around 3:30 and after a short nap, he had to check in with the Chamber of

Torture, headed by Ozra. She had all the books for certain subjects opened and ready and would anxiously wait for the exhausted Majid to open his eyes. The hot cup of tea seemed to find its way to Majid in no time after he gained consciousness.

Ozra was in charge of all the subject material Majid had to memorize, while Ali and Mahmoud covered mathematics and science respectively. Majid's schedule consisted of two years of school work cramped in ten weeks or seventy days, followed with three days of testing. Majid was promised a bike after successful completion of the task on hand. The heat was on, and that did not take in the daily 90-degree Fahrenheit summer temperature.

After three weeks of taking the minibus to school and back, and staying up until midnight, Majid's body completely collapsed. Majid became very ill and had no desire to eat and lost much weight. It was more of a mental and emotional breakdown followed by physical loss of weight. The medicine was to stop the madness and let the poor kid rest for a couple days.

During that time, Ozra had to come up with a change of strategy. The morning school was not an option anymore. Everyone was in agreement that the back and forth traveling to school and the hot days were taking its toll on Majid. Majid was given eight hours of sleeping time per day, and more of his favorite food was being served for lunch and dinner.

The new schedule seemed to work better, but Majid had to supplement his night sleep with multiple naps hiding under different wooden bed frames, about a foot above the ground, in different rooms. He also found many hiding places so no one could find him. Looking for Majid in all corners of the house did not amuse the stressed out family, and Majid would get minor beatings for such behavior.

The one time Majid received a bad beating was the time he hid on the side of the bed and the wall next to it. It was an act of genius; no one would believe that he was in the same room as everyone else. After over one hour of calling for him and looking everywhere, Ozra and Mahmoud were nervously discussing what if Majid has run away? This made Majid crack up and come out of hiding, probably not at a good time, to say the least!

After the ten weeks of torture, the big day was upon the whole family. It was a big test not just for the exhausted Majid, but for the whole stressed out family, in particular Ozra. Everyone in the extended family was questioning the decision and was waiting for the result. Failure was not an option for Ozra; it was she against all the unbelievers. So Ozra did what she could only do while Majid took the test, she prayed for hours.

Within the following week the scores were out. Majid did not seem to be as anxious as the rest of the family. He was thinking more about the summer vacation he never had, and even if he passed the test, he would never have time to enjoy the bike ride. His overall score was 17.21 out of 20, well over passing grade, but by far below Majid's standards. Ozra had achieved her goal and was looking tall in front of her family. She was convinced her son would not be the victim of the new system, even though she had no idea what it was!

Majid for the next few days waited for his bike to arrive, but it never did. Akbar who did not support this irrational behavior of having a kid going through three years of school in one year opposed the purchase of the bike. His valid reasoning was that the street next to their house was highly traveled by cars and riding a bike there was not an intelligent decision.

Majid was too exhausted to fight his father's decision or even cry over it. He was more concerned about the high school and starting the seventh grade. His father had already signed him up in a top private high school by the name of Margan. It was a good mile and half from their house, and Majid had to walk back and forth everyday.

Considering the demand for the top rated engineering schools and the seat limitations for such schools among millions of people taking the National Test, attending a private high school was considered as a must for Majid. Akbar did not seem to have any problem spending money on Majid - as long as it pertained to his education!

On the first day of high school, Majid was amused, shocked, and felt very small. Most children entering the old system of high school were twelve years or older, but Majid was only ten and from a family that were considered below average height. He was probably the smallest student in that school. All the students looked at him as if he did not belong there, and that's how he felt.

Majid's height was not the only problem, while intellectually he was very advanced for his age; he had no common ground with other students. Most students came from very rich families, some of whom the family chauffeur dropped them off from one of the latest cars in the market at the time. Some of the students were not very talented, but their parents had deep pockets. Majid did not like to associate with them.

Majid's quick pass through fifth and sixth grades also did not allow him to retain much of the material he memorized. The private school was demanding and Majid for the first time ever had to play catch up. Akbar demanded ninety percent or better in the test grades which meant at least 18 from a total of 20. This was also a back breaking demand that Majid had a hard time fulfilling.

Within the first three weeks of school, Majid, as if he had entered a prison cell, had to fight one of the tallest boys in the class. That student was from a rich family, or should I say he was the son of one of the Shah's ministers. He was a rude spoiled arrogant brat who was fourteen years old. Because of Majid's size, he decided to rub Majid on his private area, without being concerned about the consequence. Unfortunately for him, and considering Majid's fist not being far from his private area, he was on his back within a minute gasping for air.

During the next class break, Majid had to run up and down the six floor building chased by the tall brat. Majid did get a good beating that day when he was caught by the bully, but no one again picked on him because of his size.

There was another student, not much taller than Majid that came to help him from the floor. His name was Mehrdad, a very polite gentle student who asked Majid if he was alright. While Mehrdad was taller than Majid at age twelve, he seemed to be another outcast like him.

Mehrdad was a Zoroastrian (or Zartoshti) which meant he was a follower of perhaps the oldest religion practiced.

The best historical data indicates that Zoroaster (the prophet) lived about 1,500 B.C. While the origins of this religion can be traced to modern day Greece, it was highly practiced and rooted in Persia and later India. Zoroaster lived in Persia or modern day Iran.

Zoroastrianism or Mazdaism is the religion that can be considered as the mother of all modern day religions, which believed in God (Ahura Mazda), or the one Creator of the Universe. Zoroaster preached righteousness in thoughts, behavior, and words, by thinking, acting and saying "Good."

Zoroastrian's religious book Yasna (or Avesta) opens with praise of Ahura Mazda on the first chapter of over sixty. Also included in Avesta are five hymns called the Gathas which are all examples of abstract sacred poetry supporting the common theme of worshipping one God. This old religion currently has around 200,000 followers. After Muslim Arabs invaded Iran, a large number of them fled to India where most are residing today.

Avesta emphasizes the understanding of righteousness and cosmic order, the elements of social justice, and our choice of choosing between good and evil. While Ahura Mazda is the God of goodness, Angra Mainyu is considered the Lord of evil spirit.

It was a Zoroastrian belief that a savior (Saoshyant), born of a virgin from a lineage of Zoroaster will come to raise the dead on the judgment day. Evil and its spirits are considered to be completely destroyed at the end of time. Then the occupants of hell will be purified and be released.

Considering Mehrdad was the only Zoroastrian student in that school of over one thousand students, besides his older brother, he felt like an outcast. Yet with the teachings of his religion, he was the only righteous soul in the school to help Majid stand up, and that meant a lot to Majid.

Majid and Mehrdad became each other's best friend. While the two did not form any gang, that's how most modern day gangs formed. **The unwanted find each other's pain of rejection as a strong bond of connection and survival. When the system overpowers the weak into demise, elements of**

weakness become the bridge between them, only to help them survive. Majid and Mehrdad formed the strongest bridge during the six years of high school.

That was Majid's first exposure to another religion. Majid was very open- minded for he had met many closed-minded people and he did not want to be like any of them. **I guess the best way to become open-minded is to live in the midst of closed-minded people, for the parameters of their ignorance can help fuel the rays of intelligence.**

After a few months into the school year, Majid was invited to his best friend's apartment. His family liked the unbiased nonjudgmental Majid. Ozra did not feel at ease for her son to go to someone's house that was not Muslim.
She did not want her son to be associating with people that praised fire instead of God. But why did Ozra believe such baseless nonsense? The same reason as everyone else does.

People believe in what makes them comfortable with their own structure of thinking. Breaking through the paradigm of thinking requires much dedication to finding the truth if ever, and many years of hard work, that's simply too difficult for the modern day Joe. **It is normally much easier to listen to the people of authority and to the voices surrounding us. This is why sometimes we allow the truth to be reshaped until it resembles the lies we are used to hearing!**

Majid that day took another step to breakdown fear. He walked tall against the devil of ignorance all the way to his friend's house. He agonized that the people that love you and want the best for you, do not necessarily take the steps to achieve these goals. He realized the **devil is not a stone** in Saudi Arabia **that people throw pebbles at, but exists in the ignorant minds made of stone!**

Did **Ozra** know the first thing about the Zoroastrian religion? Did she understand it was the heart of her own beliefs? Did she have a friend who was Zoroastrian? Did she ever talk to anyone who was **Zoroastri**an? No! But that did not stop her from telling her son what to do. It is amazing to know Ozra (Ezra) was an old name going back to the same time era.

Why are we so afraid of unknowns? Why are we afraid of learning? Why do we consume all that science has to offer, yet fight the logic behind it? Why do we study history but never learn from it? Those were not the only questions in Majid's mind.

The 10-year old Majid was also very upset with the Shah and all the money he was spending on the 2,500th year celebration of the Persian Empire, by inviting all the heads of states to the Persepolis ruins.

People were getting very upset with the Shah and all the horror stories about SAVAK, the secret police. SAVAK was very much like the FBI, but with no control and accountability to the people.   It was perceived as an organization to protect the Shah and suppress anyone who questioned the establishment.   Due to perceived lavish spending of the Shah for the 2,500th year festivity and some of the pro-communist students who were also against the monarchy, many students demonstrated against the Shah and his policies on a regular basis.

SAVAK was very active on the college campuses at the time, and the **daily** events taking place at Iranian campuses resembled much of what happened at Kent State University in Kent, Ohio.   SAVAK was not the students' best friend and students paid a heavy price for expressing their opinion against the Shah, and in some cases they even lost their lives over it.

But why were these students opposed to the Shah and his regime?   What was motivating these top-rated students, graduating from highly respected universities to speak out and be willing to lose everything?   There must have been something deeply rooted to account for this level of hostility.   Indeed, there was much below the surface. The 2,500th year celebration simply broke the camel's back for them.

This is not a simple question, and there is no simple answer.   However an attempt to understand some of the root causes may bring an insight to many of the issues at hand in the region even today.

The pride and shame, the innovation and dark ages, the culture and poetry, Zoroastrian or Manichaeism religions, humanity and savagery, saving the Hebrews and defying them, and much more are all part of Persian history which dates back to the beginning of civilization as we know it.   All these bring complexity and confusion to the new generation of young emotional minds.   Iranians like any other society like to remember their rich past, but down play the internal problems that resulted in its downfall.   Let's call those feelings as the **Pride of the past that the present can never match.**

For over thirteen centuries Islam has played an important role in the country.   Much like Christianity and Judaism, the stories and events share many things in common.   However, the difference is that Mohammad is considered by Muslims as the last of God's main five prophets, following Jesus in fourth place, and about six centuries after him.   In Islam there is a heavy emphasis on the equality of people and how in God's eyes, everyone is seen as equal.   **In Islam, the main issue is not so much to be saved but to fight for social justice.**   Actually, heaven is almost guaranteed if you lose your life for justice and the right causes.

Islam seems to be very popular among poor nations and those that feel justice is not done to them.   In many cases, Islam has become the bridge between those groups who feel suppressed. This is also why in many Muslim nations Islam is not just looked at as a religion, but more like an ideology, much like Capitalism, Communism, and Socialism.   This is how and why there were many underground organizations during the Shah's reign that were advertising Islam in an unusual way to the young generation, much like an ideology.

Dr. Ali Shariati (1933-1977) was one such person leading the way at that time.   He, in his forty-four year life span had a significant impact on students' thinking throughout the nation. His opposition to the Shah and the establishment, his teaching at universities which was stopped constantly, his continuous detention by SAVAK, his definition of Islamic faith as an ideology, and his numerous books which were considered as anti-regime finally earned him a fatal so-called heart attack in England three weeks after his release from prison in Iran.

His books were perhaps very fundamental for recruiting college students by Mujaheddin-e-Khalg, an underground political group that defied the Shah and the United States' presence in Iran. Mujaheddin-e-Khalg was considered a progressive Islamic front and equivalent to some of the communist movements in Iran such as Sia-cal. Mujaheddin-e-Khalg however, at that time, did not work closely with fundamentalist Muslims such as Ayatollah Khomeini who was in exile in Iraq since 1964.

But the 800-pound gorilla in the room was always the way the Shah and his father came to power. His father's sixteen year reign was believed to be under British influence. Considering the British role in India and Iraq, that does not require much debate. However many people respected his father and attributed much of the modernization to a number of the projects he had undertaken.

The Shah on the other hand, did not have the respect of too many Iranians. After the Shah was sent into exile by the very popular Prime Minister Dr. Mohammad Mosadegh in August of 1953, it was common knowledge that he was reinstalled the same year by a military coup orchestrated by the United States (CIA) and England (MI6). However this was believed to come with a high price tag for the Iranians.

While Mosadegh had nationalized the Iranian oil, it was perceived that the Shah agreed in 1954, to allow an international consortium of British (40% of the shares), American (40%), French (6%), and Dutch (14%) to run the Iranian oil facilities for the next 25 years. It was also believed that Iran was not allowed on the board of directors for its own oil, was not permitted to review the reporting on the profits, and was only given 50% of the profit on its own oil. No citizens of any country would be happy with such an arrangement, and nor were the Iranians!

And now the Shah was deficit spending money for the 2,500th year festival - of exactly what? While people were afraid of SAVAK and few people would talk badly about the Shah, the general feeling toward him was not good. Everyone looked at him as an American puppet, and felt some members of his family were involved with drug trafficking and corruption.

That was the feeling in Iran, and the following are the documents released at the same time in the United States:

Source: National Archives, RG 59, Central Files 1970-73, POL 23-9 IRAN. Confidential. The lavish 2500th celebrations, held October 1971 at Persepolis, commemorated the anniversary of Cyrus the Great's founding of the Achaemenian Empire.

On November 19, David Abshire replied to a letter of concern, forwarded by Senator Lloyd Bentsen, that the Shah had pre-emptively rounded up 39 dissidents on August 23, and sentenced most to death. Abshire wrote that "The Iranian government has acted energetically to round up the terrorist groups, as would any government in similar circumstances. In our opinion these dissident elements in Iran ... are in no way representative of the views of the great majority of the Iranians, who support the Shah and his government."

(NEA/IRN, Office of Iran Affairs, Lot File 75D351, Box 6, POL 23, Internal Security, Counter Insurgency, Iran 1971.) On December 21, the Embassy expressed the view that a campaign against the death sentences was communist-organized. (Donald Toussaint to Jack Miklos, NEA/ARN, Office of Iran Affairs, Lot File 75D365, Box 7, POL 29, Political Prisoners, Iran 1972.)

The Shah did celebrate the 2,500th year of the Persian Empire in October of 1971 at Persepolis, Pasargad, Shiraz, and Tent City.

The events included celebrations on the streets, banquets at the Tent City, Light and Sound Show at Persepolis, Military Parade of the Persian Dynasties during the previous 2500 years, and a major tribute to Cyrus The Great opening with "Cyrus, rest in peace since we are awake,...".

Perhaps, the Shah wanted to use this event to place Iran on the map, and get its population to look back to its rich history, and create a rising nationalism.

In the world's history, perhaps there have not been many people more prestigious than Cyrus the Great. He has been loved by the people of the Jewish faith, and his name is even mentioned in the Bible several times. After all, Cyrus was the man who founded the first recorded human rights principles.

The Shah also felt his White Revolution, which included land reform, increased literacy, a higher living standard, roles for women in industry, as well as freedom of religion, was making him very popular within his nation. With increased deficit spending for the military, and aligning himself with the United States, the Shah was trying to play a major role in the Middle East. This is perhaps why he wanted to put himself on the same platform with Cyrus the Great to gain respect within the society and in the world.

The Shah maintained an open invitation to President Nixon, and through Ambassador McArthur, he kept up insistence for a visit. The Shah was also interested in hiring American Generals such as general Twitchell against much opposition by General William C. Westmoreland, the Chief of Staff of the United States Army.

As documented below, Mr. Henry Kissinger, a long-time friend of the Shah, advised President Nixon to attend the celebration.

---

156. Memorandum From the President s Assistant for National Security Affairs (Kissinger) to President Nixon, Washington, December 28, 1971

Kissinger advised the President that Ambassador McArthur and Secretary Rogers both urged Nixon to make his long-awaited trip to Iran, both to assuage the Shah's pride and to ease the Shah's concerns over long-range Soviet objectives in the region.

President Nixon visited Iran in March of 1972. This was the Shah's moment of glory to be seen with the President of the United States on the streets of Iran. Streets were closed off and many people were cheering the Shah and President Nixon. Majid was one of the students cheering in the crowd - but why?

Prior to the visit, SAVAK made sure all the stores adjacent to the travel route had their Iranian flags displayed. Schools on the route were closed, and students were in the streets cheering. Also, many people out of curiosity were standing on the side of the road. Most people being afraid of SAVAK kept their mouth shut, but were probably thinking "this is just great, an American President with his puppet King, in an American made car, driving on the streets of Iran."

Inability to speak freely within the society had caused an explosion of Abstract Poetry within the country. Poetry in the Persian culture is deeply rooted within the body, blood, and imagination of every individual, whether living within or outside the country. Through thousands of years of history- good, bad, or ugly, it was the great poets that gave hope and direction to the people.

Ferdowsi, about 1,100 years ago, wrote his masterpiece, the Shahnameh. For over 1,000 years, this book has remained very popular among Persians, and by many he is considered as the father of the Persian language. His poetry book written in Dari Persian narrates the story of old Persian kings starting 7,000 years ago. This book was written after the Arab dominance of language and culture a few hundred years after the advancement of Islam in Persia. His poetry helped maintain the Persian culture, heritage, and language.

A hand full of other famous philosophers and poets are Molavi, Khayam, Saddi, and Hafez. These poets are the pride of all Persians, defining people as humans first before any religion and nationality.

Omar Khayam is probably the most well known in the West for his contributions in poetry, astronomy, and algebra.

Modern day poetry was led by Nima a number of decades ago. While old poetry required and forced poets to maintain the rhyme within the poem, the new poetry does not require that. Modern poetry is more of an abstract writing with a rhythm but mainly focused on the message. The majority of these poems have a political message hidden in them, much like a parable.

Majid enjoyed old poetry, but he really loved modern poems. It was just like a puzzle to solve trying to understand what the poet was actually aiming at. With his great sense of composition, he started writing modern style poems at the age of eleven. The following is the first poem he wrote:

The Genie, The Old Ugly Genie

Days are not bright any longer,
No light dares to flicker in our night,
And if a candle is lit,
The Genie, The Old Ugly Genie,
Comes and blows it right out!
The Genie, The Old Ugly Genie,
Does not like mothers to tell stories,
About this land, and other lands,
About the Genie and his dark clouds,
He loves it when children are asleep!
But the good little ones,
Must sit by their Grandma's bed,
So that she can tell them stories,
About the big black crow,
Did you say - you would like to know?
There was one, and there was no one,
Under the dark sky of the universe,
With a big black crow holding on,
To all the food that sparrows brought home,
Or they were the food, if nothing else!
All the birds, even the insects,
Had to go to work everyday,
To bring their food to the King, Mr. Crow,
They never had enough for their own,
Even the little ones left at home!
The Crow felt that was his right,
He was the biggest, he had the might,
The silly birds who hardly could sing,
They had no brain, and they had no feeling!
But one day, an eagle flew down,
In his sharp eyes, Crow had the sign,
He grabbed the Crow with his talons,
Singing was everywhere, insects and sparrows!
If you liked the story,
Don't let The Genie,
The Old Ugly Genie,
Turn your light Off!

In the above poem, the reader had to understand that "Old Ugly Genie" meant the regime and the fear of SAVAK which most people were afraid to express their opinion against. King, Mr. Crow was of course the-"Shah" that by dictatorship and unilateral decision making had an impact on people's day to day life. Eagle was the symbol of Freedom that would eventually take away the dictatorship and would allow people to speak freely.

Majid, who was deeply influenced by his political environment at home, never shared his poetry with anyone except his family members. Majid's father prohibited his son from writing political poems, for this would have endangered the family members. Majid's poetry has been mostly in the Persian language, and it is only during writing this book that it is being translated.

Before the summer of 1972 began, Ali finished up his master's degree with the highest point average from University of Tehran. Also at this time, there was another student demonstration at his college. SAVAK was getting very bold in taking the student activists out, by calling all of them procommunist, which was not correct. Many of these students were calling for a western style democracy with more of Dr. Shariati's teaching. Shariati's books had much more influence on the college students than any other ideologies.

Students were being chased by the police and SAVAK agents on a continuous basis. Some were even going on so called mountain hikes, never to come back or often falling off the cliffs. This was at least people's perceptions, and who could challenge the masses that believe something, whether true or not. That summer, two of the opposition leaders by the name of Vatan-Khah (Nation-Desire), and Mihan-Dost (Country-Love) were executed and many students were chased off the campus all the way to the metro buses. Luckily, Ali came home safely through all that turbulence.

The summer of 1972 was very uneventful for Majid. He had nothing to do at home. There was no TV, for Akbar did not want his family to waste their time in front of it. Majid did not have a bike or any games to play, except the ones he made up. He spent most of his time solving puzzles and math problems, and reading and writing compositions. He also played a lot of chess with his older brothers- the only game they had at home.

By this time, Ali had already started a job with the National Steel Company in the suburb of the ancient city of Esfahan. Mahmoud was attending medical school and spent the rest of his time at home. Mahmoud loved philosophy and poetry and always listened closely to Majid's compositions and poems.

On occasion, Mahmoud treated Majid to a movie. A few weeks into the summer, Mahmoud took Majid to a movie and a surprise treat thereafter. Compared to the previous summer, this looked like heaven. **Everything in life is relative, even our agony and joy.** Considering the traffic in the streets of Tehran, walking a couple of miles to a movie theater was a no-brainer. Even though the difference in age was ten years, Majid enjoyed talking philosophy, history, and poetry with his older brother.

At this particular time in the city of Tehran, the population was about four million, so every square inch had to count for something. There was one park and a number of stores on the pathway to the movie theater. There were two movie theaters next to each other; both seated about 1,500. Majid and Mahmoud had to stay in line like most other people for over an hour to get the tickets, unless they wanted to buy the tickets at three times the price from people on the side of the road giving coordinated hand and mouth signals.

Shahreh Farang (Western City) Theater had four doors opening to the panorama screen on each floor. Each ticket had a number indicating the seating arrangement; some people had to get help finding their seats. Before the movie started, everybody had to stand up and honor the King's anthem, while the screen showed all the Shah's great achievements. People normally murmured something quietly, but mostly did not care one way or another, and could not wait to sit down.

That day, the movie being featured was a translated version of a Woody Allen movie. The Persian version was just as good, or should I say just as insane. You could not tell whether the movie was made in Hollywood or Tehran-wood. Majid could not stop laughing and being happy, not all because of the movie, but also because Mahmoud had promised him dinner after the movie.

The movie was over around 11:00 p.m. and the two started walking back home. On the way back there was a large crowd at a fast food restaurant. Fast food did not mean anything like McDonald's or Burger King, just a place that quickly made small sandwiches like hot dogs (called Sosis) and Olevieh Salad (similar to potato salad). The place also served a selection of imported beer, and it seemed like a large number of people ordered imported varieties.

Majid ordered a hot dog, some potato chips, and a soda. Mahmoud ordered the same thing. That was the first time Majid was watching people consume alcoholic beverages. Majid asked Mahmoud if the owner was a Muslim and Mahmoud responded that he was probably a Christian man. The Shah did respect the people of different religious backgrounds and so did most educated people.

While that night was great, the next day Majid was very excited and dreaming about visiting his brother Ali in Esfahan. Ali was working there for a short period of time and asked if Majid wanted to visit that city. I guess the memories of the earlier summer, the one from hell, was fresh in everyone's mind, and the family wanted Majid to kick back and relax. The next three weeks, to Majid, seemed to pass slowly, until he was ready to go on the trip.

Locals refer to their city as Esfahan nesfeh jahan, which means Esfahan is half of the universe. With all the ancient history and monuments, it definitely looked like it to Majid.

One could say the city, culture, and monuments of Esfahan were all the creation of one man and that would be Shah Abbas the Great (of the Safavid Kingdom).

Born and raised in Harat, the great cultural and intellectual of Persia, Shah Abbas was crowned in 1587 at the age of 17, in the city of Qazvin. From a young age he was influenced by painting, calligraphy, and magnificent building design. The Shah Abbas wanted to make a brand new capital city with a grand concept in his mind. With the help of his Grand Vizier, he moved the capital city to the unknown small town of Esfahan.

Shah Abbas was a skilled craftsman with expertise in making scimitars, bridles and saddles for his horses, and he possessed many other artistic abilities. He took great interest in learning about foreign lands and enjoyed exploring ideas from people coming from Europe. He was also interested in discussing religion with Christians.

Under King Abbas, Esfahan changed from a small town to the Imperial Capital, becoming the center of art, and one of the most beautiful cities in the world. This opened the door to the new comers who were highly skilled artisans. A large number of Christians moved to this area, for commercial reasons, while some, due to the King's personal interest were moved and relocated to the city of Esfahan from the northwestern parts of Iran.

King Abbas wanted Esfahan to be the preeminent multi-cultural center of the world, hence he utilized and empowered Sheikh Bahai, born and raised to age 13 in Lebanon. Sheikh Bahai was one of the few Sufis who was a true globalist of his time. He had great knowledge of different sciences and was able to take on the task of major projects in that city. Some of his work included having a role in the design of the Royal Mosque and Garden, building a large bathhouse that was allegedly heated by a single candle, and designing the system of water distribution in Esfahan and Ardestan.

By the end of the Safavid Dynasty, by some descriptions, Esfahan had 162 mosques, 48 schools, 1802 commercial buildings, and 283 large public bathhouses. To this day, Esfahan is internationally known for the artistic hand works and beautifully crafted wool and silk carpets.

For the first time ever Majid was watching and enjoying centuries of cultural exhibits and not just reading about it in a book and memorizing it for a teacher. Majid kept thinking **how a long trip can make a man much wiser than sitting at home and imagining what he was told by others.** Majid simply was fascinated by everything on that trip.

On one of the days Majid went to work along with Ali. Ali was proud to show off his little brother to the group of engineers at work. Soon after they arrived at his place of work, three engineers on one side (not including Ali) of a chess set were challenging the little Majid. The game was all started in fun by Ali who was bragging about how well Majid could play the game of chess.

Majid was playing but was relaxed and did not expect to win. The three engineers' pride was on the line, for they could not possibly lose to an eleven year old kid. The game was about an hour old, when you could feel the sense of relief on the three engineer faces. They could see within the next two steps Majid would be checkmated, and they were wiping the sweat off their faces. It was Majid's move, and they were so concerned about Majid not making one move to take away their plan of execution.

Majid kept looking at and touching the part that they did not want him to move. He even picked it up and lightly banged it on his forehead and placed it back at the same position to their relief. Then he moved his hand to the opposite side of the board, moved his long forgotten bishop to check their king, and in a crackling voice, Majid proudly declared, "Checkmate".

There was not enough ice water in the world to put out the fire from the three engineers' brains. They looked at each other and started blaming one another, as losers always do. **When you are so focused on how many ways you can win by defeating the unworthy enemy, you sometimes forget in how many ways you may lose by lowering your defense and end up hurting yourself.** That was a big lesson for the three engineers staring at the chess set in disbelief.   There was also a big lesson for Majid that day; **no matter how big the challenge may be, patience and logic will always prevail.**

No one knows how many people have teased those three engineers about that game since that day, but one thing is for sure, that the memories of that game will be buried with Majid for eternity.   Since that day, Majid's desire for logic and mathematics multiplied by an inconceivable number, and produced great positive results in his life.

The summer of 1972 came to an end and Majid had to start the next school year.   This time he was not tired, the school was not new, and he could not wait to get back and take on the challenge.   Besides he could not wait to tell his best friend Mehrdad about the chess game!

As usual, Majid walked to his high school everyday; he passed through a number of traffic lights, and even sometimes jay walked across four lanes of traffic. On one of those days he saw a camel for the first time ever, with his owner crying for help.   As he got closer, he realized the camel's hoof was stuck in a hole on a sidewalk right over a water drain area.   While it looked strange and somewhat enchanting, it was rather uncanny to see such a thing that early in the morning.   Majid had no clue what to do to help the poor man, so he continued walking.   He did not even know if he could get close to a camel in pain, so he did nothing.

As Majid kept walking to school he kept thinking about the man with his camel and what business he could possibly have in that part of the town.   He was near the school zone when a student's chauffeur blew the horn at him to get out of the road. The latest light green BMW with its big horn just sounded like the poor camel in pain, and the spoiled kid walking out in fear of getting a bad grade for not having his homework completed, looked like the old man fighting for his life and livelihood.   What a contrast and what a tragedy!

That day after Majid went home, he kept thinking about the old man and his camel.   He did not see them on the way back, but the images were drawn on his memory cells for ever.   Where did he come from and why? What was he doing there?   Asking those questions from Mahmoud that night, Majid realized the level of poverty in the south part of Tehran.   He discovered that people had to wash their clothes in the stagnant dirty water, and sometimes boil it to use for the drinking water. None of the answers Majid was finding was favorable to the Shah and what he stood for.

To Europe and the United States, the Shah had started to play a much more important role than just access to the oil. With the strong support from Mr. Henry Kissinger, who had visited Iran a number of times, the Shah had become a great ally in the region. His purchase of American made aircraft fighter planes helped build up one of the most advanced and disciplined militaries in the world. The Shah's spy network over the Soviet Union, his nation being the only non-Arab Islamic country to support and protect the State of Israel below the surface, and his control of the Persian Gulf was making the Shah invincible, or at least this is how he felt.

While Shah was flying high in American made aircrafts, his house was crumbling underneath him. His top ministers were not telling him the truth and were sugar coating the lies. The student voices were getting louder and in some cases silenced by the long term jail sentences or executions. While being afraid of the SAVAK, people were starting to become more outspoken. **Unlike the world's general perception, no one was against modernization in Iran, but many were against tyranny, and the type of changes that by far exceeded the population's ability to adapt.**

It would not take long before the discussion changed into a political form in many of the extended family gatherings. At the time, the extended family invited and visited each other on a regular basis, perhaps too often. On the father's side, Majid had seven living uncles and aunts, while on the mother's side, there were nine of them. There was at least one major gathering per month, and family in many cases, if needed, turned an extended hand to help the ones having a bit of a problem.

When everyone was invited to Ozra and Akbar's home, Majid had to participate in assisting Ozra in a number of chores around the house. Cleaning up the house and fixing food for a crowd of approximately eighty was not easy, and the fact Ozra did not have any daughters did not help her case. She had to prepare at least one week in advance, and everything had to look perfect. It was a matter of pride to make sure the visitors enjoyed all the food, were continuously taken care of, and that they were openly pleased with the hospitality.

For instance, when the guests arrived, Majid would open the door and greet the folks one by one. He had to ask them how they were doing. If everyone in their family was doing okay, he had to ask about the other family members each by name that did not show up and if they were doing well, and what was the reason that they were not able to show up. This was all new to Majid and did not seem to serve much purpose, for people were more focused on asking the question than listening to the response.

Then the guests would come inside, and women and men sort of separated themselves from one another, not by any rules at that time, but mostly because of the bondage between women and macho-ness among the men. You can also blame it on centuries of religious customs, male domination and pride in some cases that simply created an easy separation of genders by choice. However, western women residing in Iran, Iranian women who traveled abroad, and highly positioned and sophisticated ladies in the society did mix with men and their conversations on many occasions to the delight of open-minded men.

Majid never seemed to fit the mold, and he was always out of the ordinary. Ozra had to explain the proper etiquette to him continuously, one such thing was "Tarrof." Tarrof was a hard thing to understand, for if you ask someone for something and they say "No," why do you need to keep asking the same question and insisting? A groom has to ask three times for his wife's acceptance in marriage until she says "Yes."

Tarrof was played on both sides, for instance you ask the person to take some fruit from the bowl that you are holding in front of them while bending and hurting your back, and the person, while really wanting it, will answer "No," then you ask again and again until the person takes the piece of fruit they like. You could imagine how going through thirty people in a room while tarrofing can be a great workout for the day. This could be one reason for not gaining too much weight after eating all the different types of rice; you use up more energy tarrofing than maintaining the calories from the starch. Get the picture!

Inviting the guests into the reception room and even asking them to the dining table, required tarrofing. Certain places of the

52

room and areas of the dining table carried more stature and were mentally reserved by the host for the family elders or people of high influence and position. Those people were to be the first tarrofed to sit in those prime locations, over and over. The response from each individual, as expected, was to please ask so and so, instead of me. It was your job to keep asking until the person accepts the position in the room or around the big dining table. It seemed as though Ozra, generally, and Majid on occasions were involved in acts of tarrofing when the visitors arrived.

And the food, perhaps a menu from Heaven, was always exotic, colorful, and most of all, delicious. It was never planned to be just enough for the number of guests invited with just a couple of simple dishes, but it was to show abundance. The menu consisted of any food and fruit your heart desired at its best, prepared for the guests and at least fifty percent more for any uninvited guests. In some cases the excess food was eaten during the following days, some sent home with the college students and some was given out to the poor, but much of it was also wasted. This did not make Majid happy and it always caused internal emotional pain for him.

During the feast people consumed way too much food, because the host would constantly tarrof another spatula full of rice into their plates whether they had any room in their stomach or not. It was rude and mentally sinful to waste food, so people kept eating until their plates required no washing, yet to be tarrofed to have more. In one of these occasions Akbar stood up and screamed at his brother-in-law not to put any more food in his plate for he was blowing up, then he gently sat down and to everyone's surprise wiped the last grain of rice out of his plate. He simply refused to sin at the cost of staying in the bathroom for most of that day.

And when the guests left, there was another set of tarrofing such as, "Our hospitality did not match your stature and …", and the response was, "But it was well over our expectation and …" It was continued by, "Please enlighten our poor small home with your presence again, …" and the response was, "We are in debt to your generosity and kindness" Sometimes it took fifteen minutes with each family before they departed.

Perhaps the Shah of Iran simply tarrofed the 50% of Iranian oil profit to the western countries for his return to Iran in 1953, but perhaps it was a demand. But on a serious note, tarrofing is very integrated into the way of thinking in Iran and all its citizens. Even among those living abroad under different citizenships, tarrofing is continuously impacting their decision making and the way they look at issues.

A Persian parable states; "An atheist believes everyone is an atheist," translating to, "**We believe everyone else at the table thinks and looks at the things the same way as we do.**" This can not be far from the truth as people of many cultures sit around the same table. While the concept of Tarrof can cause a mix-up in such settings, it can be used as a great sales tool. Tarrof is probably one of the major reasons that Iranians have done well in one-to-one trades by helping long-term business development, yet have done poorly in worldwide negotiations.

It was January 17, 1973 and as usual everyone was busy with the day to day family life. In everybody's life in the family, it was just another day, and no one really paid much attention that it was Majid's birthday. Birthdays simply did not play such an important role at the time, as it plays here in the United States. This is why Majid decided to surprise the family.

Majid had saved enough money to purchase some milk and cookies from a pastry shop on the way home from school. After he arrived home, he skillfully hid the food until everyone else arrived. He made some delicious hot chocolate milk while Ozra was in another room, and then called everyone into the kitchen. In that chilly winter day the hot chocolate milk along with the cookies tasted awfully good. After everyone was done they asked what was the occasion and Majid told them it was his birthday. Everybody held Majid in their arms and gave him a big kiss on the cheek. **That was the best birthday Majid ever had; it was in giving that he received everyone's unconditional love, the pure love that is not measured by any material possession.**

March 21st, the Persian New Year was once again approaching. Ozra started the spring cleaning about mid-February. It was not just cleaning of the house - it was every blind, every window, every wall, every carpet, and just about any imaginable location in the house. It did not look like a task to

Majid, it was a tragedy. Majid had to scrub all the outside walls to the house- every inch of the walls separating the whole house from the world outside, the boundaries between Majid's home and the rest of the universe, or at least that's how Majid felt about it.

All things considered, Ozra could not take on the rest of the cleaning all by herself, so Akbar had to bring Hossein, one of the gentlemen at work to come and help. Hossein's job at work was mainly to serve tea to all the employees during the work hours; that is, about 4 to 5 tea cups per day for over 50 employees that had desk jobs. He did not make much money and a number of employees who could afford to, gave him some odd jobs to do at their home.

Ozra needed all the blinds for both floors to be cleaned, or shall I say, soaped, rinsed, and dried, slat by slat. Dust had no place in Ozra's home, above all at the New Year celebration time. Hossein spent about two weeks cleaning up all the blinds, after work and during the weekend, which was only Friday. Poor people never took a break from working; they simply took on other tasks to help feed their families.

Hossein with his wife and four children had no choice but to work. He had a small motorcycle that he drove all the way from the south of Tehran where mostly the poor resided, to the northern part of Tehran where the rich lavishly spent their money. While cleaning the blinds, Majid would serve him tea off and on, which is the proper etiquette, and deeply rooted in the Persian customs. During that time Majid would ask questions of Hossein and he would share some of the pains and sufferings that the poor people had to go through on a daily basis.

Many people had made mud homes in the southern parts of Tehran without any engineering approval. Not surprisingly, during any earthquake, the structures would crumble and sometimes bury their families within. This happened in many of the poor regions of the country on a fairly frequent basis. In most areas, the drinking water was the rain water coming down from the northern slopes, which was boiled and used for cooking and drinking.

Listening to the way people were living their lives and watching the Shah's Ministers talking about his White Revolution on the radio was a huge contrast for Majid. It seemed like the two worlds were not engaged; rich people saw the poor and ignored them as if it was all their choosing, and the poor man had no voice for he was lost and shuffled between the day to day challenges of middle class folks.

Religion always finds the hopeless, since for the weak, it is the vacuum between reality and what they wish for. Religion takes away the pain of the poor by becoming the bridge between them with no control, and God with absolute control. This is how **they can wake up and walk on a dead end road, day after day, with a big smile on a starving face.**

Hossein, like many folks in the south part of Tehran, was wearing a holy Shia name, the name of the Third Shia Saint, the one who fought injustice until he was beheaded by his enemy. The poor could not fight the poverty and social bias, but they could name all their children, in many cases five or more, with those holy names. This shows how people that continuously deal with pain and suffering, whether financial, mental, or physical, find a way to utilize religion in their lives.

Sometimes one's mental and/or physical health is the result of his or her financial status, in which for most cases, is tightly controlled by the economic welfare of that part of the society. **As the poorer sect of society grows, so does its voice of pain and suffering, and along with it the voice of religious clerks that represent the union of the poor, suffering, uneducated in many scenarios, and the globally ignorant in most cases.**

Hossein was a single dot in the sphere of poverty in Iran. **The center was the deeply unquestioned religious beliefs that were unifying, controlling, and maintaining all those dots in its orbit.** The sphere of poverty was expanding, and the religious clerks, within and outside the country were making a note of this. This is when the Shah was looking for an international recognition of his country and his status as its King, and seemed to be lost within his circle of "Yes Sir" generals and senators.

Hossein's work came to a completion after the second week. Ozra made sure to give enough money, some old clothing, and some excess dried vegetables to him before he left. But **Hossein left much more behind with Majid and that was the cry of the poor. It was the cry of the insignificant, the decimal**

error that we are willing to ignore, and the imaginary answers to an equation that have no real roots.

That New Year, Majid was not happy, for both he and his old friend Jamshid were mourning the accidental death of Hossein. The week before the New Year began Hossein had a crash while driving to one of those odd ball jobs after work. He died in search of hope for his family, he died before he could be the dot at the end of his own sentence, and he died as an imaginary answer to a confusing equation with no real answers. His dot was gone, but his wife and four children were the new dots on the sphere of injustice and hopelessness.

However, the New Year started very promising for Ali, for he was accepted with a full scholarship by a number of top rated universities in the United States, such as Berkley, Harvard, MIT, and Stanford. He had saved over ten thousand dollars in his bank account and was eager to make the trip and obtain his PhD in Mechanical Engineering. The family, in particular Akbar, was beyond himself with pride. He was looking at this as an opportunity for all the family to move to the United States at some point. Ali, his oldest son had proven to be extremely bright, and this could help his dream come true.

The only problem was that Ali politically spoke his mind and he had no respect for the Shah whose SAVAK had executed a few of his friends while attending Tehran University. This is why Akbar and Ozra recommended that Ali get married before leaving for the United States. This way he would stay out of politics and hence out of any trouble by following his path.

In Iran marriage between the first cousins was not a taboo, and Ali chose to marry one of them who was available and also liked him. Despite the fact that Akbar and Ozra's marriage was arranged and Ozra had not seen Akbar prior to the date of marriage, the new generation of people dated for a short period of time. Ali and his fiancée dated for a few weeks and went to a few movies together before setting their wedding day for the early part of November 1973.

With the social problems rising, and the reports in the White House and elsewhere indicating over 13,000 political executions in Iran, and understanding the value of the Shah over oil, in mid-1973, the Shah was allowed to return the oil industry to national control. This was designed to help reduce the poverty within the nation, strengthen the Shah, and have the Shah's Iran as a close ally in any future conflict in the region.

Considering how well the Iranian National Oil Company was beginning to do, and the fact that Ali's fiancée was residing in Tehran, he decided to move back to Tehran and get a high engineering position at this company while waiting for his wedding date to arrive. During this time, the bride's family was working hard to get the remainder of items needed for the dowry.

While Ali and his fiancée were waiting for their big wedding day, there was another war in the region, from October 6 to October 26, 1973. This war is known as the Yom Kippur War in Israel, as the Ramadan War in Arab countries, and as the October War to the West. From the Israeli point of view, the war began with a surprise joint attack by Egypt and Syria against Israel on the Jewish holiday of Yom Kippur. These two countries crossed the cease-fire lines on the Sinai Peninsula and Golan Heights which were captured by Israel in 1967 during the Six-Day War.

However, the continuous movement of Jews from the Soviet Union and other countries had many Arabs nervous in the surrounding countries, and with the support of Soviet Union Arms, these countries were trying to stop the flow of people to Israel. An example would be the September 28, 1973 attack and incarceration of an Austrian train carrying Jews en route to Israel by the Soviet Palestinian guerrillas.

While this war like any other war took a number of lives within that short period of time- 2,400 Israelis and many tens-of-thousands of Egyptians and Syrians, at a cost $5 billion for the State of Israel alone, it resulted in a number of peace treaties later. Israel, with some help from the United States, and perhaps even from the Shah of Iran, was victorious in the war. However, the two Arab States, with the help of the Soviet Union, were able to fight Israel for 20-days this time rather than the 1967 Six-Day War, which was considered an emotional victory by many.

It was almost November and the big wedding day was approaching. Unlike the United States, the wedding in Iran was thrown by the groom's family, either in a hotel or a spacious house. Since Akbar was not ready to waste any money and his reception room at the house was large enough to handle a few hundred people, choosing a location was a no-brainer. The next task was to hire a professional cook for this event, and Akbar once again struck gold by choosing the cook from his place of work.

Majid was a couple months short of his 13th birthday, but he was in charge of a number of responsibilities. These tasks ranged from purchasing blocks of ice and cases of beverages from nearby shops within a mile of the house, serving food, and keeping an eye over all the children attending the wedding. Majid had great amount of respect for Ali and was committed to doing everything right that night.

On the day of wedding, the bride had an appointment with a beautician around the noon time-frame. They worked on her hair, face, dress, and anything and everything needed. The cook was at the house early in the morning and in addition to a helper, Majid was used as a gofer. Around lunch time Majid had to bring two large blocks of ice that he carried on his shoulders. This took two trips. They were bulky, heavy and worse of all, cold, but somehow he managed. Majid probably walked ten to twelve miles that day, back and forth, to get any supplies needed by the cook and all the other immediate family members, but it was all worth it.

While normally Aghd or official marriage took place at the bride's house, all things considered, it was agreed to also have that at Akbar's house, so additional long distance traveling for the wedding celebration was avoided. The traditional Aghd room is well-lit, and the ceremony is performed during the day time when the room is full of light. This requirement goes back to the Zoroastrian weddings where the darkness was associated with evil spirits.

The bride arrived around 5:00 p.m. and was led to the Aghd room, where Ali was patiently sitting and waiting in the right hand side chair. Not everybody was participating in the marriage ceremony, only about thirty people who were the immediate and extended members of the family. The bride, wearing a white dress much like the ones here, sat next to Ali in front of "Sofreh Aghd," which is an elaborate white cloth almost matching the bride's dress.

While the room was decorated with the most breath taking flowers, positioned on "Sofreh Aghd" were two candles in ancient holders, a large mirror in a gold frame, flowers in glass vases, different types of candies (Noghl and nabat) and pastries, and most importantly, a Koran facing the direction in which the clergyman or Mula held the official ceremony.

The one hour Aghd ceremony seemed a bit long to Majid who kept going in and out of the room. Two of bride's sisters were holding a fine white cloth on top of the bride's and groom's head while two other ladies were rubbing two sugar cones eight inches tall on top of it. During this time the Mula was reading the wedding versus from the Koran, leading to the major question to Ali first, if he would agree to this marriage, and the amount of "Mehrieh."

Mehrieh was the amount of money or gold set in advance in case of a loss or break up that would belong to the wife. After Ali responded positively, the Mula asked if the bride would agree to the marriage. This was repeated three times. The first two times the bride is supposed to be thinking and not responding, and only respond to the question when asked for the third time. She responded yes, and Monir in an instant became Ali's wife and part of the family.

Ozra was wearing a delicate white chador with small blue and black dots on it, looking absolutely gorgeous and extremely happy. She never had a daughter and Monir by saying yes, instantly became a daughter to her. Ali was twenty- seven, while Monir was only twenty years old. In Iran men normally married someone five to ten years younger than them during that time.

It was about 7:30 p.m. and every light was shinning in celebration and the house looked like a bright moon in the beginning of the night.   At least seventy to eighty cars were parked on both sides of the street, with a light green BMW decorated with flowers in front of the house, and three other cars with flowers parked right behind it.

The menu for the dinner included shirin-polo or rice which is slightly sweetened and mixed with shredded almonds, white rice with saffron, bagheli-polo or rice with lima beans and dill weed, marinated shish-kabob and chicken-kabob.   The cook was placed in the huge basement and had all the food prepared.   He had three additional people attending the wedding to serve all the food and beverages.

That night ended with the bride and the groom sliding into the backseat of the decorated BMW, with about fifteen other cars following it as they rode through the busy streets of Tehran.   It was about 11:00 p.m. and all cars randomly used their horns in celebration.   After returning home, Majid did not go to bed; he almost fainted out of exhaustion.

While that day was great and was followed by another three days of jubilation, the major topics of conversation were the Arab-Israeli war, and its long term impact on the region.   While no one agreed with anyone else, everyone behaved as if they were the most knowledgeable about the topic.

Three Army Majors attending the wedding that night were surrounded and were bombarded with questions about the war in which they really had no answer.   One of the Majors went on to explain that President Sadat of Egypt, who took office after the death of Nasar in September of 1970, struck Israel first on October of 1973 in an attempt to return the Sinai lands back to his country, but they did not discuss or talk about anything else.

After the 20-day war and with no backing from the Soviet Union, Sadat in January of 1974 reached an agreement with Israel, requiring the troops from the two countries to be separated in the Sinai by a UNEF-manned buffer zone.   The war with Israel seemed to appease the poor in Egypt, and it generated internal and external support in the Arab world.   However, the loss to Israel along with the peace settlement seemed to have an adverse affect.

While the Persian race separated the majority of the Iranians from the Arabs, it seemed as though the dragged out war between the Arab States and Israel had a unifying effect between the voices of the poor and the voices raised against the West and the United States for being unfair to the Arab claims. In the view of many people in the region, it seemed there was only communism and capitalism, and there was no room for any other ism. This was probably the beginning of Islamism merging as an ideology and as a voice against all other isms.

Following this war, Iran did not join the Arab oil embargo against the West and Israel. The Shah however used the inflated oil prices to increase defense spending and bring about much more change within the nation, viewed by him and Western nations as modernization, and by the poor people in Iran as the end of the world. The changes were rapid, and in many cases had negative impacts in the life of the poor. This is why Majid continuously felt bad for the poor, and in December of that year wrote the following poem:

Poor & Rich

Small home with broken lantern,
    The door is open to the hungry eyes,
        Dusted dreams in shadow of the night,
            Home of the poor, lost in the pattern!
There is a castle not far away,
    Locked up inside in fear of losing,
        Frowning at the mirror, hating to see,
            Food left on the table, rotting away!
Smiling in pain, begging for love,
    The orphan child with tear, in his eye,
        Holding two hands toward the sky,
            Giving all glory, to God above!
Toys on the floor, no one to play,
    The spoiled child who hates to share,
        Crying for more, without having to care,
            For all God's blessings, no one to pray!
The dark clouds bare the rain,
    The light fluffs have no shame,
        The poor carry a heart of gold,
            The gold blocks the rich man's vein!

The population of the Jewish faith in Iran, even though supported by the Shah and having ownership of many of the lucrative businesses in the nation, was starting to feel discomfort within the country. This was probably one of the reasons that most Jewish students attended different school systems, and did not mix well with the rest of the society.

There was only one student of the Jewish faith in Majid's school. He was not one of Majid's friends, however he had many other friends in his class and he was very popular among everybody who knew him. Though not many, to some ignorant people, he was representative of the State of Israel. This type of feeling was more visible among the poor, and people that did not travel far from their homes.

According to many of the Old Testament biblical books, in particular Ezra 6:14, the Persian kings were credited with permitting and enabling the Jews to return to Jerusalem and rebuild their Temple. Jews have resided in Iran for over 2,700 years, ever since Shalmaneser V conquered the Northern Kingdom of Israel and sent the Israelites into captivity at the state of Khorasan in Iran.

At one point during the peak of the Persian Empire, Jews were estimated to comprise about 20% of the population. This population over the centuries, much like Zoroastrians, culturally and linguistically integrated into the rest of society, and the percentage of believers dropped by introduction and influence of other religions, peacefully or otherwise.

The Jewish population in Iran enjoyed a good bit of freedom. The Shah respected all religions and allowed their holy celebrations within their own communities. While it was good for the new generation to be exposed to other religions, the older generation was still hanging on to their own view, for and against other religions.

It was June of 1974, when Ali received an extended renewal for his acceptance to attend the American schools with full scholarship. However, at that time Monir's father was a victim of a stroke, and for that reason and perhaps others, she did not want to leave the country. While this did not seem to have much impact on Ali, it had a severe impact on Akbar.

Akbar kept smoking cigarettes during the night and walking back and forth in the yard in middle of the night. It was not Ali's dream, but it was Akbar's dream falling apart. Akbar's brother, a medical doctor who was 26 years younger than him was residing in the United States, and Akbar had a similar desire. Akbar was 61 years old and the stress was causing him to develop an ulcer.

To make Akbar's mind rest, Majid went to Mashhad with Ozra and Akbar and stayed with relatives for three weeks in the summer of 1974. During some of the days, Reza, one of Majid's cousins would take him to his father's shop. In the back of their shop, there was a knitting machine where much of the fabric was produced. In the front part of their store they sold shirts of all different colors and sizes. Most of the customers were the visitors to the Imam Reza Shrine which was less than a mile away.

Reza's parents were doing very well and on occasion Nayreh, Ozra's sister, would invite her relatives to her house for a few weeks during the summer. Majid always looked up to his cousin Reza who was a year older. He was very bright and made decent grades in school. During the summer he also enjoyed working for his father and had been helping out since age eleven.

Reza rode his bike to work everyday and if Majid wanted to go along, he had to sit in front, while Reza skillfully paddled his bike in the crowded streets. While a large number of older people drove a car, riding a bike by younger people and many of the poor folks was a common practice.

One day, on the way back from work, Reza asked Majid if he knew how babies were made. With no school sex education, and Majid's parents feeling odd to talk about it, Majid was clueless, but he acted as if he knew something. There it was - for the first time, to much amazement and disbelief, Majid learned how babies were made, from his cousin. Majid could not wait to get back to Tehran and share that knowledge with some of his other male cousins.

This was the extent of sex education at the time, and most grownups did not talk about it, as if this was a taboo and not part of God's intent for reproduction. After gaining that knowledge and returning back home to North Tehran, Majid was not feeling comfortable looking at the girls, especially his female cousins, as if they were a different species.

During the period of the Shah's reign women did not have to wear the chador or the piece of garment that covered their body. As a matter of fact, North Tehran seemed like it was a western nation, with women dressing up in the latest European styles. The change in women's attire between the north and south part of Tehran was drastic and this was sending a wave of emotion, like a dart in the heart of men's pride in South Tehran.

In cultures where the male gender had dominated the females for centuries, this dominance had become an acceptable behavior by the members of that society. Over a period of time, this has resulted into an integration of this view into the religion, as if God's female population was inferior to the male by design.

The modern day women, such as Majid's aunts from the father side, were well respected judges, lawyers, teachers, senators, and anything they desired to be. They drove cars, attended colleges, and worked in factories. This however did not sit well with the poor, uneducated, and the angry part of the society, and hence it caused a split between women in southern and northern Tehran. The northern side found themselves free of obedience to their male counterparts, while women in southern side viewed that as a sin.

The dress code was very different among women in Iran. When walking on North Tehran streets, on occasions one could see women's underwear as some wore mini skirts. Considering the traveling abroad by the wealthy being a common practice, it was not unusual for some folks to continue wearing European style clothing at the time. On the other hand, on South Tehran streets and all other cities in Iran, just about all the women wore their chadors before they left their homes. Older women even covered their faces to make sure no amount of sin was committed. In many cases, young girls did not cover their faces, perhaps to reject the old way of doing things or maybe to indicate they are ready for marriage.

The clash of cultural values was playing an important role on the movie screens within Tehran. Some of the smaller theaters were showing X-rated movies which were packed by high school boys missing their afternoon class sessions. The adjacent streets to these theaters smelled like urination and trash if one passed through them.

In the opposite side of town, some of the mid-sized theaters over the weekend were enjoying large crowds of people watching and yelling in pride for Fardin. Fardin was the hero, the "007" in a lot of the movies - the person who was strong and someone that normally fought for the poor man's pride. For instance, in one of the movies, he was the man who was prepared to die for the pride of his sister who had committed suicide after being raped. In that movie, everyone in the theater was patiently waiting for Fardin to find and kill the guilty men, all three of them and take their lives even if he had to lose his. This type of movie was very popular among people that were feeling the society was moving in an opposite direction to their values, and God was under attack.

Ozra and a hand full of other women were the only ones still wearing their chadors when they left home in North Tehran. Ozra was born and raised in the holy city of Mashhad, and no one could change the set of beliefs she was accustomed to all her life. She had read the Koran from the first page to the last, at least once a year since age 14.

That year during the holy month of Ramadan, Majid escorted Ozra to a large mosque. On the 19th day of Ramadan, the first Saint of Shia, Ali (the 1st Imam), was stabbed by a sword during prayer, which took his life within two days. That was a very important day for all Shia Muslims. Ozra like many others had to remember the injustice done and cried her eyes out, and once in a while smacked herself on the head with the palm of her hand.

Considering Majid's age, he could not sit too far, but far enough not to be mixed with the women in the crowd. Majid normally tried to listen to the clergyman but there was too much distraction. Perhaps the biggest distraction was the young pretty girls that pretended to cover their faces but were not very successful, and Majid somehow could hear their giggles through all that noise.

That day was the highlight of the Shia religion, much similar to the other holy days when some of the other saints lost their lives by poison or simply were killed in a battle. This is probably why Shia religion is such an emotional one, since one continuously is reminded of the injustice of the past.

Ozra, among her friends, was highly regarded and she was placed right in the center to recite the Koran proudly with a loud and bold voice. It was all in Arabic and no one really understood what it meant but everybody chanted after Ozra while moving their bodies back and forth. No young children were allowed to sit too close to these women for they were all cleansed (**Pauk**). Children for not properly cleaning themselves after defecations or touching uncleansed material were considered **Najest**.

Majid who had taken a shower that very same day was considered Nagest by many of these older women that had not bathed for weeks in some cases. This is why Majid could never make any sense out of Najest and Pauk. Nor did he ever understand why anyone would read something that had no meaning to them. This was perhaps the reason why the new generation liked Dr. Shariati's perceptive of Islam rather than the old fashioned blind faith.

That summer was coming to an end and Majid had a big decision ahead of him. He would be entering the tenth grade which was the first of the last three years of high school. He had to decide what area of study to choose among Biology, Mathematics, or Literature. This was a major decision since the classes that followed would prepare the person toward a profession related in those areas.

Majid loved modern poetry, philosophy, and political debates, hence he chose Literature. This decision was quickly vetoed down by Akbar and everyone else in the family, simply because it was considered as a dead end street with little return on years of private school investment.

Pursuing a future in political poetry could have literally resulted in a dead end for Majid, a young emotional man. While easier to obtain a college degree in literature related fields, there was barely any money in those jobs to support a family. A degree in literature was no match to Ali's master degree in mechanical engineering, Mahmoud pursuing a doctorate degree in medicine, and Ahmad obtaining a degree in physics.

Akbar and Ozra both only having elementary school education degrees, and more so Ozra, were in competition for the first place among all the extended families to deliver the most educated children to the society.   On the surface, this seemed to be the case, but in reality the higher level degrees in engineering or medical field meant the higher the social status and financial rewards.

So Majid ended up majoring in Mathematics rather than Literature.   This however did not stop him from writing poems. He wrote as a hobby and for self-fulfillment.   He also recited poems in his single Literature class that everyone had to take regardless of their majors.   We will find the huge impact of his poetry on his life in the next chapter.   A month into the new school year, and being a spectator to the political tension between the so called freedom fighters and the Shah's regime, Majid wrote:

My Wishes...

How much would I wish,
    To be a dove and know how to fly?
        And to be free of the two dimensions
           Holding me down from the open sky!
How much would I want,
    To lose the earth, behind my wing,
        And find home in the clouds of justice,
           Rising above fear, and once again sing!
How much would I like,
    To stroll on a beach, in a sunny day,
        Walking at night when the shadows bite,
           In the light of the moon, finding my way!
How much would I desire,
    To smell the roses in the spring,
        And cut the thorns that stab me,
           Leave them behind, and none to bring!
Wishes are the poor man's dream,
    How could he fly? He has no wing,
        Moon never shines, and roses die,
           Gold and silver, belongs to the King!
Hope and wishes are the ink,
    A dance of colors on the paper,
        Majid's rhymes, for hearts to sing,
           Poems are written, today, for later!

This time period coincided with August 8th, 1974, when President Nixon resigned due to the Watergate scandal and Vice President Gerald Ford took the office. This was not very good for the Shah for he had built close ties with the President Nixon in his earlier trip to Iran. The Shah of Iran wanted to stay a major power in the Middle East and Watergate had a huge impact on watering his dreams out of the nation's gate!

President Ford had to pay all his attention to the internal affairs and uniting his nation together after Watergate, and this was the time that the opposition voices in Iran were perhaps falling on deaf ears at the White House. While Watergate left a few scars internally, it possibly had the most significant impact in the Middle East, and perhaps was the beginning of the end for the Shah and his dominance and control over the region.

With the increase in oil prices and Iran being free of the old oil treaty, the Shah was enjoying the increase in the oil revenue. While spending much of the money on the US made aircrafts and tanks, he was also trying to bring about huge changes or so-called modernization within the country. **The problem was that the rate of change was higher than what a large sector of society could handle, and the pain of change was mostly impacting the way of life for the middle class and the poor.**

The last three years of high school in a top-rated private school proved to be very difficult. Six days of school, six hours of lectures per day, with very well known and respected teachers that demanded perfection and infinite amount of homework was back breaking. Majid had to stay focused and work until the late hours of the night to get all his work done.

While the Shah had created the mechanism for many students in villages and rural areas to learn how to read and write and more public high schools were built, there were not too many colleges for higher education. Only several hundred students in a country with around a 40 million population attended medical schools, and a few thousand could end up in the respected engineering schools.

Not having enough colleges caused a large amount of dissatisfaction among the youth that could not obtain a higher degree to improve their lives, and created a huge competition among those who had the means to do so. This is why Akbar who was a long term visionary had no problem spending the money on Majid's school tuition to improve his chances for a brighter future.

While Majid only paid attention to studying during the next few years, the only thing that seemed to relax him was poetry. He wrote some of his own and read a number of modern and old style poems. He appreciated the work of old poets such as Khayam, Hafez, and Saadi. Majid was most taken by Khayam and his Rubaiyat, which was a selection of two lines or quatrain poems called Rubai.

Khayam after Abne-Sina or the mother of modern day medicine was perhaps the most respected and highly regarded person in Persian history. He was born in the State of Khorasan in the eleventh century and is believed to have lived over 80 years. While he was a mathematician and astronomer and the father of our modern day calendar year, he is known in the West for his Rubaiyat which was translated by Edward Fitzgerald (1809-1883), an English poet and translator.

Khayam did not want to be considered as a poet but a scientist who wrote a few poems. His Rubaiyat has been restored by a number of people and there are only a few hundred in existence today. His views regarding the universe, evolution, and even God were well beyond his time, and even the center of modern day debates. Here are a few modified translations of his Rubais, to the best of one's ability:

| As the Cock crows, those who stood before, |
| At the Tavern, shouted, "Open the door"! |
| You know, little time; we are given to stay, |
| When - gone, no one returns once more! |

| Come with Khayam, and leave the wise, |
| One thing is for sure, that life flies, |
| One is the fact, and the rest - all lies, |
| Once blown flower - for ever dies! |

| O Mullah, we work much harder than you, |
| Totally drunk, and still more sober than you, |
| You suck human blood, and we do grape, |
| In fairness, who is more immoral, than you? |

70

> If you are totally drunk, enjoy it,
>   If you are sitting with a beauty, enjoy it,
> For the universe ends in nothing,
>   Imagine you are gone, since you are, enjoy it!

> Secrets of universe, you don't know, nor I,
>   Solving of this puzzle, you don't know, nor I,
> Our dialogue stays behind closed curtains,
>   If the curtain drops, you won't survive, nor I!

> My friend, let's not worry about tomorrow,
>   Value the moment, enjoy it, and let it grow,
> Tomorrow, when we leave this world behind,
>   We are in journey with those, 7000 years ago!

Khayam's Rubaiyat shows his view of the world, the clergymen, and to some extent, his life style. While Khayam did not have much following through the mosque-goers, his poetry could be heard among people that enjoyed life for what it had to offer them, and among the scholars that read between the lines of his poetry.

Persian poetry was so deeply rooted in Iranians that some people met on a monthly basis to recite poems. There was even a radio poetry competition that the best were selected to compete. This radio program was based on many rules. Folks could not just recite a verse of a poem from memory but they also had to do it within a time constraint. Akbar knew thousands of poems by heart, and in many occasions he used it as a way of giving advice to his sons. Most of the poems he recited were from Saadi (119?-1292).

Saadi is one of the most famous Persian poets during medieval period. Ralph Waldo Emerson, an avid fan of Saadi, compared the wisdom and beauty of Saadi's poetry to the writing of The Bible. This is why at the United Nation's main entrance Saadi's translated poem is summarized as a mission statement:

> Of one Essence is the human race,
>   Thusly has Creation put it in the Base;
> One Limb impacted is sufficient,
>   For all Others to feel the Mace

The actual Farsi or Persian writing is written from the right to the left. In many cases, in translation of a poem, to make the verses hold its rhyme, the actual meaning and cultural values of the poem are lost. This poem has been recited by every Iranian over centuries. It has become the foundation of Persian kindness and compassion for the least among the population. The actual translation of the poem, to the best of one's ability is:

> Everyone in the human race are the members of one body - created from the same precious marble,
> If life brings a member pain - then it transfers to all the other members,
> If You ignore other people's sorrow, You are not a member of Human race!

Saadi's two famous books to humanity are the Bostan (The Orchard) and the Golestan (The Rose Garden). The Bostan is a set of stories written in verse promoting high virtues such as modesty, proper behavior, and elements of justice for living a spiritual life. He mixed humor and philosophy throughout the Golestan and always gave glorious praise to God in his works. Here are a few small selections from Bostan and Golestan:

> World has turned, and will turn many more,
> The wise never puts love, in this world's core,
> If you can give a helping hand to others, do it,
> Before it is too late, for nothing is for sure, ...

> The green leaves, in the mind of the Wise,
> Each is a book, God's blessing for its' Size!

> O' Saadi, man of greatness, never dies,
> Dead are those, whose life, are all lies!

Akbar, in particular, loved to recite the above verse to Majid since he was a young child. One can probably say Saadi was the spiritual side of Islam in Iran throughout centuries, for it was much easier to recite Persian poems to young children as a code of conduct, than reading the Koran in Arabic in which many did not know the meaning and the translation.

Another famous and influential poet from the same time frame, who was also born in Shiraz several decades after Saadi, was Hafez (1320-1389). The book which is a collection of all his works and is known as Divan-e-Hafez consists of 500 of his Ghazals and 42 of his Rubaiyats. Ghazal and Rubaiyat are simply a different way of reciting poems and each have a different rhyme scheme. At a young age Hafez was forced by his father to memorize the Koran. Later on in his life, this led him into memorizing the work of famous poets and scholars such as Saadi, and Attar who was heavily influenced by Rumi.

Hafez had lost his father at an early age and had to leave day school to work at a bakery in his early teens. When he was twenty one, while delivering bread at a rich part of town, he fell in love with a young woman of incredible beauty known as Shakh-e-nabat. While this love did not lead to anything due to the clash of classes and he married someone else, throughout his life his poetry was heavily impacted as a result of his pain and sorrow surrounding this matter. Here is the translation of some of his work, to the best of one's ability:

I've nothing to show for my life but sorrow,
My love, good and bad, all has been sorrow,
My cheating companion, was none but pain,
My lovely fiancée is no one - but sorrow!

My friend, why hurt the foe, let go!
Drink wine with a beautiful face, let go!
Be engaged in a dialog with intelligence,
And stay away from the ignorance, let go!

The following is the modified translation of Ghazal 79 by Shahriar Shahriari, as a sample from Hafez's 500 Ghazals:

1	The heavenly breeze comes to this estate,
	I sit with the wine and a lovely mate,
2	Why can't the beggar play the king's role,
	The sky is the dome, the earth is my state,
3	The green grass feels like Paradise,
	Why would I trade this for the garden gate?

4	With bricks of wine, build towers of love,
	Being bricks of clay, is our final fate,
5	Seek no kindness of those full of hate,
	People of mosque and church, they debate,
6	Don't bad mouth me, using my name in vain,
	Only God can choose, my story narrate,
7	**Neither Hafez's corpse, nor his life negate,**
	With all his misdeeds, heaven for him awaits.

At the time, and for most of the time after Islam became a dominating and influential religion in Iran, Islamic clergy frowned upon Khayam and Hafez, for their type of poetry. They did not like the words such as wine, talking about the beauty of opposite sex, and the philosophical discussion of the universe. For this reason when Hafez died the orthodox clergy opposed an Islamic burial for him, which created an atmosphere of conflict and debates in Shiraz.

To solve this problem, much like Este-khareh, it was agreed for a young boy to open one of the pages of "Divan-e-Hafez" for guidance. It was verse **7** of Ghazal 79, which not only cleared Hafez's name with the clergy, it made the use of his book as a way of predicting the future. This is called "Fal-e-Hafez", and it is used by many people, in particular the ones in love, as a guidance.

During this time frame, religion in Iran seemed to play a complementary role to one's way of life, but Persian philosophy and poetry both old and modern played an ongoing role.

It was March 19th, 1975 and two days before the Persian New Year. Majid was done with the first half of his school year, and everyone was ready for the New Year. It was early in the morning when the phone rang and Ozra answered. Not long after, as expected in the culture, Ozra was crying very loudly by the phone for hearing about the loss of one of the family members.

It was her youngest sister's husband, a Major who was ranked very high for his age. He had a heart operation at Cleveland clinic in Ohio two years earlier which resulted in prolonging his life a few years. Her sister had two young children ages four and six, and this was difficult for everyone to watch. In Iran, due to the importance of virginity before marriage (mainly female gender), barely any widows with children ever married again.   Ozra's sister was only 25 years old and this made everyone sad in many different ways.

According to the Islamic rules, he had to be buried within a day, and hence all the family gathered to pray for the soul.   Being a Muslim did not guarantee the gates of heaven rolling open; it was the deeds and one's way of living that was considered to play an important role.   The dead body was to be covered with a white garment and then placed in a coffin after the proper washing and cleaning process was performed.

The burial ceremony, once again had many similarities to the Zoroastrian religion which originated over 3,000 years ago. The center piece of Zoroastrian religion is Good Thoughts, Good Words, and Good Deeds, so for three days after death, one would be evaluated on these merits to allow the soul to enter heaven or hell.   It seems many of the concepts in one religion are similar to the others, their origins sometimes being hundreds and in some cases thousands of years apart.

That year, New Year went fast, without much celebration within the family.   Young children still received presents but not too many families visited one another during the 13-day holiday season.

It was summer of 1975, and the Shah, with the additional oil revenue was committed to modernization and cleaning up of many areas in Tehran and other major cities.   It seemed as if he was trying very hard to improve the country's image in the world, and to increase tourism.

One of the major projects the Shah took on was the area around Imam Reza's Shrine in Mashhad.   It was not the immediate area around the Shrine that had people upset, but complete destruction and renovation of the stores in the surrounding area.   Considering the size of Imam Reza's Shrine, the number of stores demolished were several hundreds if not more.

Reza's father was one of the victims of this financial massacre.   In over two months he lost his entire savings and business, his expensive equipment used for knitting fabrics and making sweaters had to be sold in a fire sale for a dime on a dollar. When the Government made a move, SAVAK made sure to do away with anyone who was a potential concern for them, as a function of homeland security. Not too many people have much to say in a dictatorship, and Reza's father with a wife and five children did not have much to say either.

Reza's dad with no government assistance had to rebuild his future at age 50. Like Akbar, who found his future in the city of Tehran, he had to leave his family in Mashhad to start over again in Tehran. Family elders, mostly old established men, had a meeting and lent some funds to the newcomer. He was able to start over and pay everyone their money back, and then some.

While beautifying Mashhad was a success, the number of people losing their livelihoods and even some losing their lives either by heart attack or suicide, did not paint a pretty picture in people's mind. It was the general perception that the Shah either did not know, or simply did not care about the impact of his course of actions on these victims. Many of these folks, some with deep pockets, and some connected to the deeply rooted clergy establishment in the Shia holy cities, made a note of this. This even angered many of the major Ayatollahs outside the country. They either resided outside the country by choice or had been exiled.

All these discussions at home, with Majid's ongoing anger toward the Shah and reading of some of Dr. Shariati's books, made Majid more interested in Islam as a way of change in the existing conditions of the people. While boys had to start learning how to pray on a daily basis by the age 16, he was committed to an early start. Ozra, who did not like to drink a cup of water without the approval of Mullahs, did not like her son breaking the law by praying at an earlier age.

This however did not stop Majid. I guess he needed to channel his dismay into something other than his poetry. So, like anyone else who prays globally, he learned how to pray in Arabic which was not his native language. After a couple months, Majid realized, after all that - he was not a common Joe and he needed to understand the meaning of what he was praying. Here is the meaning of the first prayer in English, to his understanding at the time:

Ozra did not like to be challenged by her own 14 year old son about the meaning of the daily prayers, nor would anyone that had prayed all their lives without a comprehensive understanding of it. Majid, after all those years of education and knowing 2 plus 2 must result in 4, was not letting this go. **One must apply logic to anything in life, especially if it does not make any sense.**

So Majid who tried to look at things from another dimension, decided to learn the complete meaning of the prayer in Farsi. During the prayer, he first said the prayers in Arabic and then Farsi, all by and from heart. This was a big sin being committed by Ozra's definition. But by Majid's definition **God wanted to help us improve our way of life by prayers and morality, and not just praying for the sake of being forgiven by God.**

After that summer, Majid started the eleventh grade. The national competition for entering highly ranked universities in Iran was very tough, and only the tough could prepare for such a monstrous challenge. It was the beginning of the two years of hell on earth to prepare for the national exam. Since Majid was only 14 years old, Ozra became the chairman and CEO of Majid's day to day activities, which were mostly studying, and not a whole lot of other activities.

Within a month into that school year, Akbar who was studying, memorizing the signs, and preparing to get his driving license at age 62, decided to buy a one year old Iranian made car called "Paycaun." He got a good deal on the car, and to surprise the family, he decided to drive the car home without a license and having little driving experience.

It was about 11:00 p.m. that night when he arrived home with no car. On the way to the house he was in a major accident and the car was almost totaled.   Luckily, he was not hurt and he did not go to jail for driving without a license. He had skillfully paid off the officer attending the accident, for not having a license. This amounted to about $500 in today's market value to let him go free.

Akbar studied two months to pass his written exam and tried over six times to pass his driving test, which he eventually did.   After being in seven accidents within six months, the family decided for him to quit driving before someone was hurt.   With around 4 million people and major traffic jams, Tehran was not a place for a 62 year old man to learn how to drive.   This is why once again Akbar began taking the bus and occasionally walked for an hour to his place of work.

Since Akbar did not drive the family car any longer, Ahmad would take the car on occasion without Akbar's permission to give rides to the public and make a few tomans (seven tomans per dollar at the time).   Majid also took the car in and out of the house and drove it around a few blocks after school. On a few instances he even drove Ozra to her sister's house, upon her request.   This however was not a wise choice, considering that he did not have a driver's license!

January of 1976 proved to be a very cold month that year. There was a tremendous amount snow everywhere, and the rooftops carried a big load. It was Majid's job to shovel all that heavy snow from the rooftop.   The roofs were flat and required much work to shovel the snow off of them.   While Mashhad was as cold as Cleveland, Ohio; Tehran's climate was more like Columbus, Ohio.

Cold or not, there was not too much to do, other than studying.   All seasons had the flavor of books, days and nights went by as fast as turning another page of a chemistry book, or solving another math problem.   It was not Adam and Eve, but math and science thrown out of heaven to create hell for Majid on a daily basis.

A month before the eleventh grade was over Akbar who was under pressure from Ozra finally purchased the first family television set.   It was elegant and somewhat pricey, with only one problem- Majid was not allowed to watch it until the school year was over.   It was toward the end of the school year, and Majid had to study for all his comprehensive exams.   Majid could not understand the timing of this purchase, as if he did not have enough to be worried about.

And there it was - the last exam in eleventh grade, and Majid was finally done. Now he had only one more year of high school to finish up after that summer.   On the way home the only thing he could think of was sitting in front of the television set and enjoying it for a few hours.   At that time, Iranian TV offered three channels, two in Farsi and one in English.   The programs did not start until late in the afternoon, and Majid was planning to catch the first show.

The English TV channel showed some American football and programs geared to satisfy the Americans living in Iran.   Of course, it was being televised in English, and Majid once in a while tried to watch it to improve his English, but the game of football was too harsh and meaningless for him to watch.

The other two TV channels in Farsi had a variety of shows and commercials.   Commercials were only at the end of each show and not during it.   Programs included celebrations, new and old American movies and even some funny shows with its Iranian dialect, and some Iranian made movies and serials that lasted for one year and beyond.   Iranian programs followed a very similar format to the American produced programs.   Majid's three favorite American shows were "The Six Million Dollar Man", "Iron Side" and "The Three Stooges."

Majid, at last was at home.   Studying so hard during the school year had placed him in the second place in his class of 42 with all the tough competition in this top-rated private school.   He was very happy to be done, and finally grab a snack to enjoy in front of the TV, that Thursday afternoon.   One of Majid's uncles (by marriage) was in the reception room talking with another relative when Akbar came home early from work.   Akbar without any hesitation or even asking turned off the TV while Majid was watching it.   Majid felt insulted and protested this decision by saying "What is wrong now?   I am done with all my exams".

Akbar paused and said, "You need to go and purchase your books for the next year and start studying."   Majid felt as if someone spilled a gallon of ice water on his head, and with a shaky voice shouted, "I can not take this anymore.   I suppose if I am

dead, you would make sure I am buried with a bunch of books."
While this comment sounded funny to Majid's uncle, a high school
physics teacher, it was very insulting to Akbar.

Majid started to walk away but Akbar caught up with him
and tried to slap him across the face. That was the first time he
was doing such a thing to Majid and for multiple reasons.
Education was everything to Akbar, and talking back to one's
father while walking away was considered a major disrespect. He
was not ready to take that from his youngest son. Majid pulled his
arms up in the air protecting his face from the abuse. This even
made Akbar angrier while Majid's uncle was playing a peace
making role. Akbar did not speak with Majid for three days
because of his rude behavior, and Majid did not watch much
television that summer either.

I guess at that age, Majid could not realize that something
else was really bothering Akbar. Several months earlier, Akbar
the capitalist, had purchased 16 tons of rice, two brands, Basmati
and Rose, and had stored the cache in the basement of the house.
This was to satisfy the businessman inside Akbar and to help him
with additional income. His marketing strategy was to sell the
rice to the local shops on a monthly basis.

Local shops were spread out in every corner of every block
in large cities, and Akbar knew the owners. However, there were
two problems that Akbar did not put in his equation. First, that 16
tons of rice was about 10-fold too much to satisfy the required
demand, and second and most critical, was that the biggest
consumers of rice were the neighborhood mice.

A couple weeks after the incident with Majid, Akbar sold
all his rice to a major distributor in that type of business without
much loss. However, he was not very nice with the mouse
population in the basement. Let's just say this time all the cats in
the neighborhood had a mouse party.

A big burden was removed from Akbar's back and he
seemed to be much happier. To everybody's surprise, a couple
weeks later, Akbar came home for lunch with three American
Hippies. At that time, there were some Americans that did not
have much money, yet they traveled the world, ate anything, slept
anyplace and let each day surprise them in a different way.

Akbar knew a few English words such as "Food, My house, etc.", and that was good enough for the three strangers to get off the bus and follow him to the house. Ozra was ready to have a heart attack after seeing all those people in her house. She brought Akbar to the kitchen and angrily asked "What am I supposed to feed them?" How do you know they like what we eat?" In the meanwhile Majid was entertaining the long blonde haired guys wearing raggedy tee shirts with his broken English.

That day the family did not share their lunch with the strangers, they simply gave them all their food, that is, rice and chicken kabob. The hippies seemed to be very hungry, and with her sense of hospitality Ozra did not have the heart to send them away starving. The family ate some bread and cheese as they always did for breakfast. In the Persian culture, and culture of Tarrof, you feed the guest before thinking about taking a bite yourself, and that truly was a good example for Majid.

While that was an interesting experience for Majid, the following week, he encountered one that had a gigantic impact on him. Majid went on a trip with Ali to a brick factory, or shall I say just a place where they made bricks. While Ali was talking with the person in charge, Majid was sitting on a chair viewing a row of 15 shacks. Each shack was a place for one family to live, a space of 100 square feet with no water, no electricity, and barely anything else.

Some women were cooking food in a pot, mostly water with some beans and potatoes, on the fire and attending all the children left behind. There was one child in particular, a two year old girl that stole Majid's heart for life. She was sitting on dirt with a small bowl of yogurt in her hand. With her dirty hands she was wiping the tear from her beautiful brown eyes and then adding dirt to her bowl of yogurt. Majid did not have the heart to watch the flies all over her, while she was putting the yogurt in her mouth. **He turned his face around for he had no heart to see, yet opened his heart to the face of hunger, in the brown eyes of an angel, ever unseen!**

Majid noticed most of these children had large stomachs, but why? This did not make any sense to him and it seemed like a good question for Mahmoud who was finishing up his medical school. Mahmoud explained to him that it was due to the amount of rice, potatoes, and starchy foods the poor people consumed. That made sense, for poor people did not have the means to purchase meat, but rice and potatoes were very cheap. This in turn was causing diabetes and other problems for them in earlier ages. Some would lose their vision in their early forties and it was common for some to lose their lives in their fifties.

It is always easier to attend one's holy sight, like a mosque or a church and pray for the poor, and in the process feel righteous. Though, it is by far harder to go in the midst of the unfortunate and lend them a hand out of their difficulties, and to shower them with God's unconditional love. This was Majid's first experience seeing the absolute pain of poverty in the eyes of the poor, while they were baking the bricks for the rich man's home, in their hunger and suffering. Majid wrote the following poem within that week from his visit:

"Closed Doors"
How do you open the closed doors?
The door keeping my heart in pain?
How long is the secret in my heart?
The story of rich man, gone insane!
How do you grow crops and plants?
When there is no water, and no rain?
How could I look at the hungry eyes,
And leave them - - - with no shame?
Lord, open the closed door of minds,
Lead us – so your love will remain!

While poverty seemed to be the way of life on the south side of Tehran, the north side seemed to be a different country all together. European style stores, multiple floor shopping centers, and even American style supermarkets were everywhere. Some of the supermarkets were designed to serve the Americans and European customers with the cashiers speaking in English.

Many companies like General Tire and others had subsidiaries in Iran. Also, a large number of Americans worked with the National Oil Company, and many had an occupation as training personnel for the military. As one observed certain parts of the country, to a large extent Iran seemed like the 51st State of the United States, except it was not listed as such. As the number of Americans was on the rise in Iran, so were many other service providers such as Indian doctors and Philippino nannies. Many of these changes were creating a level of international exposure and diversity, bringing a breath of fresh air to the youth. Yet at the same time it was causing much disorder for the older generation who were clinging on to anything, whether religion or old cultural values, to defy change.

The summer of 1976 was coming to an end and Majid was anxious to begin the last year of high school. At the same time, people in the United States were getting ready to vote for the next president. President Ford, with much support from the Shah of Iran, was running against Governor Jimmy Carter. The public disgust with the political corruption following Nixon's resignation helped Jimmy Carter, the unknown "fresh face" with barely any exposure to international politics, to become the next elected President of the United States. This occurred in November of 1976.

Carter becoming the Democratic nominee, and the victory of Ford over Regan with the smallest of margins among the Republican candidates, played an important role in the selection of the American president, one of the major leaders in the world. While Americans, or about 4.2% of the population of the earth, chose the next American President, the world watched the election with much anxiety. This is because the **American Foreign policies had, and to this day has, a major impact on the other countries, especially in the Middle East.** Carter's election was probably the beginning of the end for the Shah of Iran. This will be explained in the next chapter.

Twelfth grade proved to be every bit of what Majid had imagined and more. While classes began at 8:00 in the morning, on Thursdays it started at 6:30 a.m. due to one teacher's time conflict. The general classes included Literature and Composition, English, History, Physics, and Chemistry. However, there were six different classes in mathematics, and they required much homework.

The only fun activity for Majid was to watch people while walking back home from his school. Sometimes the high school girls from a few miles down the road would be walking with the boys from Majid's school. One could hear them from a distance cracking jokes and giggling. While Majid passed by the crowds, and enjoyed many of the pretty faces, he was too shy to speak with anyone, and too determined to do well in his studies. He was simply not looking for any distractions.

In many instances, a lot of boys were smoking cigarettes to act cool in front of the girls, and in some cases, they were even smoking illegal drugs. Using opium in a moderate manner by the elders for pleasure, or being used to remove pain by the sick was not frowned upon. Yet the young generation's use of hashish to simply have fun was a new trend on the rise, and to many people it was a troubling sign. Many people believed that one of the Shah's sisters was behind the drug trafficking, and that was not sitting well with the people either.

Three months into the school year, Majid was enrolled in additional private classes to increase the odds of getting into his favorite college, which was Tehran University. Three days each week, after he arrived home from school at 3:00 pm, he had a late lunch and then took the bus through the congested streets of Tehran to go to those classes, take more notes and yet do more homework. These classes were so packed that at times students had no place to sit and they had to take notes while standing.

The Persian New Year of March 21st, 1977, passed Majid by extremely fast that year while he was studying during the days and nights. The Shah was also very busy modernizing the city of Tehran by destroying the old shacks in the south part of Tehran and replacing them with new homes. The poor people could not afford the new homes, and in some cases would not leave their shacks. After a number of warnings, the order was to bring them down with or without people in them, even if the tenants refused to cooperate. While the mud on the poor man's head took a hand full of lives, the perceived and frequently repeated stories of those unseen events continued softening the dirt under the Shah's feet.

While the voice of poor and weak did not reach the Shah's ears hidden under his crown which was worth over 50 million dollars at the time, it did resonate in the public domain and with the story tellers. The Shah had been the King since 1941, and even with a bit of an interruption during 1953, he was returned to power by the CIA and MI5. As an old statesman, surviving all his adversaries, it made the Shah look invincible in the eyes of the White House, and the new President.

Majid did not have much time to follow politics or watch the news since he had to study for two major exams, one, a National Exam on all the twelfth grade core classes, and another one several weeks after that called Conkour. Conkour was a comprehensive exam testing one's knowledge in national and worldwide science, mathematics, English, geography, history, etc. The score from the two exams were added using a formula and then each student was rated among several hundred thousand people or possibly in the low millions that took the test.

Before knowing the rating results, students had to pick their top 10 choices of universities and programs. Students with the highest grades would be the first to fill up the open positions for those programs if the accepted students actually signed up in that program. There were too many students, and too few reputable colleges, hence tough competition. The top 1,000 had a chance to attend the medical school, and the top 5,000 had an opportunity for one of the engineering schools. However, in order to be accepted by the highly rated engineering colleges, one had to place in the top 2000.

The final exams were held during May of that year. The 16-year old Majid felt very confident about his abilities, and with an air of superiority took the exams, rushed through them because of his youth, and turned them in before anyone else. He had completed his test in half the allotted timed! This proved not to be an intelligent decision due to his minor silly mistakes, or maybe it was meant to be!

While Majid scored fairly high in the national exam, he knew it was not high enough. You could compare it to scoring between 1,450 and 1525 on the SAT out of a possible 1,600. Majid had to pull off magic during Conkour to improve his total grade. The already exhausted Majid slept about 5 hours a day and the rest was studying, memorizing, walking around the house holding a book, and falling sleep with a pencil in his hand.

Majid was able to do very well in the Conkour, but was it good enough? Majid only applied for top rated universities such as Tehran and Poly-Technique with his ten choices. While his overall rating put him in the top 2,500 nationwide, he was not in the top 2,000 which was required for the programs he had applied for. Therefore his name did not appear in the national paper as being accepted by any of those universities. This by far - was Majid's biggest failure in life - shattered pride - and a family devastated by the outcome.

Pride in Iranian culture played an important role, and the 16 year old Majid felt he had let everyone down. A couple times he considered jumping off the roof top to end the pain inside, but his logic held him back. He even out of anger hit one of the expensive dining room chairs against the floor and broke it in pieces. Every person in the family felt his pain but no one could offer him any cure!

There were a few choices to consider. One was to wait another year and take the two national exams over. This was Majid's last choice. Next was to take other small tests for some of the private colleges that required significant college tuition, and the third choice was to apply for universities in the United States. Majid loved the last choice even though it was the most expensive one, for every affluent student of his age group wanted to go abroad, in particular the USA.

Majid was a nervous wreck for his eyes blinked at a rate of 20 times per minute. It was determined by the doctors that this was a nervous behavior due to the circumstances and mainly lack of sleep. Sleeping was the last thing he worried about, for his future was at a cross section.

As usual the head of the household, Akbar had to make a decision on how to proceed. Akbar was ready to hand down the decision to and for Majid. The Day of Judgment had finally arrived. Waiting for another year and taking the exams over was a choice from hell for Majid. Studying and passing the requirements of private colleges in Iran, as recommended by many of the family members, was not his top choice. Majid's dream was the unimaginable dream of going to the United States, but how? And how could the family afford it?

Akbar had all the members of the immediate family gathered and gave a short speech about Majid's future. He rejected Mahmoud's idea for Majid to take the exams over, or the option from hell as Majid called it. His preference for Majid was to take the exams for some of the private colleges, and also to apply for some of the universities in the United States, in particular the University of Akron which was less than half an hour from his brother's house.

Majid could not be any happier with his father's decision. Not only did he did not close the door to the idea of continuing education in America, but he also had him sign up with the Simin Organization to improve his English. Simin only offered English classes in Comprehension, Grammar, and Speech. His Grammar teacher was Iranian; his teacher for Speech was British, while his Comprehension teacher was American. Attending those classes was the pre-requisition for taking Heaven in the following semester, or that's how it looked to the 16 year old Majid. Majid would walk home speaking English to himself, and singing "I've seen fire, and I've seen rain, I've seen sunny days, etc" by James Taylor. While Majid was no longer depressed and looking to his future with much hope, hope did not seem to play a role for the poor in the south part of Tehran, and their children.

It was August of 1977 and Majid was signed up to take the test with RCD, an American-based University in Iran that mainly offered economics. It was one of the new and highly respected universities in Tehran. All the teachers were assumed to be Americans and all the subjects were covered in English. It was an opportunity for the students to learn about the American world of economy or where the perceived global economy was heading.

Only 3,000 applications were accepted which enabled the students to take their test. If Majid could not go to USA, this looked like the next best option to him. The test was all in English for each subject matter. When the test was completed, Majid felt good about his performance on it. But, Majid badly wanted to be accepted by the University of Akron to improve his chances of going to the United States, for obvious reasons.

The phone rang - it was one of Majid's cousins who took the same test and unfortunately was not accepted. She told Ozra, Majid's name was 21st out of the 50 students that the University accepted and his name was listed in the national paper. Many of the students accepted were either the children of American citizens residing in Iran or had English speaking parents that resided in the United States for a while. Majid's pride was finally back, and now he had some options.

In the meanwhile Majid was also accepted by all the universities he applied for in the United States. Being accepted at the RCD University would help Majid fluently speak English, and make it much easier for him to complete his graduate studies anywhere in the world. Therefore, the key question became "why send him to the United States and spend all that money for his education?"

While everybody was in favor of Majid staying and attending the RCD University, there was only one person wishing for Majid to go, and that was Majid himself. Majid never asked his father to send him to the America, but his actions were louder than his tongue and his face revealed the story of his heart!

From a young age, Akbar treated Majid with much love and respect, for he believed that Majid brought much needed change to his life. Also considering that Ali never went to the United States despite all the scholarship opportunities, Akbar did not mind his youngest son doing so. However, Akbar was 60 years old and sending a son to the United States meant at least $8,000 per year at that time, while his annual salary was only $18,000. So what was there to do to make a wise decision for Majid's life and his future? Akbar decided to do the "**Este-khareh**".

The selected room, the place for Este-khareh was cleaned in advance and the house was very quiet when Akbar started the "Vozo" or the process of self cleansing. Majid had to do the same and enter the room with Akbar while Akbar cleansed his soul through an hour of reading the Koran and at times having tears coming down from his eyes. Majid's life and his future depended on it as well, so naturally tears were falling off of his cheeks at a much faster rate.

Akbar started reading the Koran at a faster speed and chanting. Majid knew in a few minutes, his destiny would be written in the book, literally. Then Akbar started a separate prayer while holding his arms toward the sky and asked God, the God of Universe, if it was a wise decision, with all things considered to send Majid to the United States. Then he skillfully, while praying, opened the Koran and started reading the top verse. Majid's eyes were glued to the top of the page - it indicated "Good."

Akbar for the second time, and after praying for another five minutes, challenged God with the same question and once again randomly opened the Koran. Once again, it opened on a page - saying "Good." For the third time, Akbar followed the same routine but asked God, if it would be in Majid's best interest to stay in Iran and attend the RCD University. The reply from the Koran -was "Bad."

Majid's body was as cold as ice, the hair on his body was pulling from his skin and jabbing him everywhere, his heart was full of unimaginable joy, and through all the tears dancing in his eyes, he could only stare at his father and was speechless. That was the moment of truth, and who could deny - God. Akbar after completing the prayer, very calmly squeezed his son in joy, and asked him to prepare for the journey. He was the head of household, and no one at that point could deny his judgment, especially after his Este-khareh.

Majid left the room with a big smile on his face, and in much excitement, shared the news with the rest of family members. Ozra was not happy to let her baby move thousands of miles away. His other brothers were puzzled with their father's decision, for he had never wasted a penny in his life and now was willing to spend thousands. But the bigger question in everybody's mind was that, "How is he going to pay for it?"

The next day Akbar called Ali in one of the rooms at the house and had him close the door. Ali, his wife and their two month old son were residing in the second floor saving their money to buy their first home in cash. Majid knew the discussion would be about him, so he put his ears close to the door to listen to what was being said.

Akbar had a plan to send Majid to the United States and he wanted to bounce it off his oldest son Ali, then about 31 years old. Considering the family structure and behavior in Iran, and the level of expectations from the oldest son, Ali proudly offered to pay about $150 per month toward Majid's expenses in the United States. Akbar rejected that and said, "I am an old man, but I am not a dead man, and I will have a second job to support my son's expenses without any need from another human being."

Akbar paused for a second, while Majid was sweating behind the closed door and pressing his ears further into the door to hear the rest of what his father had to say. He continued, with a bit of a tremble in his voice, "However, considering my age if I happen to pass away while Majid is attending his school, you will be in charge of managing his expenses with what I leave behind and you must support your brother with whatever financial shortcomings there may be." Ali, without a second ticking away took on the responsibility while Majid's sweat and tears were joining on the palm of his hands.

Majid had to hurry up and get his visa to travel to the United States before he turned 17 years old. He only had three months left. If he did not have his visa and his letters of acceptance by the University to prove the continuation of his education, then he would have to serve in the military for two years - that was the law. Since Majid was already accepted by The University of Akron, he simply had to make an appointment and get in the line at three o'clock in the morning at the American Embassy gate with all his documents.

While Majid's mood was jubilant after obtaining his visa, that was not the case in the streets of Tehran. The opposition to the Shah's regime was building up and in some instances a few theaters were burned down to the ground for showing movies with too much sexual content. Students attending the universities were causing a lot of pain for the establishment, and none of this was good news to the Shah of Iran.

On November 15, 1977, the Shah and his wife, Mrs. Farah Pahlavi, visited the United States, and had their first meeting with President and Mrs. Carter. The following is from the Collection of public papers of the President; book II by President Jimmy Carter:

The President began by expressing his personal pleasure at meeting His Imperial Majesty for the first time, noting that this visit will enable them to establish close personal ties of friendship. The President expressed his appreciation for His Majesty's message of condolence to the families of those who lost their lives in the recent disaster in Georgia.

The President reaffirmed to His Majesty that he fully supports the special relationship which the two countries have developed over the last 30 years and gave his personal commitment to strengthen further our ties. The President emphasized the broad mutuality of our interests in the region and globally, and expressed appreciation for the support which Iran has extended in achieving our shared objectives. The President reiterated the importance that he attaches to a strong, stable, and progressive Iran under the leadership of His Imperial Majesty. To that end, he emphasized that it remains the policy of the United States to cooperate with Iran in its economic and social development programs and in continuing to help meet Iran's security needs.

Nowhere in their public discussions, was there a mention of the unrest among the population in Iran. Nor was there any discussion about the political prisoners and executions in the follow up meeting in Iran on December 31st of that year. Here is another piece:

THE PRESIDENT. Your Imperial Majesties, distinguished officials, and citizens of Iran:

My own Nation has been blessed this year by an official visit of His Imperial Majesty, the Shah, and by the Shahbanou, Empress Farah. This was a fine gesture of friendship. And we also benefited from extensive discussions between the Shah and myself of important issues for Iran and for the United States. I am proud and pleased to be able to come to Iran at the end of this year, my first year in office and, I believe, your 27th year (37th year)[1] as a leader of this great nation, and to begin another new year with our close friends and allies.

[1] Printed in the White House press release.

When President Carter said 27 years in the above speech, he did not realize the Shah was the king during the following American presidencies; Franklin Roosevelt, Truman, Eisenhower, Kennedy, Johnson, Nixon, Ford, and now him. Did President Carter question the Shah of Iran about "Human Rights" violations behind the closed doors? This remains a good and viable question for him.

By January 17, 1978, Majid had already purchased his plane ticket to the United States. His plane was via Iran-Air to London, England, and from there to JFK, in New York, on March 3rd of that year. Seconds did not seem to go fast enough for a young man in search of his future. He was the second member of his extended family after his uncle, to go to the United States. It seemed as though everybody was happy for, yet jealous of him, for being able to go to the United States at such a young age.

Majid was having a hard time finding his old friend Jamshid. For the last two years of high school, he was too busy to give attention to Jamshid. The three inch Jamshid who resembled the Walt Disney Mickey Mouse, with a name that represented the Persian Kingdom was nowhere to be found. Days were passing by, and Majid wanted to bring his old friend along on the trip, but where was he?

After much search, Majid found Jamshid below the bottom drawer in his desk, where he did his homework. It was not a pretty scene, for the hat was missing, and Jamshid's head was barely holding on to his body. Jamshid, the representative of the Persian Kingdom as the name suggests, was Majid's best friend through the good, bad, and ugly. What happened to Jamshid - and how would that impact Majid, in the years come? Majid was heart broken and made sure to give Jamshid a proper, well deserved burial, in a five inch deep hole next to a rose in their garden.

Ozra was also filled with sadness, not because Majid was upset about losing his 3" plastic toy, but because his son was leaving her beyond the mountains and plains, lands and oceans, and would be about 10,000 miles away. Would she ever get to see him again, will he be able to take care of himself? She had many questions and no answers. The only comfort was that Majid's uncle was not living far away.

The last two days before Majid left for the United States, their house was full of guests, many of whom Majid had never seen before. It felt as if Majid was preparing for a trip to the moon. It seemed as if folks saw their own reflections in the eyes of a young man leaving for an industrialized nation, where the sky was the limit to the new innovations, and freedom actually meant something.

The night before the early morning flight, about 20 of the guests stayed over to go to the airport with the family. Ozra cried for two days in a row, and had two asthma attacks that night. Majid did not get much sleep, but when he woke up at six o'clock in the morning, he found himself tied to Ozra by two pairs of pantyhose. It looked funny, yet painful, for Ozra was not taking the separation well.

At the airport, Majid kissed everyone on the cheeks, and everyone passed on their love back to him in the same manner. Each member of his family had the last word with him before he waved good-bye to over 50 people.

Akbar kissed his son and said "Study every page in life, and make sure you understand what it means." "Write to me twice a week if not more," said Ozra with tears crackling her voice. Ali said, "Make sure you obtain your PhD in Engineering," Mahmoud followed that with, "You will enter the land of equality, work hard, and you will be anything you wish to be." Ahmad, the jokester of the family said "Remember all the money you had in your desk last week and you could not find it; I already put it to a good use."

And with that last statement, while everybody was laughing, Majid left for a new beginning to unknown horizons. Majid left for America.

Turbulent Years

It was early in the morning of March 3rd, 1978 when Majid entered the 747 Boeing aircraft for his final destination point, Cleveland, Ohio's Hopkins Airport. That was the first time Majid was traveling all alone, the first time on an airplane or perhaps the largest bird in the sky.

Before the airplane took off, Majid kept looking out of the window as if he was looking at all the ropes connecting him to his past, and he could hear the engines of life running to connect him to his future. His heart was filled with sadness and his mind was full of joy; was that two people in one? He was breaking from the past that had delivered him to that day, yet excited to meet the challenges of life ahead and the promises of a bright future. Majid had a great plan for his future, yet life would have a few surprises of its own.

The second the airplane left the ground at Mehrabad airport, Majid felt like a child in the womb that had to survive the new challenges and yet to be born again into a new life of unknowns.

Imagine moving to a country where so many aspects were different – the language, its values both cultural and social, the religion, its variety of races, and most importantly, the way of life. While these differences would present big difficulties for people in their mid-thirties and above, they were only another page in Majid's book of new things to learn and enjoy.

Iran Air at that time had a direct flight to New York via London, so after a couple of hours of refueling time, Majid was on his way to his dreamland. Majid always had a roadmap in his life; it very much began when he jumped from the 4th to 7th grade, and now it was wide open for imagination. He was determined to get his masters degree in one of the engineering fields, return to Iran to get married, and go back to United Stated for his PhD and residence. Would he ever achieve that goal or any of it? That was the big question that was laid in front of him.

It was early March and the weather was not friendly. The flight from London to NewYork was bumpy, and a blizzard in New York State had JFK airport shut down. Majid by now had a total of three hours sleep within the previous 36 hours. All the excitement for a young man did not allow him to get more than a wink of sleep. Finally the plane landed after circling in the air for hours before permission to land was granted, but at LaGuardia instead of JFK airport.

I guess this, in the total picture, was a great beginning to over 4 years of turbulence in Majid's life. The confused Majid with some ability to speak English with perfect grammar but with no knowledge of any slang was having difficulties understanding the people's accent. Somehow with much help from the folks in the airport, he was able to find his way to JFK.

Majid was too exhausted to admire the size of the airport and the diversity that existed among different races. On that cold night, just about all the flights were cancelled. Majid looked like the only young man wearing a suit and a tie and walking around the airport aimlessly. His flight from JFK to Hopkins was cancelled and the next available one was the same time in about 20 hours. It took Majid over an hour to figure out the mess he was in, but that really was not too bad for a brain which was not functioning on any food or sleep, and was operating in the same manner as a zombie.

After one hour of sitting anxiously, Majid had a bright idea in his half dead brain. He walked to the ticket desk and asked the lady if there was any quicker way to get to the Hopkins airport. She felt sorry for the young man staring at her in desperation and went out of her way to help him out. After a few minutes, she said weather cooperating, he could take the flight to O'Hare airport in Chicago, and from there to Hopkins airport. Majid, who was functioning at half-brain at the time, considered that flight change a no-brainer.

During the flight from JFK to O'Hare, Majid sat next to a professor who was originally from Israel. He was teaching at two universities and he had to fly back and forth twice a week. That was very intriguing for Majid, and the professor found the young Majid in search of his future very admiring. The professor had a few good pointers for Majid and his education in the United States.

Majid's flight landed at O'Hara airport around 4:45 a.m. O'Hara at the time was the largest airport in the nation, and after getting off the airplane, Majid was desperately walking through long hallways looking for something to eat. Majid's next flight was before 6:00 a.m., and when he left the inspection gates to get some food, the tall black gentleman (David) kept pointing at his ticket and telling him something. Majid could not understand the local and vocal accent, so the appeal for the food on the opposite side of the gate, by far exceeded his other senses.

After Majid had his badly needed coffee and his first delicious donut, he did not waste much time and was ready to go back through the inspection gate to take his next flight. Majid had already checked the gate he needed to get on board and he only had 20 minutes left. Trying to go back through the same gate, David who was about twice the size of Majid blocked his way. Majid was panicking and kept showing his ticket to him. Majid kept pointing at 6:00 a.m. flight to Cleveland on his ticket, and David kept pointing at the time when the inspection gate was open for travelers, which was also 6:00 a.m. The bright intelligent Majid with all those years of education, within 24 hours of being at his dreamland was down to his knees begging for mercy, to make his flight. David felt sorry for him and went through his small carry on bag and let him off the hook.

Majid had the fastest marathon of his life against his shadow to make the flight and he made it at the very last moment. It took about five minutes for his heart rate to get back to the normal level after he found his seat and laid his head to rest. When Majid landed at Hopkins airport, he called his Uncle Massood to pick him up after the 12 hours of delay. It was about 9:00 a.m. on March 5th, and no one in the family, including Ozra knew of Majid's whereabouts until now, and this had everybody concerned.

Massood, who was a psychiatrist, was not only respected by the hospital community and his office patients, but also by all his brothers and sisters in Iran, as well as the extended family. He had been in the United States for about 11 years, and after he finished his advanced medical training work in the New York City, he had moved to Cincinnati for a few years, and now he was becoming established in the Cleveland and Akron area. He was also a professor at Rootstown Medical Center.

After another hour of waiting, Majid could see his uncle with a big smile covering his face. "Where have you been sir, we have been worried about you," said Massood. That was enough for Majid to start moaning and groaning about all the pain and suffering he had experienced for the past couple of days. At least they had something to talk about for the next 30 minutes in the car before pulling into the driveway at Massood's house.

Snow had covered the entire landscape and Majid's brain was just as icy as the ice shingles hanging from the trees. When the 1975 model two door Mustang came to a halt in the driveway, Majid tried to pull the handle upward to open the door. This was the wrong way and he was left with the broken handle in his hand. This was not the kind of impression Majid was hoping to leave behind on the first day. Massood, looking at him with a big puzzle on his face, and holding himself back from saying anything hurtful said, "Here in the United States, if something does not work in one way, do not force your way upon it." Majid made a note of that in his memory or whatever was left of it.

When Majid entered the house he was greeted by his Aunt Sima, and the two younger daughters, Dora and Sarah, four and six years old, respectively. His cousin, Mojee, age thirteen, was still at school, and she arrived home a bit later. Majid was absolutely in no shape to talk and he was dead tired. Massood's small office with a sofa bed was shown to Majid as the bedroom to use during his stay until he learned about his new environment.

Before Majid aimed for the shower, Sima asked him what was his favorite dish. Majid in a shy voice responded "Ghormeh-Sabzi" which was the stew with beef and vegetables. After the shower Majid laid on the bed and before he could count to ten, he was gone. When he woke up, it was time for dinner so he headed directly to the kitchen, for he was starving.

To Majid's surprise, the food was rice and eggplant, and it had nothing to do with what Majid had asked for. The food was delicious and Majid was thankful. Sima was wondering if Majid was going to ask about the food and how come it was not what he had asked for. Since Majid was too shy to ask such a question of his hosts, Sima and Massood with a big smile covering their faces told Majid that he had slept for about thirty hours, and they did not have the heart to wake him up.

After dinner Majid had a tour of the house. Their home had a good sized family room, a master bedroom and two other bedrooms. The office was not far from the kitchen, but Majid loved the large basement the best. Their house was located approximately half way between Cleveland and Akron, a nice location in Stow, Ohio.

Majid, who had three older brothers always wanted to have a younger sister. Over a three day period, it seemed like Majid had traded his three older brothers for three younger sisters - what a change. The family could not wait to show Majid around, and Majid could not wait to learn all about his new environment - what a trade off!

The following weekend, the forty-one year old Massood took Majid to one of the local malls, Chapel Hill Mall. In the mall, there were several stores in a closed setting; this was different from the thousands of stores in an open space, which was what Majid was accustomed to in Iran. Massood was a very busy man yet very calm and focused. These characteristics to a young emotional man who was used to tarrofing, were a bit odd.

Majid followed his uncle's lead through the stores without any agenda. His uncle pointed out a few items Majid needed and purchased them for him. Majid was more interested in the store signs, the cleanliness and organization of the stores, the politeness of cashiers, etc. He was mostly fascinated by all the pretty blonde girls, for he was not used to seeing that many in the city of Tehran.

Majid had great amount of respect for his Aunt Sima, since Ozra always spoke very highly of her. At the time that Ozra had moved to Tehran and the family was not doing well financially, Sima had surprised her with much kindness. Sima had made Ahmad and Majid two nice warm winter coats and Ozra was forever in debt to her. **The level of kindness is always measured at the time of need**, and while Sima was her sister-in-law, Ozra always looked at her as a daughter she never had.

Majid was signed up for a ten-week English class at Akron University. Massood's family asked Majid to stay with them while attending the English Language Institute (ELI), and he gladly accepted. Everyday except weekends, Massood dropped him off at the bus station around 6:30 a.m. and Sima picked him up around 3:30 p.m. It worked out great, for Majid was being dropped off and picked up at the same time as their children.

It was a bit too cold for Majid waiting for the bus to arrive during the month of March, especially in a place that was not far from Lake Erie. Majid was not much bothered by the close to "0" degree temperature, as much as the cold wind blowing at his face, and leaving him with red cheeks and a frozen nose. It was not half as bad at 3:30 p.m. when the bus dropped him off, for now and then Sima stopped at McDonalds and Majid could enjoy a Quarter Pounder sandwich.

Majid was once again the curious kid. He was just like a sponge absorbing everything in his new environment and spitting out what he did not like. That's an opportunity that many folks do not have in a lifetime, and Majid was following his father's advice before he left Iran, which was "**Study every page in life, and make sure you understand what it means.**"

At the bus station Majid made many friends, for his accent and usage of words was just too cute for people to resist. There was a sixteen-year old blonde girl, perhaps a bit on the heavy side, who enjoyed talking with Majid and giggled continuously during and after Majid spoke. Majid's interest was to improve his ability to speak English, and she was perhaps enjoying the alien from Mars.

Another time Majid sat next to a Texan, and he was absolutely clueless of the conversation, but to be polite Majid nodded his head in agreement and even smiled a few times. It did not take the Texan but three minutes to move to a different location in the bus. The big lesson for Majid was not to nod in agreement with the things he could not understand, and simply ask them to repeat what they had to say.

Majid was at ELI about an hour before the classes began at 8:00 a.m. every morning. During that time he reviewed and tried to speak English with anyone in the building. That early in the morning there were only a few people finishing up mopping the floors and cleaning up the bathrooms.

Majid wanted to carry on a conversation badly, so he cleared his throat and translated one of the Iranian slangs to English, while trying to get the attention of the person mopping the floor in front of his feet. "Your hand, not to be tired," Majid said in a kind voice, while the person was staring at him in confusion. What that slang meant was "I hope you are not too tired from doing all this hard work."

Majid had to stop translating the hundreds of Iranian slangs into English, and start learning the English slangs. That's probably the most difficult part of learning a new language, not so much speaking the correct language but learning the one spoken in the streets. The first time a person asked Majid "What's up," he looked at the sky for an answer.

Languages constantly change as a function of cultural values and social behavior adjustments. This is why English is spoken differently in many English speaking countries such as England, Australia, United States, etc. This is why when Mojee's friend asked Majid if he was gay, he answered positively, thinking that she was asking if he was happy. When Majid learned about the prank pulled on him, he was not happy or gay about it, but he let it go. This is when he learned that a word used in the street language can have different meanings, some of which he had never heard before.

While attending ELI, Majid met a lot of other Iranian students among people of other nationalities, attending the same program at different levels. Out of 13 students, 6 were Iranians. There were about 220 Iranians going to Akron U, among over 27,000 students, and that was by far larger than any other nationality.

Considering the political environment in Iran, there were a number of anti-Shah Iranian political organizations and activists at Akron University. While Majid did not care for the Shah's regime, he had no interest and knowledge of any of these groups. This however did not stop these organizations from continuously trying to pass their publications to him and the other students for free.

Majid only had time for his English classes and he had to immediately leave school to make the bus back home to his uncle's house; therefore he did not take part in any of the political activities. Considering his level of effort and resolve, Majid was able to pass the English entrance test within the first term and start his education in the upcoming summer session.

While attending ELI, Majid made a number of friends with some of the Iranian students attending the same class, among who were Esi and Mo. It was time for Majid to move closer to the college; therefore Esi, Mo, and he decided to move to a four bedroom house within walking distance of the university. The only other room in addition to the kitchen was occupied by the owner's son who also attended Akron University.

During the summer of 1978, Majid took a pre-calculus class that he passed with a grade of A since he already knew the material from his high school years. The 24 year old Esi took another term of ELI, while the 26 year old Mo had to work somewhat longer on his English. The big soccer fields at the university seemed like a great place to hang out when everybody was finished studying.

During that summer Majid and Esi made friends with two of their neighbors. The two ladies, Mary, in her late seventies and Thelma, in her early eighties, were originally from Scotland. Mary and Thelma lived across the street in a small home. Thelma just loved to talk about all her life experiences. Majid benefited from the never ending, going nowhere conversations which improved his listening and speaking abilities. Also, the two ladies needed some mental stimulation. On occasion, Majid and Esi were also invited for some good old-fashioned American or perhaps Scottish cooking.

Fall semester was about to begin and Iran was making the national news, not the part where the Shah was approved to purchase the American made F16 fighter airplanes, but about the unrest in some of the major cities in Iran. At Akron U, the three Iranian political organizations on the campus were trying to recruit both new and old students by simply passing out publications. However, the majority of the Iranian students were not involved with any of these groups.

The communist group probably had two to three members, and it was not popular at all. While communist ideology was appealing to a small group of intellects in Iran, the majority of people rejected it, because the emphasis on God was missing. While all the political groups in Iran played behind the scene, that was not the case in the United States where there was freedom of speech. These groups were closely monitored by the FBI, yet left alone.

Two other major parties Majid came to learn were - the Mojahedin and the Islamic Counsel. The majority of students that had read Dr. Shariati's books were leaning toward the Mojahedin, and the ones with more Islamic roots with a fundamentalist way of thinking had a tendency to support the Islamic Council.

Akron U, while smaller than Ohio State and many other universities, was believed to be the head-quarters of the Islamic Council in the northeast with about 20 members. This organization was led by one of the Iranian students who was getting a PhD in sociology and had a limp when he walked around the campus. The Mojahedin had about 7 or 8 followers but were not very committed. They normally had philosophical discussions about the creation, read some verses from the Koran and then tried to analyze them.

Considering that Majid had read a few pages from one of Dr. Shariati's books while in Iran and since he was a poet, he found the discussions about the origins of humanity and the universe intriguing. For this reason he attended a couple of sessions of the small pro-Mojahedin group, lasting over two hours each. The discussions were more philosophical than political and were held in one of the campus classrooms during the weekend.

But the majority of the Iranian students, about 200 in all, did not get drawn into the politics. Some of these students were pro Shah, but they were not led by anyone; and they consisted of a circle of friends that wanted the monarchy to stay in power. The majority of these students, through their parents, had close ties to the regime in Iran. Others were simply from very rich families that in most cases were taking seven years to obtain a four-year college degree. In some instances, some of these students got high on illegal drugs, drove the latest sport cars, and hung around the most beautiful girls.

This was also around the time that President Carter was departing from the long-held policy of containment toward the Soviet Union and promoting a foreign policy that put human rights at the front. This change in policy was a break from overlooking the human rights abuses by the nations allied with the United States. This shift in the policy created a perfect storm for all of the oppositional voices against the ailing Shah at age sixty.

The angry voices were becoming louder and louder on the streets of Iran, demanding Human Rights and an end to the monarchy. The Shah made a few changes in the government, but it was too little too late, especially with little backing from the United States. On September 8, 1978, after declaring Martial Law, the Shah's security force fired on a large group of demonstrators at Ghaleh Square, killing several hundreds and wounding thousands.

This news exploded, nationally and internationally, in the face of the Shah and his regime. President Carter, with limited understanding of the Shah's strategic role in the region, could not support such a violent act and had to distance himself from the Shah of Iran. Majid and many other Iranian students were following the news, and discussing politics in the campus hallways, and were anxious to find out what would follow next. Majid, being emotionally impacted by the death of many people during this time wrote the following poem:

Blood of Justice

Darkness, take away my life, but my way,
    Not a chance, for it leads all those in chains!
Place your feet on my chest, but within my heart
    Is a road map, beyond any misery and my pain!
Lighten my night, with the fire of your guns,
    Shower me in your bullets, or those drops of rain!

Wash away our sins, in the blood of justice,
    Is the King knocking - or his guns, gone insane?
Are we just an image, in a broken mirror?
    Spirit is beyond the blood - in one's vein!
Lord, Give us the courage to run the path,
    In this we pray, once again, in your name!

Prior to this time Majid and many Iranians had not heard from Ayatollah Khomeini who had been in exile in Iraq for about 15 years.   Khomeini always spoke against the Shah and how corrupted his regime was; hence he was sent into exile, for the Shah was afraid of executing any Ayatollah (Word of God) because of their stature.   A. Khomeini was turning up the heat on the Shah under the human rights umbrella, and the United States and the West seemed to be quiet and at times very cooperative with the movement.

About this time, there was a call for a demonstration in front of the United Nations by the Islamic Council to shed light on the human rights violations in Iran.   Infuriated Majid had to go along in a carpool to the location.   Majid had never been to a demonstration, nor had he seen New York City other than the airport, and all the tall buildings.   There was a lead person in front screaming the slogans, and a crowd of young emotional people screaming back, while the policemen on their horses were guiding them through the busy streets.

Majid could not believe the level of free speech, and kept thinking how great it would be to experience this in his country. The tall buildings were absolutely beautiful and beyond his imagination.   This trip was giving him an insight about large cities in the United States, and he was really enjoying it.   When the crowd reached the front of the United Nations, some of the Iranian students - to Majid's surprise, started praying which seemed a bit odd.   The guy with the big speaker started chanting "Iran becomes Vietnam, US get out of Iran."

Majid was surprised with the level of boldness of the statements and to some extent he was uncomfortable.   This was his first experience in such a setting which was driven by the feeling of human loss in his homeland and perhaps by some peer pressure.   On the way back, the driver fell asleep for a short period of time.   That almost resulted in a major disaster, but luckily one of the passengers was paying attention and saved everyone's life.

Majid's first fall semester had begun at Akron U, but it seemed far from the way many other students began their college year.   The challenges were not just the classes he was taking and not so much the cultural differences, but it was more the language barriers, and definitely what was going on in his homeland.   The only factor that brought a separation from the reality was learning about the environment surrounding him.

It was the day before Halloween and the landlord's son Mike was getting his costume out from the closet when Esi and Majid arrived home late that evening.   Mike explained the Halloween celebration to the two roommates while Mo was sleeping in his room.   It was getting dark outside and Esi, looking at all of Mike's Halloween costumes, had a scary prank in mind.

Mike, Esi, and Majid quietly walked upstairs, and Mike, with a master key, skillfully opened the lock into Mo's room without making any noise.   The three quickly entered the room and closed the door behind them.   There was however, a bit of light penetrating through from the outside.   All three had white sheets covering their bodies while holding on to some fake glowing hands sticking out of the white sheets.   The masks covering their faces did not look friendly at all.

Mo repositioned his head on the pillow but did not open his eyes while the three ghosts positioned themselves around the bed. Esi sat right in front of Mo's face.   Now was the moment all three were waiting for, the time of a real Halloween scare.   Esi very gently caressed Mo's hair with the glowing hand.   Mo simply put his hand through his hair and turned his face.   Mike was on the opposite side to welcome him in case he opened his eyes.

Mo refused to open his eyes until Majid at the bottom of the bed started pulling the hair on one of his legs.   This time he jumped up in the air thinking that something was biting him and actually ran into one of the ghosts.   By now his eyes were wide open and he was screaming from the bottom of his lungs.   The three ghosts started laughing and turned on the light, but this time Mo was the one who looked like a real ghost.

The door was quickly opened and the three ghosts started running away from Mo, the real Halloween monster. They quickly dropped their sheets on the way out of the house, while being followed by Mo in his underwear. Esi had to yell "You fool, you are in the street in your underwear," before Mo realized it and quickly turned around and ran back to the house. The three ghosts did not return home until midnight when Mo had cooled off.

Though what was going on in Iran was not a Halloween celebration, it was incredibly scary for most of Iranian students in the United States, considering how it might impact their lives and their future. This was about the time frame when thousands took to the streets of Tehran, rioting and destroying the symbols of westernization, such as movie theaters and liquor stores. The very first university attacked and closed as the result of the uprise, was none other than RCD, the American university Majid was supposed to attend.

The riot seemed to have a domino effect, and the soldiers providing their two year military service were refusing to shoot at the angry mob. The army was placing the soldiers in those states where they had no relatives and in places they could not understand the native language, so it would be easier for them to follow orders. This did not help the regime much, for the soldiers were leaving their post since they did not want to open fire on their own people.

Ayatollahs from different states with millions of followers started following A. Khomeini's lead to ask for the Shah's departure. When a **Fatva** or a religious order was issued by the Grand Ayatollah, the true Muslims had to follow. Majid did not know the meaning of all the Islamic terminologies at the time, yet while talking to the students in the Islamic Counsel, he behaved as if he knew all of them. He was probably not the only one, for the youth in Iran, unlike their parents, were not as much into religion or fundamentalist behavior.

Ayatollah Khomeini, originally born in the small town of Khomein about 180 miles south of the capital of Tehran, was leading the movement against the Shah. The Persian students in different parts of the world were uniting under the same flag to support the change in Iran. **While the majority in Iran desired**

106

the change, the type of change was not the same in each individual's mind, yet they unified to ensure the revolution was successful.

While people were sacrificing their lives in Iran to end the monarchy, the only lives sacrificed here in the United States were the turkeys. It was Majid's first Thanksgiving in the United States and he was invited to his uncle's house. Majid soon learned about the celebration and the origins of it. Sima had prepared the turkey and Massood skillfully was cutting it in somewhat thin slices. Mashed potatoes, green beans dipped in mozzarella cheese, yams, and cranberry mold were just a few items on the dining table.

To Majid's surprise, rice, the most important item in Persian gatherings was missing. Then again he was not in Iran, and learning about other cultures was just a breath of fresh air for a man consumed with politics. Majid had not heard of A. Khomeini but for a few months, although he talked about him so patiently, as if he had known him for years. Massood listened to Majid who was in defiance of the Shah and the state of Iranians as a result of his policies.

Massood did not say anything and looked at a young emotional man who had just discovered the world and the solutions to every problem. Massood was a psychiatrist and his young nephew was no different than any other emotional 17 year old kid who knew everything. Very calmly Massood said, "I suppose you prefer Theocracy over Democracy." Majid without understanding the two terms; and what they really meant, responded "I guess I do."

It was not long after Thanksgiving, on December 11th of 1978 that a group of soldiers mutinied and attacked the Shah's security officers. The Shah was fighting cancer within, and without any external help, he was losing the war outside. While President Carter during the 1978 New Year celebration was served by the Shah in Iran, for the 1979 New Year he was nowhere in sight.

The first day of the New Year of 1979, Majid along with his uncle's family, were invited to the home of one of his friends from the hospital. Sheila who had one of her legs amputated when she was young, had prepared pork and sauerkraut for the main dish and different desserts. Majid never had pork in his life for he was a Muslim, and now he was between his religion and tarrofing.

To be polite and not to hurt his host's feeling Majid placed the first piece of pork in his mouth. With his mind playing tricks on him, it felt he was like biting on a live snake, since it was forbidden to eat pork in Islam. He quickly shoved a spoonful of mashed potatoes in his mouth and without chewing the meat he swallowed everything. He then drank a whole cup of Coke to wash away the remainder of any particles, as if his sins would be forgiven.

I guess what one eats from early childhood, and how a person looks at different aspects of life, has a lot to do with his or her up bringing. Majid stared at his plate trying to find something wrong with the meat in his plate, but it looked like a piece of turkey or chicken, and did not taste much different. The second piece did not have the same mental impact on him as the first one. This time Majid was able to actually taste and enjoy the mashed potatoes and the sauerkraut.

Majid was told by her host that on New Year's Day, people serve ham or pork to bring them prosperity and better way of life for the incoming year. Majid did not ask the relevance between the two, for his culture was filled with many similar cases. While Majid was trying to be attentive that day, he could not wait to return home and follow up the news about the changes in Iran, on his 19 inch black and white TV.

Factories in Iran were shutting down due to the strike by the workers, even the oil industry was shut down. People were marching in the streets on a daily basis, without worrying about SAVAK, security forces, or the military for that matter. The Shah was not getting much support from the outside, and one day shy of Majid's 18th birthday, on January 16 of 1979, he fled Iran. Not only did the United States not intervene when the Shah was overthrown and sent to exile, but he was refused entry to the United States even though he needed medical assistance!

Majid, like much of the Iranian population, was following the events and could not get enough news in one day. While a few months earlier, he did not know A. Khomeini, now Majid was following him on the news, as he traveled from Iraq to France, and later on to Iran.

An older Grandpa figure who spoke with much simplicity, A. Khomeini seemed like the right choice - an old and wise man, for a large population who had enough of the Shah and his family.

Majid, at the time was no different than the rest of the Iranian society and as an emotional poet wrote the following poem:

Who was the one?

Who was the one, who delivered the dawn!
Watering the flowers, in the heat of the sun!
Who was the one, who wiped the dark cloud!
Lightening the nights, leader of the crowd!
Who was the one, in the killing and violence!
Blessing the dead, in a moment of silence!
Khomeini was his name, and truth was his faith! ...

Two weeks after fall of the Shah, on February 1st, A. Khomeini entered Iran, and the speculation that Shah's air force would shoot down his airplane, did not materialize. A. Khomeini's arrival was celebrated by many in Iran and closely monitored by other folks that did not know a lot about him, including Majid and his age group.

After landing at the Iranian airport on that day, A. Khomeini made a number of promises to the Iranians, two of which were:

- To have a popularly elected government that would represent the people of Iran and with which the clergy would not interfere

- No one should remain homeless in Iran, and everyone should be given free telephone, heating, electricity, bus services and free oil at their doorstep

Majid was promised toys when he was five years old that he never received, he was promised a bike when he was ten years old and it never materialized, so at age eighteen, as much as he believed that people can not have something for nothing, with some level of doubt he remained cautiously optimistic about his hero's promises.

In the early part of 1979, the Internet did not exist and there were no blogs, therefore it was much easier to believe the stories about the legends and assumed heroes. It was critical for Majid to learn about the person who had just entered the country and was ready to take a leadership position. To this point he was a blind follower, a person of faith, someone who fasted during the month of Ramadan and prayed regularly. But now, it was time for him - to open his eyes to what the blind faith had delivered him.

A. Khomeini was a seventy-six year old man, a Sayed from a religious family who lost his father in a local dispute when he was five months old. He was then raised by his mother and one of his aunts until age fifteen when they both died. After this he was under the guardianship of his brother, Ayatollah Passandideh. At age 18, he joined the Islamic seminary in Esfahan.

A. Khomeini completed his religious studies at the Dar al-Shafa school in the city of Qom. After graduation at age 23, he taught and wrote a number of books on Islamic laws (Sharia) and Islamic philosophy. He continued as a lecturer and teacher for decades at Najaf-Iraq, and Qom-Iran and became a leading Shia scholar. Many of his students later became leading Islamic Marja such as Ayatollah Motahari.

A Marja possessed a large following, normally millions of people from the same region. A Marja or Grand Ayatollah had the power to issue a fatwa, in which his followers were obligated to follow. That included the issue of a Jihad against the establishment, if deemed necessary.

After the death of the most followed Ayatollah Burujerdi, in 1961, at the age 59, the time seemed right for A. Khomeini to take a leadership position. Since 1920 when Reza Shah (Shah's father) had assumed power and took a secular position, and led an anti-clerical modernizer role, the clergy were trying to find their way back. A. Khomeini found strength and popularity in opposition to the Shah, especially after the Shah's re-installation back into the kingdom in 1953 by the foreign sources.

The Shah's introduction of his "White Revolution" in January of 1963 seemed to be a defining point for A. Khomeini. The "White Revolution" included six programs: land reforms and nationalization of forests, profit sharing in large corporations, national literacy initiatives, privatization of national owned ventures, changes to allow women to vote, and allowing non-Muslims to hold office.

Since many people did not trust the Shah due to the 1953 coup, most of the religious leaders considered his "White Revolution" a dangerous turn away from the traditional and religious values and a move toward westernization. This is when A. Khomeini called for a meeting of all the senior Marjas at Qom to persuade them to boycott the Shah's "White Revolution."

On January 22, 1963, A. Khomeini denounced the Shah and his initiatives, and took a leading opposition role with the kingdom; something that no one had dared to do in the past. A. Khomeini closely worked with other senior Iranian Shia leaders to condemn the Shah and his regime for moral corruption and submission to Israel and the United States.

On June 3rd of that year, A. Khomeini gave a fiery speech calling the Shah a "wretched miserable man," among many other remarks. On June 5th, he was put under house arrest which caused a riot and the loss of over 400 human lives. A. Khomeini remained under house arrest for another eight months.

Later, in November of 1964, A. Khomeini denounced the "capitulation" law, which was a diplomatic immunity for American military personnel. This meant that these individuals could only be put on trial in an American military court. Prime Minister, Mansur, had A. Khomeini arrested for disapproving the Shah's decision. Later, during a furious request for an apology, A. Khomeini was slapped by Mansur. This act cost Mansur his life two weeks later on his way to the parliament, and caused A. Khomeini to be sent into exile to Turkey by the Shah.

A. Khomeini was now back and had the backing of the youth, and all those college students that led the revolution. Dr. Shariati's books indicated a revolution would only succeed if there was only one leadership, and A. Khomeini was in complete agreement with that statement. Since students blamed SAVAK for the killing of Dr. Shariati, they were willing to put their support behind Khomeini, and follow a fundamentalist Islamic movement which was popular among their parents and grandparents. This was all in the hope of the change for a democratic government that would allow freedom of speech.

S. Bakhtiar was the provisional government put in place by the Shah before his departure on January 16th. A. Khomeini appointed his own interim government on February 11th, and with much support from the population, he stated that his appointed government was "God's government" and any disobedience against his appointee was a "revolt against God."

I guess one can draw a conclusion that God had just entered Iranian politics. To the majority of people, such a statement was fine, since the goal was to remove the Shah at any cost. Such remarks simply skidded off people's ears without much attention to its impact in the long term, but at the time it created much emotional fuel needed for the revolution to succeed.

By this time the soldiers had begun to defect and a jihad was declared against any soldier that did not. Therefore the Shah's old military leaders claimed neutrality which caused the Shah's interim government of S. Bakhtiar to fall. This was clearly the end of the kingdom in Iran, and the start of something new, something that many people had waited for since 1953 - or was it?

While the Shah, his family, and a number of his top ministers had left Iran in a hurry, a large number of his generals and majors were left behind. Those who stayed behind were either too stupid, or too proud to leave. Ex-prime minister Hoveida and one of the most famous and proud generals, General Rahimi, along with hundreds more ranking officials met the firing squads.

Two of the majors that had attended Ali's wedding were placed in a prison. They had to stay in prison for a period of time to verify they were not involved in any of Shah's brutality against the people throughout the uprising. If two or more people claimed their involvement in firing against the people during the revolution, then without a court and a jury, they were met by a round of bullets from the head to the toe. Luckily they both survived and were later discharged. However, listening to the firing squads, day after day, had broken them mentally and emotionally for the remainder of their short lives, thereafter.

The March 31st referendum to replace the monarchy with an Islamic Republic was an absolute success with a 98% "Yes" vote, for A. Khomeini. The population was madly in love with this grandpa figure that could say or do no wrong. The 2% perhaps included people that still believed in the Shah and expected his magical return and a large number of Marxist and Socialist university students that at one point had supported A. Khomeini against the Shah.

It was mid-May 1979 and Majid could not wait to finish school and go back to his country during that summer. He was in the United States for over a year and he was looking forward to visiting all his family members. Ozra also could not wait to see her youngest son, and she was standing in front of everyone at airport that Friday night when Majid returned.

While many people sacrificed a sheep right in front of the feet of a loved one returning from a long trip, the family knew better. Besides, Majid had told the family if they did so, he would shorten his 10 week stay to only 4 weeks, and that had resulted in his favor.

Considering the instability and the rapid changes in the political atmosphere within the nation, there was a large increase in the price of food and other goods; hence Majid had also boycotted any large festivity due to his arrival. This did not stop Ozra from inviting all the relatives, but it also did not stop Majid from refusing to eat any of the fruit and cookies. Majid made sure everybody noticed his dismay, much to Ozra's dislike.

Majid was invited by many of his immediate and distant family members within a couple of days of his return. While he enjoyed the attention and the exotic food, he was shocked by some of the questions asked behind closed doors by some of his male cousins. The question topping all the other questions was- how many girls did Majid have sex with during the previous year in the United States.

While Majid was puzzled with such questions during the time that the country had just gone through such transformation, the "None" response by him seemed to have a more surprising effect on his audience. Such questions seemed to carry no weight and often were overlooked by a simple silly response; however, they were an indication of a much deeper social problem and a wrong perception of the unknown.

An Islamic Republic meant the clock was turned back to 1920 or prior to that for the women's movement in Iran. Women once again had to cover themselves from head to toe, wearing no perfume and makeup. This did not just suppress the women's freedom, but the partition of the two genders in the public place through such scrutiny, caused more sexual appeal toward the opposite sex.

On the other hand, years of watching movies made by Hollywood during the Shah's regime, had left a perception that most girls in the west would jump in the sack with any guy after a couple of dates. Hollywood for decades had painted the picture of people from the Middle East as oil rich, with little or no brains, and mostly being camel-jockeys. In reverse, to the people in Middle East, the western societies seemed violent, yet intelligent. They also thought westerners constantly consumed alcoholic drinks and randomly had sex as they pleased.

This is why Majid's age group of friends and relatives had those perceptions and way of thinking. **When you are thousands of miles away from the source, truth becomes an insignificant matter lost in the noise. Those capable of making the loudest noise which has nothing to do with the facts, become the perception makers, and the rest will repeat and defend those viewpoints.**

It was early June when Ahmad took Majid and two of their cousins on a trip to the mountains. It was about a six hour drive starting on a highway, changing to two lane state roads, and then followed by gravel roads into the mountains. For a couple of days they spent time in a fairly cold climate, but nothing in comparison to the cold temperature in Akron, Ohio during winter months.

This was the first time Majid could truly share some of his experiences he had in the United States with the group, while he learned about all the stories of the revolution. One of the stories was about how people saw the picture of A. Khomeini in the moon on one of the nights before his arrival and so forth. Majid was amazed by the size of the human imagination, and was shocked on

114

how the common Joe would believe anything in a time of desperation.

Early in the morning on the next day, the group decided to have some fresh hot mountain milk after a cold night and before they left for hiking. They were staying at one of the two rooms owned by a family of seven, for a very reasonable amount of money for their two-day stay. The middle-aged lady served them breakfast with fresh eggs and hot milk, again for a very little price.

Majid asked the lady about the revolution in Iran and what she thought about it. The set of answers were completely shocking to Majid, for she had not heard of any revolution, nor did she know what it meant. In the mountainous areas, they mostly spoke their own local language which made the conversation very brief with the people from the cities. She did not even understand where Iran was, and what being an Islamic Republic meant.

On the way back, since Majid could not get any answer from that lady, he started to think what did it really mean to be an Islamic Republic and why? What if the leader of the revolution was a funny man, would it make the nation a Comedian Republic? How about the Shia Islamic Republic of Iran? With over 2,500 years of being a kingdom, the country was never called "The Monarchy of Iran" or anything else. It was either referred to as Persia or Iran, which meant land of Persians or Iranians, respectively. There seemed to be too many questions and far few answers in Majid's mind.

In the Middle East, Israel was labeled as a Zionist nation, which people in the region believed was a raciest view; for the landmark created by Zion over a century ago, indicated a part of the Arab land was promised to the Jews. So, does this mean Iran was only promised to the Muslims? What about the Zoroastrians that pioneered religion in Persia, and the Jews that at one point were counted as 20% of the population. None of this was making much sense to Majid on the long drive back home. Why would a country like Iran, so diverse in its way of thinking, religious roots, cultural values, and philosophical view points limit itself to one set of values, and disconnect itself from its own rich heritage?

A. Khomeini was an honest man with an honest answer responding to Peter Jennings of ABC News on the airplane flying back to Iran after 15 years in exile. Peter asked "How does it feel to return to Iran?" and the response was "I don't feel a thing." A. Khomeini was a dedicated Shia Muslim spending all his life in Najaf, Iraq and Qom, Iran in pursuit of his religious views, so the answer was absolutely correct. It was all about his views of Islam and its promotion, and the need for a strong holy puppet in the region.

But what did the Islamic Republic of Iran mean to the rest of the region? Iran was not the birth place of Islam, Saudi Arabia was; and Prophet Muhammad was an Arab with the Koran being written in Arabic. This is in absolute contrast to the fact that in Iran people spoke Farsi and were from the Aryan race. A major problem was that Iran, with a majority Shia, was different from the rest of the Arab world with mainly majority Sunnis. This dynamic set the stage for potential new problems in the region. No one was ever a challenge to Saudi Arabia for being the heart of the Muslim world throughout the centuries, and no country ever imposed a threat by claiming to be the center of Islam in the world until now. The main question was - how would this all play itself out?

The new Islamic Republic did not respect and recognize the state of Israel, so how would this impact the regional Arab-Israeli conflict? Would a rise in Islamism in the region cause a rise in Hedonism, Buddhism, and Judaism? And would this ultimately cause tension between Christians and Muslims? Once again, he had **many questions, and this time, fear of giving any answers.**

Before returning back to the United States, to continue his education, Majid and two of his cousins took a trip to the city of Mashhad. It was during the month of Ramadan, and unlike previous years, no restaurant could serve food during this month until sunset. A. Khomeini had declared the last Friday of Ramadan as International Day of Quds and the birth week of Prophet Muhammad as the Unity Week for all the Muslims.

Upon Majid's request, the other two cousins agreed to get a place for a week in one of the small towns, about 30 miles away from the city of Mashhad, a place called Torghabeh. While the entrance to the town square had electricity and running water, within a couple miles from it there was no power, and people had to walk for at least a mile through the mountain trails to a water

116

spring to fill up their jugs.   Majid, from a young age, had an intuitive connection with the underserved in the society and wanted to feel their pain for at least one week.   This was a great opportunity to do so, and also experience the natural beauty of the region.

Taking a bus ride to Torghabeh, Majid had an opportunity to talk with some of the local residents traveling back after they had voted for their favorite public officials in local elections. They looked like a set of hard working farmers that had never visited any large cities until then.   After talking for a few minutes with one of the farmers, Majid asked him, "Who did you vote for?"   The response was not exactly what Majid was looking for, it was, "I do not know."

Most of the elders from that village did not know how to read and write, nor did they know any of the candidates.   They were told it was their religious duty to vote and the round trip bus ticket to and from the city was paid for by the state officials.   At the voting booth, they were told who A. Khomeini would vote for, and if they were in agreement, placing their finger print on the form was sufficient.   Majid was quickly learning about the meaning of democracy offered by the theocracy.

In the world, there is a big confusion between the ability to choose and the meaning of democracy.   Many governments like us to believe that democracy is when the population votes freely and the votes are counted fairly – or is it?   Majid did not believe that was the case; for voting freely is only a component used in the process of democracy, and if voting is the only factor, it would end up to be nothing but an uninformed choice with an unknown result for the uneducated and/or ignorant societies!

In a democracy, not only do people respect the differing points of views, but they welcome them.   It is in this diversity of opinions that democratic societies have found greatness, and not in monolithic thinking processes.   **Democracy relies on an informed population about the issues, and candidates that are not owned or paid for by any special interest group. Democracy thrives on a set of rules and laws that are defined by a written constitution to protect all its members despite their religious beliefs and political affiliations.   Democracy is**

117

the respect for the individual's civil rights, and is without harassment and persecution of those differing from the governing body.

Majid was not sure that the farmers, or for that matter the population really understood what they were standing and fighting for. The week earlier and right before the day of election, there was a call for a demonstration near the Imam Reza Haram by one of the religious leaders. Over a hundred thousand people marched down the streets, walked over the grass the previous regime had seeded, and destroyed it, while chanting, "Death to the three corrupt ones, Carter, Sadat, and Begin."

Toward the end of the bus ride, Majid was very concerned about where the country was heading. Millions of hours that could have been used to cultivate the ground to make the nation independent of food from outside, was wasted through useless marching. Why would anyone desire the death of any other human being, especially in a holy city? Wouldn't that be a sin? Why would anyone vote for anyone without even knowing the candidates and what they stood for?

A couple of nights later the three cousins decided to walk to a restaurant after sunset to break their fast. Majid was in a heated political discussion with one of the cousins when the other one screamed, "Look, look," pointing far into the distance, perhaps ten miles away. There was a huge source of light, a half circle with the rays of light extending to the image of the moon in the sky. Everyone froze in their steps, noticing the locals standing on the roof tops and people praying in the streets. Some were claiming the end of the world had come, some were claiming the 12th Imam Mahdi's return to earth, and some were just speechless.

A few minutes later the source of light began to reduce in intensity while the radius of illumination continued to increase. After half an hour the light was completely gone and the moon returned, but Majid and his cousins, continued walking with a body temperature well below freezing point, due to the scare, in that hot summer night. The world had not ended that night, as many locals believed, and no one claimed to have seen Imam Mahdi the next day. Since the Iranian Air Force, during the Shah, had encountered UFOs in at least one occasion, Majid believed this was just another similar experience.

Shortly after that trip Majid once again was ready to leave his beloved country to continue his education. This time, Ozra did not seem as anxious to see her son going away, and was happy for him. There were not as many people at the airport this time or as much sadness as the first time when he left home. However Majid was leaving with a different attitude than the one when he arrived.

Majid visited Iran to come closer to the changes caused by the revolution, but now he was flying away from it faster than anyone could imagine. He was looking for answers, and he was leaving with many more questions. He had looked for a clear voice, but he only heard the crows singing and the people chanting in frustration. He was looking for hope and he found disparity. Majid was confused and he had no road map, with a long journey ahead of him!

After returning from Iran, Esi and Majid moved into a different apartment location. One of Esi's old friends had a two bedroom apartment on the 12th floor of a building not far from Akron U. His roommate had left and he needed a new roommate. Considering the cost, Majid and Esi took one of the larger bedrooms and were able to meet the rent payment.

Esi's friend Mo was a long term student, trying to finish a four-year degree in six years, and he had resided there since 1975. He had a beautiful girlfriend and a side dish who visited him right after church just about every Sunday. Mo's favorite pass time was to get high on pot and become delusional. None of this behavior made any sense to either Majid or Esi, so basically they stayed at the university campus most of the time and only returned home to sleep.

It was the beginning of the new school year and Majid had to pay attention to what was important in his life and future. The classes were not too difficult, but trying to compete for excellence with barely any family support in a different culture, and with all the language barriers was not easy. However, the person who had a much bigger problem on his plate was President Jimmy Carter, whether he realized it at the time or not.

President Carter was facing the same type of problem, but on much larger scale. His concept of "Human Rights" was great in theory, but it seemed to invite a number of problems due to the social and cultural differences in the world. This was a major policy shift from "Containment" to "Human Rights". U.S. backed governments that were normally overlooked for abuses committed against their population, became exposed by this policy shift. Introduction of "Human Rights," while very attractive in a general sense, made these regimes very vulnerable, and allowed the opposition groups in many such countries to become much stronger. Somoza from Nicaragua and the Shah of Iran were perhaps the victims of this policy shift.

With the Shah being overwhelmed with internal problems in 1978, and the Soviet Union having a pro-Moscow government installed in Afghanistan, the Carter administration began supporting the anti-Soviet Islamic factions in July of 1979. Perhaps the irony was that the USSR was afraid of Islamic expansion into its borders, while the U.S. was afraid of Soviet access to the warm water in the Persian Gulf, and the control of oil fields in the region. To avoid such a threat, and curb the Shia uprising in Iran, by some suggestions, the $40 billion covert program to promote Vahabism (a fundamentalist sect of Sunni Muslims originated in Saudi Arabia) in Pakistan and Afghanistan seemed like a great alternative.

The United States was busy fighting Communism, and supporting Islamic fundamentalists through the Vahabist movement in the region, when the power grab for the high office began in Iran. While A. Khomeini was considered as the father of the revolution by most everybody, the young generation had other ideas for the presidency of the nation. However, A. Khomeini had his own concepts of an Islamic Republic in mind, as stated in his book in 1970 "Authority of the Jurist (Velayat-e Fagih)". Velayat-e Fagih basically meant the highest position in the nation must be a Marja. This was in contrast with an agreement made among all the revolutionary forces prior to the fall of the Shah. Many Marja and highly influential Ayatollahs such as A. Taleghani, that Majid respected passionately, did not approve of such a position, for they believed in separation of state and religion.

In the meanwhile the Shah, living in exile and suffering from lymphoma, was finally allowed to enter the United States on October 22nd of 1979, on a temporary asylum for medical treatment of his cancer. This was a big emotional upset to many of the Iranians, both within and outside the country.   There were a large number of Iranian students demonstrating in front of the hospital where the Shah was admitted.   The same was happening in Iran but on a much larger scale.

The society seemed to be breaking down between logical thinking and the power of emotion.   Lines were being drawn between one's blind faith and the logic required to shed light on the major issues of the society.   The battles were being shaped between ignorance and intelligence - the conflict between the meaningless words of the past and the new world that could promise a brighter future.   The war has always been between the forces of "Hate" and the army of "Love." While "Hate" prevails in the short run, "Love has always been the long-term solution.   "Love" requires building and creation, which takes time, where "Hate" is in destruction and demise, requiring little time.   This is why most scholars, engineers, doctors, and the country's educated started to leave the nation, since the power of "Hate" was much stronger than the seeds of "Love".

Being informed on such large "brain drain" (currently estimated 150,000 to 200,000 per year), on October 31 of 1979, A. Khomeini made the following observation and assessment to this potential problem facing the nation in years to come:

They say there is a brain drain. Let these decayed brains flee. Do not mourn them; let them pursue their own definitions of being.   Is every brain with - what you call - science in it honorable?   Shall we sit and mourn the brains that escaped? Shall we worry about these brains fleeing to the US and the UK? Let these brains flee and be replaced by more appropriate brains. Now that they are filtering, you are sitting worried why they are executing? Why are you discussing these rotten brains of lost people? Why are you questioning Islam? Are they fleeing? To hell with them. Let them flee.

The youth, in particular the college students, seemed to be chasing their tails, some denying and some fighting for the new regime in power.
With the emotions running high, on November 4th, 1979, the United States' embassy in Tehran was seized by a number of students who were committed followers of A. Khomeini, taking 63 American citizens as hostages. While the eleven black hostages were immediately freed, the following demands were made for the freedom of the remaining 52 hostages:

1. The return of the Shah to Iran for trial,
2. The return of the Shah's wealth to the Iranian people,
3. An apology from the United States for its past actions in Iran,
4. United States to promise not to interfere in Iran's affairs in the future.

Considering the political climate in Iran, with a large number of people supporting the students, and with organized demonstrations around the embassy, A. Khomeini decided to support the hostage-takers actions while the world was condemning it. Many scholars believe this was used by A. Khomeini's supporters to bring their theocratic constitution to the people's vote. Since elections were to take place about a month after the hostages were taken, A. Khomeini supporters felt that with the current emotional state of the people, they would gain enough votes to successfully pass and carry out the elections. **It is always easier to catch the fish when the water is muddy. It is effortless to persuade emotional people to favor an irrational idea when the tempers are running hot.**

With hostages taken in Iran, the Iranian students and the majority of the Iranian-American population in the United States found themselves in a very awkward position. Majid was completely confused and discombobulated by the action of some of his own people, and regularly watched Ted Koppel on ABC Nightline News. Majid was free to move about, but for the first time ever, he felt like a hostage within his own body and completely speechless. To separate himself from the atrocity committed by his nation, he was more inclined to introduce himself as a Persian than an Iranian.

Why was the country called "The Islamic Republic" and not simply "Iran", was no longer the only question in Majid's mind, but the new question was, "What happened to the Persian culture of hospitality and all the values it represented for thousands of years?"   Understanding the fact that one's embassy is considered as their land, this act of violence was as if Iran had declared war against the United States. What if the United States decided to retaliate?   What would happen to the status of Iranian students in the United States, and their future welfare?

As if these questions were not enough to depress someone, a student from India was attacked by someone who had lost his job at a gas station.   In the attacker's strange mind, there was a connection between him losing his job and the hostages, so he retaliated by putting an Indian student in a coma.   This created much fear among the foreign students, so they began walking in groups to and from the university for protection.

Majid did not remember his 19th birthday on January 17th of 1980 for he was upset with just about everything happening back in his homeland.   He could no longer support a revolution that had nothing to do with the values of his nation.   Iran, throughout the history of mankind, was a beacon of tolerance for many religions, cultures, and languages; and now, it was anything but!

In the meanwhile, the new Islamic constitution generated a position of Supreme Leader and a Council of Guardians who could veto any perceived non-Islamic legislation and could eliminate candidates running for office.   Naturally, A. Khomeini became the Supreme Leader but amazing enough, a non-clergy man by the name of Banisadr, an economist, became the President on February 4th, 1980. It appeared as if the clergy were gaining more power while the rest of the society was being considered as non-Islamic or not as Islamic as those wearing a turban on their head.

Prior to the revolution A. Khomeini's ideas seemed to be progressive and pro reform; however, once in power his philosophical views of an Islamic state were in opposition to those of modern and secular intellectuals.   A. Khomeini truly believed that those seeking freedom of speech were against his principles, as stated below:

Yes, we are reactionaries, and you are enlightened intellectuals; you intellectuals do not want us to go back 1400 years. You, who want freedom, freedom for everything, the freedom of parties, you who want all the freedoms, you intellectuals; freedom that will corrupt our youth, freedom that will pave the way for the oppressor, freedom that will drag our nation to the bottom.

Such comments were not the freedom of speech and the press promised by A. Khomeini, and nor was it what Majid had hoped for. Free services such as water, gas, and electricity were just a pipe dream and never happened. **It first appeared as though people had traded their "King" for an "Ace," but they ended up with nothing but a "Jack."**

Majid's only outlet was his poetry, and again he found himself behind closed doors with a pen and a pencil. While he wrote, rehearsed, and delivered to an audience of one, the opposition papers and protesters in Iran were coming under attack by club-wielding vigilantes, one by one. This behavior which was a state run operation was once again defended and explained by A. Khomeini as stated below:

The club of the pen and the club of the tongue is the worst of clubs, whose corruption is 100 times greater than other clubs.

Around the same time, many scholars and opposition groups had begun to review many of A. Khomeini's books, and perhaps the club of his pen. The book that the Iranian constitution was mainly derived from was "Velayat-e-fagih". The three main topics for running the nation, in a simplified version were:

1. The laws made for society must be from the laws of God (Sharia or Islamic Law) which included every aspect of human life,

2. The country leaders should be Fagih or people that are knowledgeable of these detailed laws for every topic,

3. The clergy shall prevent injustice and corruption, to provide protection for the weak, and most importantly destroy anti-Islamic influence and conspiracies.

A. Khomeini's other two books defined the aspects of human lives and how people should conduct themselves. These books even covered issues about incest, aberrant sex, and details about appropriate ways of defecation and urination.

There it was - an ancient society with great national treasures such as Khayam and Saadi, with the origins of perhaps the oldest known monotheistic religion to humanity known as Zoroastrianism, with Kings such as Cyrus that freed the Jews, and perhaps a culture seven thousand years old - and now it had to relearn how to speak, dress, eat and drink - according to A. Khomeini's understanding of the Islamic laws in his books.

The new laws enforced a new dress code for both men and women in public places. Women had to cover their body completely, including their hair, and were not allowed to wear make up, while men were banned from wearing shorts, short sleeves, and tie. These major changes in social behaviors were monitored and corrected by imprisonment if necessary, by the Islamic Revolutionary Guards, and in some cases by heavily armed teenage children below age fifteen.

Every aspect of human life was measured as a function of Islamic Laws defined by the Supreme Leader. There was even a committee for redefining the universities under Islamic Laws. Luckily, the metric system and the laws of physics remained the same, but the earth once again seemed to have become flat and there was no room for evolution in a revolution that defied logic.

At the same time, the opposition against religious life styles was largely increasing among women and was being met with harsh punishment by majority of the ruling clergy. The opposition however, was not limited to the women, but also by some highly influential Ayatollahs such as Montazeri and Talleghani, and other major organizations that supported A. Khomeini prior and during the revolution.

While immediately after the revolution, hundreds of members of the military and the monarchy lost their lives to the firing squads, now was the time for the guns to turn toward all the opposition groups and university students who opposed losing their freedom of speech and one's ability to choose.

The news from Iran was at best confusing and perhaps disappointing for Majid. **He could not understand what gave the right to one set of people to re-define the life style for another set of people. He could not understand the purpose of all the rituals that followed his religion to the point of confusion. Did God even have a role in the religion or was God just being used as a tool to promote a set of behaviors?**

In the meanwhile, President Carter was becoming very frustrated with the regime in Iran. The Executive Order 12170, issued on November 14th of 1979 to freeze the bank accounts of the Iranian government located in the United States in the amount of $8 billion, was not showing a sign of hope. Since this bargaining chip was not bringing about the release of the 52 American hostages, a rescue mission attempt was made on April 24th of 1980 with no success. It was to Majid's surprise that the United States did not take a much stronger position toward Iran and play a military option at the time.

The lack of action against the government in Iran, and the promotion of the Vahabist movement in Afghanistan as a counter measure to Communism, was probably the reason for the start and growth of the two fundamentalist movements in the region at this time. The Vahabist movement, probably and in large part, was the result of Iran becoming the Islamic Republic of Iran.

The government in Iran was always afraid of outside forces, some with merit and some used as an excuse to further promote their behavior. For instance if the price of the Toman dropped in the international market, somehow it was to be blamed on the United States and not the actions of Iran in the worldwide community - such as taking the American hostages. It is very much like when a student receives an "F" and blames it on the teacher; while an "A" indicates how intelligent the student maybe.

Iran at this time was a country in turmoil both internally and internationally. The only way for the ruling party to stay in power was to suppress the voices within, by any means. The highly popular Ayatollah Taleghani, who was against domination by the clergy in the political system had a heart attack late that summer and died, while some other Ayatollahs went under house arrest.   The opposition voices, **though Muslims**, were declared, **"Warriors against God,"** and thus considered as **infidels**, so spilling their blood by any means was promoted.   A. Taleghani's death had a sobering and painful impact on Majid, for he had so much respect for him.   This caused Majid to write a poem in his honor:

The Sage

The candle of our lives, has lost its flame,
 And the flowers, are wilted in our sorrow;
The dancing butterflies, without your light,
 No longer fly, between the lines, so narrow;
The spring flower, is lovely when it blooms,
 But now just a picture, left in your shadow;
The red tulips, do you know why the color,
 Buried in the dirt, is a bloody seed to grow;
Life is a moment, for those with no writing,
 Legends never die, dreams are not hollow;
Taleghani, we salute you; the candle of our lives,
 The holy Sage, leaving our lives less shallow!

The death of A. Taleghani seemed to bring about much further separation between Mojahedin and the ruling party. Mojahedin, who followed A. Taleghani, had a strong appeal among the college students.   After A. Taleghani's sudden death, due to a so-called heart attack, it seemed as though a war was declared between the regime and any opposition views and ideas.

Since in most cases, one's interpretation of a religion is different than another person's understanding, the religions have constantly been altered as a result of those in leadership positions and their interests.   When religious people are in charge of a government, this absolute unchecked power becomes extremely dangerous.   Before they know it, they play the role of God and start passing judgment upon people.

During the same time frame, some of the minority religions within the nation came under harsh treatment.   While Sunni Muslims were treated with a good bit of respect, the story was different with people of Jewish faith and Baha'is.   Judaism as a religion was mostly respected; however, Zionism was considered as a secular political party and was under high scrutiny. This caused a huge migration of Jews to Israel and elsewhere in the world. It was estimated that about 60% or a displacement of around 50,000 people of the Jewish faith occurred over the next two decades. Bahai, on the other hand, a young religion, originated in Iran with 250,000 followers, was considered by the government as a political party and not a religion. Therefore like many other political oppositions to the ruling party, many of the Baha'is fled the country after a few hundred lost their lives. A large number of them are now residing in the United States.

The second year of college was winding down when Majid purchased his first car. It was a five-year old red super bug. To check the car out, Majid brought along his uncle. Uncle Massood did not know much about car engines, but he did warn Majid that the person selling the car was trying to get rid of it, after all, he was a psychiatrist. Majid was however pre-sold. In any case it was a car at a reasonable price that he could afford. Secondly it was a super bug, and it was red with stripes on it. Finally, he could not go through another summer without a car.

As soon as summer began, Esi and Majid decided to move to a different residence. They were able to rent the bottom floor of an old house over a mile away from the university. The sixty-year old lady owner had separated the two floors of a house and was able to rent them out as separate units. It had a large kitchen with a small bedroom next to it, and the large family room was attached to a sunroom next to the front porch. While Esi used the small bedroom, Majid fixed and occupied the sunroom for the year to come. Inside the house, there was a very nice and cozy gas operated fireplace, but the neighborhood had much to desire.

Howard Street, which was considered as the center of illegal commerce after dark, was only four to five blocks away from the new house. The neighbors were mostly poor black and white families, some by choice, and most out of necessity. Many of the folks seemed to be welfare recipients and had large families, in mostly two-bedroom run down homes.

For the first two years in the United States, Majid was mainly involved with schoolwork, trying to improve his English, and was deeply concerned about his homeland. While Majid was still nineteen years old, most of his friends including Esi were in their mid twenties. Their eyes seemed to be more on the girls in the library than their own calculus books. But, Majid was a poet and an emotional political junkie who was very shy around the girls.

Majid's friends were constantly trying to set him up with blind dates. A year earlier, they even managed to put him in a car with a hooker in the downtown area, and paid for the services he never obtained. Majid was far different from many of his friends, he was very expressive and he simply could not look at the opposite sex as an object of entertainment. Therefore, that scary night in a dark bedroom, all Majid could do, was to ask the middle-aged lady about her children and why she chose that profession. Through the dark hours of the night, Majid learned that sometimes people have to sell their body to feed their family, even in the richest nation on earth. She asked Majid if he wanted to get his friends' money back, Majid shook his head no. **He was speechless that night and learned never to judge anyone who is in need and never to cast the first stone.** She advised him to find himself a girlfriend that deserved him.

On his first blind date, Majid felt comfortable, for he was dating someone in her last year of high school. He was not very good at making small conversations with girls since he was too shy. There was however a world of difference between Majid and let's say Monika. The only thing in common was their height. Growing up, Majid did not like his father smoking - but at that young age she smoked. He had a very analytical mind, but she hated math. Perhaps the biggest difference was Majid was mentally from the opposite side of the earth. Even so, she was his first friend outside the circle of his Iranian friends. Majid after two years living in the United States was beginning to learn that just because you reside somewhere, you do not automatically discover everything about that society unless you are willing to mix with it and try to learn the standards and values of that society.

This relationship was very valuable for Majid in many ways. For one, his friends were not on his case anymore and they stopped teasing him. However, the best part was that Majid was invited to some of the high school baseball games and he even gave a lecture in one of Monika's classes about Iran. The teacher felt it was very valuable for the students to learn about other parts of the world. Majid and Monika's relationship was neither mental nor sexual but it proved to be a great learning experience for both young minds. She felt special in her high school prior to her graduation, and he learned so much about the folks living in rural areas and the challenges of a single mother raising two daughters on a single paycheck. Majid was like a sponge soaking all the knowledge about his new environment. The date, on most occasions, required a 45-minute round trip drive for Majid. It included a cheap dinner and sometimes a movie, frequently on either a Friday or Saturday night.

In the meanwhile, the news from Iran was at best frustrating. The small changes toward a completely theocratically run government were gaining a strong hold. The 52 remaining American hostages were being used by the media as a way of getting the poor and uninformed to rally behind the new establishment. This was carefully orchestrated to completely shut down all the oppositional newspapers and stop all the other political party activities. Majid was torn apart between his beliefs and all those that were using religion as a tool to control the people through its deeply rooted rituals. **Throughout centuries, many righteous leaders have used their religion as an unparallel unilateral platform. This has created a unique position to allow absolute control of the masses in the name of God. While religion can be beneficial if used as an individual spiritual choice, it can be highly restrictive and dangerous if used to manipulate other people.** Majid articulated his feelings in the following poem:

Love of God

My love is nothing like those in love,
    My love is not defined in a moment,
        I learned love, from your love for me,
            When love has no name, your majesty,
                Can I love you? - When you are Love,
                    Is it, Love of God, or - God is Love!

In the universal game, just as the wind, Majid's life is passing by,
The world of wonder, the days outnumbered - who knows why?

Stories are told by all the believers,
    Truth was silent in darkness of night,
        Tales of cruelties or mountains of light,
            Enlighten us Lord, lost in our shadows,
                Frightful from, all the terror in our minds,
                    Show us the way, the bridge to your love!

In the universal game, just as the wind, Majid's life is passing by,
The world of wonder, the days outnumbered - who knows why?

Clergy make a living, from Lord's name,
    Simple minds are asleep, not a soul awake,
        When they filled our glasses full of wine,
            From grapes of ignorance, there is no shame,
                Dressed like Shepard are wolves these days,
                    We are all the sheep, in the big man's game!

In the universal game, just as the wind, Majid's life is passing by,
The world of wonder, the days outnumbered - who knows why? ...

Majid was entering his third year of college in the fall of 1980. His life was becoming very stressful. Many classes in the Electrical Engineering program with a number of laboratories and extended lab reports was keeping him up until the early hours of the morning. While school work was tough enough, many of the Iranian students were being denied their yearly visa renewal due to the hostage crisis, even though that was not given as the primary reason. Luckily, Majid's visa was "During Status – or D.S." which meant as long as he was a student he did not need to renew his student visa. Just imagine after years of attending college you are thrown out and deported for some off-the-wall reason. I do not believe Mr. Ted Koppel held a single interview on Nightline with any of such students. I guess **Just and Unjust is always in the eyes of the beholder.**

Perhaps the most turbulent year in Majid's life had just begun without any advanced warning. Sometimes it seems like everything comes at you at the same time - school work, fear of deportation with no reason, feeling bad about the status of

131

American hostages in your homeland, and now it was time for the car to start acting up or should I say, breaking down. To make matters worse, that September, Saddam Hussein, or the self-promoted President of Iraq, decided to attack Iran due to Iran's internal political chaos. Saddam was believed by many Iranians to be highly supported by the United States and Saudi Arabia. Consequently, using his knowledge of all Iranian air bases and conducting a two day continuous bombing of such locations caused a crippling effect on the Iranian military. Surprisingly enough, this was followed by a massive land invasion. It was even believed that the United States, unofficially, was providing naval support to Saddam's Navy in the Persian Gulf.

At this point, Majid was completely shook up by all these events. Saddam Hussein troops had advanced and were occupying Iran's adjacent oil-rich State of Khuzestan. While this war on the surface seemed to weaken the two anti-Israel nations which had accumulated massive military buildups, it actually had an adverse effect with long-term complications. The internal chaos inside Iran due to the economy, frustration of women due to the restrictions, and shakiness of the office of presidency, was causing a huge amount of turmoil for the establishment. This war created the sense of nationalism and support from many of the people that were defying theocracy, so in this way it strengthened the regime.

Was this another miscalculation by the Carter administration?
First was the concept of "Human Rights" which was noble but naïve for its time. Second was the support and financing of one of the most fundamentalist Islamic groups in Afghanistan fighting against the Russian Army, later being redirected by one of its leaders and subsequently called Al-Qaeda. Third was lack of a direct military threat to Iran after occupying American soil (its embassy). And now indirectly favoring a ruthless dictator (Saddam) - resulting in a nationalist movement in Iran, causing a setback for the moderate factions, and ultimately strengthening the regime in power!

Hezbollah, or Party of God, was formed at the beginning of the revolution and its members were regarded as counterrevolutionaries. This group which is currently the most feared in the Middle East, its origins being in Iran, acted with no restraint or fear of persecution. While people were unhappy with Hezbollah, after the country was invaded, as mentioned, the Persian pride superseded any internal division and unified the nation under A. Khomeini.

Masses of the youth, thirteen and above, joined the Mahdi Army while wearing keys to open the gates of heaven. The young and old volunteered. Men as well as clueless donkeys were all lined up in chains to walk on mines. Tens of thousands voluntarily gave up their lives in the first few months, excluding the donkeys, while walking hand in hand over the mines and chanting "Allah-O-Akbar". The American made Hercules airplanes that flew the dead bodies back to Tehran were so packed with human remains that blood would be gushing out on the take off. Ahmad and Mahmoud had to serve in the army for a period of time at the beginning of the war, as well as a number of Majid's cousins.

Caskets of Shahids (people who willingly lost their lives for a just cause) were carried in the streets of Teheran and other cities on a daily basis. People over a period of time lost their ability to crack a joke and laughter was becoming a thing of the past!

Majid was not much into going out on dates at this point of his life. He seemed to be confused, concerned about his brothers' safety, exhausted from all the school work and frustrated with his car. It was mid-November when Majid took the twenty mile drive to pick up Monika and go out on a cheap date. There was at least ten inches of snow on the ground and the temperature was not far above ten-degrees Fahrenheit. The car started choking right after dinner and during the drive back to her house. Majid quickly pulled to the side of the road, a dark state road in the boonies lacking any sign of life. Majid was concerned and extremely nervous for the temperature in the car was dropping at a very fast rate. Majid and his companion became fearful, for there were no homes close by, there were no street lights, and worst of all there was no one with a logical mind driving that late at night.

If Majid did not believe in miracles, he became a believer that night. About fifteen minutes after the car had stalled, a red and blue light that normally means time to pay a fine, could not have been anymore welcoming. The officer's face looked like a holy man from heaven and the warm seat in the back of his car felt like a hot day at the beach. Majid's car was towed that night to his house and Monika was dropped off by the state trooper at her house which was less than two miles from the place the car broke down. That was enough for Majid to politely bring that relationship to an end, for he simply did not have the financial means nor was he emotionally prepared to handle all the car problems and the long distance commute.

It was a week before Christmas when one of Majid's best friends received the bad news that his uncle was shot by a 13- year old guard inside Iran. He was a surgeon going home with his wife in the back seat of their friend's car late at night. It was a common practice at the time for young guards to patrol the streets late at night with a machine gun. They could stop any car and ask couples for proof of marriage. Apparently the driver did not realize he had to stop and the thirteen year old guard started shooting at the car. A surgeon who had saved many lives could not save his own life. Majid was absolutely outraged with this news. As if this was not enough, supposed stories of innocent people getting executed on a daily basis, even pregnant women, was beyond Majid's imagination. The news of a woman nine months pregnant being shot by a guard for simply reading some anti-government newspaper was too much for Majid and kept him up many nights. Majid was depressed over the news, and he wrote the following poem as a healing process to his soul:

Flowers never die

Another time, I shall recite,
Yet my poem has no rhyme,
Why worry about the sounds?
When they carry no meaning!
And when every word is lost,
To tell the stories of those in pain!

Disgraced is every letter,
    Ashamed are my rhythms,
        When the 9 year old child,
            And the pregnant lady,
                With a 9 month old fetus,
                    Have to lose their lives!

Is blood the answer to ignorance?
A cover to crucify the innocents?

        Power can only bring arrogance,
        In weak minds with no tolerance!

            All those crucified will rise again,
            Seasons change, **flowers never die!**
Remember again, those in love,
    The rain once red, is coming down,
        Streets are flooded by tears of pain,
            Lambs are taken, Shepard - insane,
                Can you hear the voice, six feet below?
                    Is the nine month fetus crying to you!
The chains have closed our minds,
    The blind don't mind walking in dark,
        Remedy for every pain is more fear,
            Religion is sold in kilos and pounds,
                Losing his life to the bullets of cruelty,
                    Listen to the voices from far beyond!

Is blood the answer to ignorance?
A cover to crucify the innocents?

        Power can only bring arrogance,
        In weak minds with no tolerance!

            All those crucified will rise again,
            Seasons change, **flowers never die!**

      The war with Iraq was raging on. Many countries such as France supplied arms to both sides of the war. The West did not want the Islamic revolution to spread to the nearby oil-exporting countries in the Persian Gulf. Among Muslim nations, Saudi Arabia and Egypt supported Iraq while most anti-government

Islamic parties within most of the Arab nations supported Iran and Hezbollah. The fierce resistance by the Iranians and the incompetence by Saddam's military turned the table against Saddam and his supporters in the region. This unorthodox and unexpected suicidal behavior by Iranians was not calculated in anyone's equation prior to the invasion.

Thus soon after, this sacrificial behavior created much fear within the Arab governments, as well as the nation of Israel.

A. Khomeini's revolution was now taking a strong hold internally and becoming popular on Arab streets. **Perhaps one can say Hezbollah, which had its own flag, became an organized, well-trained, underground entity as a result of this war.**

The sense of nationalism benefited the ruling party during the time of war, but losing one's personal freedom was not what people were bargaining for. The Iranian people were concerned about the war and the drop in value of the toman against all the other currencies due to the expenses caused by the war. Outside the country however, opposition groups were concerned about losing the freedom of speech within the nation. The longer the war lasted, the easier it was for the ruling party to keep a strong hold on the power. All they had to do was to blame all the turmoil in the country on the United States, and all the opposition groups.

Knowing that the newly elected president in the United States would take direct action against Iran for freedom of her citizens and being in the middle of a bloody war, Iran was looking for a way to release the American hostages. This was made possible by an Algerian diplomat and is known as "Algiers Accords." This agreement took place one day prior to the end of President Carter's presidency. The hostages were released on January 20, 1981 immediately before Mr. Regan was sworn in as the new president. Not only did this protect the regime in Iran against a direct attack by the United States within a short period of time, it also made them look strong against a superpower in the eyes of many people in the Middle East. The 444 days that 52 Americans were held hostage against their will had a larger long-term impact in the region. **It broke the paradigm of thinking that the United States government is invincible; hence, it**

helped the Islamic fundamentalist groups in the region become stronger.

In the spring of 1981 there were many clashes within Iran that took many lives - many caused by the ruling party by means of executions, and a few by the Mojahedin which was the strongest opposition party. Mojahedin, which was once again an underground operation, was involved with a number of bombings that had taken the lives of some clergy and members of the ruling party. Majid was never interested in being affiliated with any political party, but because of his poetry the opposition political parties were interested in him. After many requests, on one occasion, Majid recited his last poem in front of a large audience of activists at another university. This was not the smartest move that Majid had made, for his poems were always written to promote the healing process for his own soul. For this one act, Majid paid a huge price.

Within two days of reciting his poem, Majid received a phone call from his father at six o'clock in the morning. It did not take much at the time to be labeled as an anti-government activist, and now Majid was identified as one. Students that passed the name of people like Majid were suspected to receive a kick back from the government in Iran. They even made money for passing the name of students that did not appear to support the government activities. That morning, Akbar asked his son to immediately cease any activity against the government in Iran. Majid was absolutely clueless, for that was the only time Majid had read his poem in front of anyone. It however cost him dearly for it meant his parents could not support him financially anymore and he would be taking a huge risk in going back to visit his family.

At this point Majid had to worry about survival. In life people can focus on many issues that seem important to them at the time, but when they lose the means to pay their bills, nothing looks the same. Majid was neither a U.S. citizen, nor did he have his Green Card or the permission to work in the United States. As a foreign student he had a Foreign Alien status. Foreign students' tuition, rightly so, was twice as much as those of local students. The biggest question for Majid in the spring of 1981 was how to pay for over $9,000 per year expenses without any money coming from his parents. Majid only had around $1,000 in his bank account and approximately one and half years of the college program to complete. What was he supposed to do?

Like anyone else trapped in a situation like that, he was awake in the middle of the night thinking about all his problems. Despite an average of "A" in math, the numbers were not adding up in his life. Since his tuition was paid for that whole semester, the $1000 was enough to carry him to the end of that school year, but what was he to do after that? Between the classes and staying up at nights, one early morning when Majid was washing his face, he noticed one of his eyes was totally bloodshot. He had an exam that day around 10 a.m. but he checked into the university medical center right away. After a quick check up, he was told it was caused by his nervous system and he needed to take it easy.

As if Majid did not have enough pain, it was time for his car to once again break down. This time however, he had to leave his car on the side of the street and simply walk to and from school every day. The two mile walk was not too bad. The only problem was that he had to walk on the ice with a hole in one of his shoes. The strong wind was difficult to deal with while crossing the bridge in early March. Majid's favorite prayer while crossing the bridge was, "**Lord I only fear you and seek strength from you**." This prayer seemed to keep Majid sane even though he had much pain in his heart.

Toward the end of that semester and before the summer of 1981 began, the stress seemed to take its toll on Majid. He was down to the last $400 in his bank account and instead of hearing the joyful songs by the birds he could only hear a screeching sound. He attended his classes but had a hard time paying attention to anything or taking any notes. During some of the classes he even had tears falling off his cheeks without even trying. He was the victim of loving his country and his country hating him in return. Majid was in a state of depression and in verge of a nervous breakdown. His pride did not allow him to call his uncle for help, and his uncle was too busy with his own family life.

As if someone was watching over Majid, other than his poor roommate Esi, who was not in much better financial shape - the phone range during the last weekend of the school year. "How are you, Majid?" said Uncle Massood. Majid was happy to hear his uncle's voice whose house was only thirty minutes away.

Majid claimed that he was just fine, but his uncle detected the sadness in his voice. "Are you sure?" he asked in a soft voice. Majid could no longer keep his pain to himself, so he spilled out all the problems he was having. Uncle Massood invited Majid to his house for couple weeks and prescribed him some mild medication. Majid also earned some money by painting the exterior of his house. One thing that helped Majid tremendously by following his uncle's advice was to **get up and get busy doing something if he could not sleep during the night.**

This visit to his uncle's house had a major positive impact on Majid's life. It turned a boy to a man. Not so much by Uncle Massood showing him the way, as much as Majid finding his way without staring at the problems that were chasing him. **When people keep thinking about their problems, not only does it not solve anything, but it also takes away from the amount of time that they can spend on finding a solution.** The two week stay gave Majid the badly needed time to first analyze where he was standing in life and then attempt to come up with a game plan that was possible to execute.

To better understand himself Majid had to look inside, and to resolve the problems facing him he had to look outside. He had lost faith in a religion full of rituals, a religion that was demanding and was offering him no long-term vision. Yet in being lost, he had found spirituality and the belief that doing good will bring about goodness to all aspects of his life. Majid began his internal trip by trusting in God in ways that were very special to him, and he knew God was watching over him in every step of the way. To better deal with the external issues on hand, he for the first time was forced to realize that life is not "a bowl of cherries." **Life was not promised to be fair to everyone but would be more promising to those that focused on the cherry and not the pit.** Winners in life are not those who are dealt a great poker hand, but those who have a lousy hand and yet they get the best result out of it.

"When the going gets tough, the tough get going," was a new slogan imprinted on Majid's way of thinking. He was no longer upset with the outcome of his immature behavior, but focused on the main issues in his life that required quick and immediate resolve. The first issue was survival and the second one was to put his parents' minds at rest, by knowing their son was not involved in anything that would cause problems for anyone in the family.

Many folks out of hunger choose the longest path to success, however if they spend a day or two to come up with a clear vision, they achieve their goals at a much faster rate. Majid spent a couple days and came up with the following outline:

a) Any solution to his problems must be ethical and legal,

b) Any grade below "C" was not a viable or an acceptable option,

c) By immigration laws Majid had to take a minimum of 12 credit hours without dropping any classes. It was legal to work at the University for $3.35 per hour. Therefore he needed to minimize the number of classes he took and maximize the number of hours he worked within the campus and the football stadium.

d) Minimize the walking distance to college and reduce the cost of living to its absolute bare minimum,

e) Tutor friends and other students in return for favors and pocket change,

f) Work outside campus during the summer with a special 3 month permit,

g) Get some assistance from Uncle Massood in the form of a loan if needed.

Next Majid had to promise his father he would not speak his mind even though he was tens of thousands of miles away. Since Majid could only express his pain through his poetry, he also declared his silence through the following poem:

"Stone"

I am that stone; the one buried,
    In the mountain of darkness,
        Trapped by a black widow,
            In the web of weak minds,
                And tired from the dust,
                    Choking my life away!

I am that stone; the one buried,
    In the fire of volcanic hearts,
        Falling from the utmost high,
            Rolling to the lowest valley,
                And leaving nothing behind,
                    But flames, fume, and pain!

I am that stone, the frozen earth,
    Confused in the quake of life,
        Deaf to the ticking seconds,
            Lost in the mist of dusk,
                Motionless in the thunder,
                    And blinded to the light!

I am that stone, the frozen earth,
    Missing my tongue, having no song,
        Blindfolded in the demon's dungeon,
            Powerless in the bottom of the ocean,
                That even Messiah wouldn't be able,
                    To blow a soul into my dead body!

I am that stone, mourning the silence,
    Of the waves after arriving the shore,
        And the sand when it is washed away,
            Heart full of pain, body made of agony,
                For I have seen more than what I need,
                    And I've heard beyond my understanding!

I am that stone, who made a promise,
    To the light that extends to heaven,
        To the mountain, valley and desert,
            To the long seconds of lonely nights,
                And to the fury of roaring waves,
                    That I lose my voice forever more!

I am that stone, voiceless,
    I am that stone, pointless,
        I am that stone, colorless,
            I am that stone, soulless,
                But I am still a stone; and,
                    That stone deserves respect!

141

After writing this poem, Majid brought a closure to his poetry writing for many reasons. Writing poems can bring healing and generate an uplifting feeling to the poet, and an escape from the folks that emotionally do not relate to the writer. Living a life of poetry keeps a person emotionally engaged, and Majid literally and psychologically could not afford that any longer. This also would put a stop to politics in his life which had only brought him pain. The fact is that he realized **singing to deaf ears is a waste of time**. This also put an end to being harassed by his conservative father that measured everything in life by tomans and dollars. But most importantly, Majid had to work hard for survival and every second had to count for something, and every minute had to be value added.

While the term multi-tasking was not even defined at the time, Majid had to start mega-tasking. To execute his master plan that summer, he did not take any classes so that he could work at the University and maximize the number of hours he could work. He also helped some of his friends that sold ice cream from their upgraded old post office trucks, and even found time to tutor college students in math. This perhaps was the best learning experience for Majid - to gain knowledge about his environment while earning a living. He found much more love in the poor neighborhoods than the rich ones, and saw surprising generosity among those that sold their body as they paid for all the children's ice creams on the entire street. He learned how drugs were changing the future of a country and the simplistic and naïve solution was to "Just say no." He learned that Americans are hardworking, peace loving, yet not very well-informed about national and global issues, for their concerns were mainly on local and day-to-day concerns. Majid was now more interested in learning about his new environment than the one that had written him off.

Majid's budget for food was about $35 per month, so the diet consisted of jars of beans and outdated hotdogs, vegetables and fruit from a local flea market, and a lot of marked down pita bread and cheese from a cheap source that baked the pita bread on a daily basis. Majid's new extended friendship with Iranians, Arabs, Americans, some Koreans, and even one friend from Israel, at times provided food and entertainment at no cost, but largely helped him change his way of thinking. For the first time, he was looking at the issues in a different way, and those issues had started to look differently. It is true to say, **if you change the way you look at things, the things you look at will change**. The challenge to his existence by losing the money from his parents proved to be the best thing that ever happened to him. **It is in breaking the ropes - - - to our past - - - that helps us find - - - the string - - - that connects us - - - to a bright future!**

After that summer, Majid and Esi moved within half a mile from Akron U. Majid only took 12 credit hours and slowed down his graduation by about one semester. With his school requirements and work hours, Majid barely had any time to pay attention to the politics inside Iran, other than some snap shots here and there.

Iran however was on the same track as before and A. Khomeini supporters continued using the war as a tool to further control the people and most notably use their power over the way of life in the nation. The nation seemed to be in constant chaos. In June of 1981 the Iran's moderate Government of Banisadr collapsed which was followed by two months of provisional presidential council. President Rajai barely lasted for a month before he became a victim of another assassination. This was followed by another two months of provisional presidential council rule, and this time A. Khamenei (current Supreme Leader) was elected as the President in October of 1981.

The major global event, under most analysts' radar, was the growth of Hezbollah in Iran and its establishment of roots elsewhere in the region. Hezbollah was loosely formed at its origins by a number of A. Khomeini's followers in the early 1980s. It spread through the young emotional minds that controlled the streets of Iran with no accountability for the taking of innocent lives. To their simplistic and unconscious view, those who were not guilty and lost their lives would end up in heaven. For the teenage militia there was absolutely no place for those who opposed such a holy movement.

Over a period of time, this Shia group, Hezbollah became more organized. It also began to utilize many features of Hamas, a Palestinian Sunni group perceived as terrorists in the West, and as freedom fighters in the Arab streets.

A. Khomeini's book by the name of Velayat-eh-Fagih (Willayat-Al-Faghi) became the guideline for Hezbollah over a short period of time, much like a new religion. The major difference between Hamas and Hezbollah however was that Hamas had very little financial support, and Hezbollah was fully supported by an oil and gas rich country. While Hezbollah's finance was covered from the top, their main supporters were from the bottom, the very least educated, the angry, and the most fundamentalist group of people intolerant of opposing views. These type of people are prepared to give their sons to fight evil and promote a just or an Islamic society. **Considering that poor people are always waiting for someone to come and fight in their behalf, the Mahdi Army was formed to fight injustice within Muslim nations.**

The Iranian alliance with Syria, a majority Sunni nation, played a role in Hezbollah's movement into Lebanon. This new coalition between the Iranian and Syrian governments was a big financial help to the Syrians by means of some free oil and support against Israeli forces in South Lebanon. For Iran, it helped spread Hezbollah internationally so that supporters developed throughout Arab streets which were in defiance with the Arab governments. One could speculate that by 1982 Hezbollah had spread out to Lebanon with a common flag, ideology, army, and most of all strong financial backing.

Throughout this time Majid focused on finishing up his degree in Electrical Engineering. He was upset about the Iran-Iraq war that took so many lives, but there was nothing he could do about it. That war did not just take hundreds of thousands of lives at that point, but it bankrupted the Iranian economy. Since it was not popular to tax people to stay in a war, the government printed more money without any backing. Over a period of time, this caused a drop in the value of currency by many fold. Just imagine one dollar was traded for seven tomans in 1979 and just after two

144

years of war it was being traded for over four hundred tomans. Many people, including Majid's parents, that had a good retirement plan, were left in the dust, for inflation was completely out of control.

1982 seemed to be full of events. That was the year that Esi, Majid's roommate of four years, decided to marry Fariba. Four years earlier, she had attended the English school at the same time with Majid and Esi. Majid then moved to a three bedroom apartment with Abbas and Siamak. While Majid knew Abbas for a couple years, Siamak had just started his Master's degree in Electrical Engineering. Strangely enough Majid and Siamak went to the same high school in Iran for six years and now they were roommates.

Finally, as May of 1982 was approaching, Majid was getting much closer to his finish line. Through all the ups and downs, late night studies, miles of walking back and forth to the University, working any odd hours, and eating plenty of old hot dogs and beans, Majid was going through the final exam week before he received his four year degree. He had no party to attend after his graduation and he was not even invited to a single dinner. He did not have any money to purchase the cap and gown for his graduation, so he could not even attend that ceremony.

After his last test Majid and one of his friends, who was in the same class celebrated his graduation by having a beer at the Chuckery or the university's cafeteria. That was Majid's second glass of beer in the United States ever, and Majid's first degree. Majid was now ready for the graduate school and he was happy to be done with four years of stress in his life.

The turbulent years were finally over, and Majid had learned the biggest lesson in life, and that was, **"No matter how difficult life can treat you, one can achieve his or her goal, if it is documented, measured, and failure is not considered as an acceptable option."** On that note, let's have the next drink to Majid who achieved his goal, and cheers to all the folks that chase their dreams, never give up, and strive for the best!

Evaluation Years

Majid, who was always interested in math, and maintained a 4.0 average in all his college math classes - decided to first pursue his masters degree in Statistics before his graduate work in Electrical Engineering. Majid's interest in statistics was the result of the second class in control systems that required some knowledge of probability and statistics. This meant it would take him an additional semester to get his degree since he had to take some pre-requisite advanced math classes. Majid was only twenty-one years old and all things considered, he was in no rush to get done. He had a scholarship that paid for his education which left him with over $550 dollars per month for his expenses. The requirement for his scholarship was to teach two sections of basic math classes for the business major students. In addition he was allowed to work eight hours on campus, which he did.

Life seemed to be completely different from a few months earlier. Majid was very natural at teaching since from age ten he was tutoring other kids in math. He loved to teach, and this was a great experience for him being in front of a class. He prepared his lectures well in advance and sometimes rehearsed them in front of a mirror. He even prepared small jokes to make sure he was not losing the students' attention during the lecture. The first half an hour of each class was a prepared TV lecture delivered by the head of the program, followed by numerous examples presented by Majid for his sections. There were probably 10 to 12 of these classes per semester for mostly students with non-engineering majors.

At this point, Majid was at the top of his game. He had learned how to survive on the bare minimum financially, how to work with friends of multi-cultural backgrounds, and now he had plenty of money to enjoy life a bit more. To keep the cost down, some of his friends, including Esi, helped him get his ailing car back on the road. One of the guys was more creative. He had Majid rent an air compressor and buy some gallons of red paint to improve the car's appearance. That proved to be a disaster of paint job for he was learning on the job at Majid's expense. There were paint drips all over the car, thus Majid learned that **in life, you really get what you pay for.**

It was a late night in September of 1982, when Siamak came home with Behroz. Behroz was a slender twenty year old student from Iran. Siamak had found him on the side of the street where he slept for a couple nights after his landlord had evicted him. Like many Iranian students, his money was cut off from Iran and he had simply run out of money to pay his rent. Siamak quickly huddled with Majid and Abbas to figure out what to do with him. Siamak had already fed him 3 hamburgers at McDonalds and was very concerned about his future. The three roommates quickly grouped together and came up with a quick solution to help Behroz out. They told him he could stay with them until he got back on his feet. During his stay Behroz managed to work at the University while continuing his education. He slept on the couch and cooked many Kurdish meals as a token of his appreciation.

After three weeks of stay, Behroz started dating a young fine girl at Akron U. that was perhaps a couple years younger than him. Behroz and Joy seemed to be made for each other. She came from a religious Presbyterian family in which her father was a preacher. The whole family seemed to be spoiling Behroz, and they even cleaned up a room in their basement for him to stay. Behroz was a simple honest man and the two had hit it off from day one. Majid was also invited over to their house plenty of times and he enjoyed sharing his experiences with the family, as well as learning much from Joy's father, or Mr. Sheinberg should I say.

It was a few months into the school year and the old car was humming again. Majid, who was impressed with the relationship, between Behroz and Joy was now ready for a girlfriend of his own. One of his friend's girlfriend set him up with a girl she knew. Jessica, let's call her, was a fine looking nineteen-year old girl who had just got out of a relationship. She was a sophomore in business. Majid who was emotional and a romantic person by nature gave much attention and respect to her and tried to spoil her with good restaurants and fine dinning. He even brought her over to the Sheinberg family right before a dinner engagement. Mrs. Sheinberg, as if Majid was her own son, did not have a positive view of her and she made sure to share that with Majid. Without getting into much detail, Majid came to that understanding a few weeks later, and he had to walk away from that relationship with a broken heart.

During Christmas of 1982, Behroz and Joy were married. Majid was happy for both of them, but very sad and confused about himself. He was at an age that he was desperately looking for companionship but he was not ready to go on another blind date. During that holiday season, Majid was also invited to one his uncle's parties. One could say when a number of doctors and their wives came together, the biggest talk of the night centered around who was wearing the largest piece of jewelry among the women and at what price tag. Majid, who could not afford a hamburger for lunch a few months earlier, watched the folks throwing plates of food into the trash. He was impressed by the classiness of the guests, yet outraged by the amount of waste when there were so many hungry.

Majid had a few weeks off before classes started in spring of 1983. He had some time to think about all his experiences in life, and to determine where he was heading in life. **It is always important to use the pockets of time that become available to people to figure out and fine tune their direction toward their goal.**

While Majid barely knew Behroz, during that short period of time, Behroz had a significant impact on Majid's thinking. The four things that grabbed Majid's attention were, a) how easily a person who runs out of money can be left by the side of the street and become homeless, b) how quickly one's life can change if the person is helped by the society, c) how people from a different part of the world can be united if they have common interest, and, d) how Behroz was at ease with the American culture and the way of life.

On the other hand, he remembered his uncle's party. People who attended were mostly doctors who earned over a quarter of a million dollars annually with some surgeons making around a million dollars a year. That created a different set of questions for Majid such as: a) what causes people to migrate and decide to stay at the new place and even change their citizenship, b) why would rich people have a higher tendency to show off their material wealth, and c) why is it so hard for the rich people to understand the plight of the poor.

Those were not the only questions, for Majid was also concerned about him being able to, a) ever go back home to visit his relatives and do some site seeing, b) work in the United States and build a future here, and, c) meet and marry someone that shared the same values and standards as he did.

While the questions were many, the answers were not as obvious. In life we first have to pose the questions to ourselves, before we try to look for answers. **At times we should simply treat ourselves as if we are an object. Since we do not move an object without a reason and a goal, we should not take the next step in life without having a clear vision.** Some folks unconsciously choose not to characterize where they wish to find themselves in life; hence, their failure to plan will most likely place them in the land of failure. This is why Majid wrote these questions in his poetry book so that over a period of time, he would find the answers. **It is always better for a person to take their time and come across the answers wisely, rather than rushing into them quickly and obtain worthless and sometimes harmful results.**

While Majid was busy articulating a new strategy in his life, Hezbollah was building strength throughout the region, particularly in Lebanon. For decades Western countries were perceived to be controlling many of the governments in the third world nations - for their own interest. But how could a third world country's creation, Hezbollah, be capable of a similar influence? Very easy - in order to get into someone's house, you either have to know the head of the household or offer their youngest child a lollipop. Hezbollah's programs to help the poor and provide free medical care, gave it the ability to warm the heart and soul of the targeted set of people. As a result, the emotional youth of these families provided the so-called freedom fighters.

There is always a place at the table for any organization that provides financial support to the poor and watches over their interest - while recruiting their children for a so-called higher cause. By Hezbollah's definition, the higher cause in this case would have been the withdrawal of the Israeli forces from South Lebanon. This was how the Iranian based Hezbollah was able to proceed in the heart of Arab lands.

With the financial support from Iran and available youth in many countries in that region, such as Lebanon, Hezbollah was ready to take charge - from the bottom to the top. Many of the kidnappings of Westerners especially Americans, the bombing of the American Embassy in April of 1983, and later bombing of the American barracks in Beirut, Lebanon were to blame on Hezbollah. There seemed to be no antidote for an organization that was popular among the Shia in the poor and middle class neighborhoods.

While from the race, language, and the sect of Islam point of view, Iran has always been different than the rest of the Middle East; Hezbollah, a fundamentalist Shia based organization was able to break those barriers down by lining itself up with the main hot issue of the Arab population. This issue was - the perception that Israel had been the aggressor since the 1967 Arab-Israeli war. Pulling the American troops out of Lebanon by President Reagan proved not to be the smartest move in the region, for it created a vacuum to allow Iran and Syria to finance and encourage the spread of Hezbollah into more Arab nations.

Thousands of miles away, at Akron University, Majid was the only teaching assistant that was offered to teach the same math classes in the summer of 1983. This time he had to prepare and teach the class on his own without any video assistance. This helped boost his confidence and improved his ability to speak English greatly. In addition he spent much time after the classes communicating with his students, many times on personal levels. This helped him better understand different segments of the society and their issues and concerns. He was finding himself at ease in connecting with all the students and the type of problems they had. Majid realized and noted that on that day, **in order to be at ease with a culture, one must engage in many common activities within that society.** For this reason, Majid not only provided free tutoring for some of the students that summer, but he also had some interesting experiences with his American friends. Some of these included bar hopping and a couple times even being mesmerized by exotic dancers.

Over that summer, Majid also went along with one of his friends that sold ice cream over the weekends. Amazingly enough most of his business came from the poor neighborhoods. On the ice cream route, one can encounter just about anything, some negative and many positive memories. He saw the part of America many choose not to look for, and the middle class that was consumed by day-to-day issues. He saw the poor, the broken families that strived for the best they could be, the separated middle-aged women looking for companionship, and drug dealers awaiting customers on the street corners. He saw the homeless and the hopeless, and he also saw many failed government programs. Some people even tried to trade food stamps at sixty percent of its value so they could use the dollars to fulfill their thirst for alcohol and drugs.

Majid never forgot the day when the four year old Michelle with her big, sad eyes and long blond hair did not raise her hand to stop the ice cream truck. She simply did not have any quarter to pay for the Popsicle. "Hi Michelle," Majid said in a compassionate voice, "No Popsicles today?" Michelle with tears vibrating her vocal cords replied, "But I have no money." Majid with permission from his friend quickly rushed to the freezer in the back of the truck and grabbed a Popsicle for her. "This is for you, the prettiest little girl on earth," Majid said in a kind voice. She may not have been the prettiest girl on earth, but at that moment she definitely was the happiest. **While there are not enough material possessions on the earth to make the rich man happy, a little bit of love and kindness goes a long way for those living in poverty.** Majid that day learned the reason why most rich folks have a hard time reaching down to help someone less fortunate. **The well-to-do population is normally within a circle of their own, never meeting girls like Michelle to understand that poverty is not a choice, but a circle with a small radius holding the unfortunate people close to its origin.** Rich folks also always look for better opportunities; hence it would be hard for them to tangle themselves up with the needy and less sophisticated.

Majid's weekend journeys through the streets of Akron had an enormous impact on him. For the first time his head was not buried in the pages of a book, but he was learning about the real environment that was shaping the minds of people and the way of conduct in a society. The ice cream truck never traveled through the rich neighborhoods for those folks had plenty of ice cream in their freezers, but Majid had already experienced their behavior. The rich, were so lost in a material world, that their principles and hence the height of their friendship, were defined by the amount of material possessions and belongings they had. God seemed to play a much smaller role among the rich than the poor. In the very poor ghettos with ravaging drug and prostitution problems, "Jesus Saves" seemed to be painted on the old run down buildings, among other writings. Majid could not understand that in a rich country comprising over 30% of the world wealth, while having less than 5% of the population of the earth - why the rich people could not save the poor folks, and why they had to wait for Jesus to do so. At the time, of course, he did not understand the actual meaning of the "Jesus Saves" statement, in the mind and soul of people within the Christian faith. Majid was never able to figure out **why societies do not realize that the strength of any union is as strong as the weakest link among it.**

The middle class, while working hard, seemed to enjoy their weekends at the park, involved in organized games for the youth. Another important weekend function was the attendance of church services which lasted anywhere between one to several hours depending on the type of church and religious affiliation. On Saturdays, ice cream trucks seemed to target the games at the parks and the kids playing games in the street all day. Some parents were friendly when they bought the ice cream for their children and some folks were annoyed by the music. One perhaps could categorize the middle class people in that region as hard-working, church going, relatively high moral people that were very informed about the local community and to some extent the national concerns, but they were much less interested in global issues. Also there was another class somewhat between the poor and the middle class, and that was the single mothers who worked hard to take care of their children. Some of these ladies did not mind flirting with the ice cream drivers for a free ice cream and sometimes other favors - even having a casual sex.

Majid was learning about America, and it looked as if the Americans, with open arms, were willing to learn about him and his experiences in life. The biggest assessment Majid had made about Americans was that they were so open to learning about people from other parts of the world with little prejudice. This was making him feel wanted and at ease to join right in. But at the same time, much like an unpleasant odor in the air, he felt there was a dark side to the psyche of some of the white, even church going, middle-class folks about the issue of race. There was not even one black family living in the middle to upper class white neighborhoods, and hardly any black folks attended white churches and vice versa. It felt like a couple that was not divorced but had nothing in common, yet living under the same roof. Let's compare it to two roommates that shared a refrigerator, but made sure their food was separated. They had totally different interests in life and did not value each other's interests much. This seemed odd to Majid who was welcomed with open arms, yet those who were born in this land with darker skin and had defended it against its enemies, did not appear to have the same sense of belonging. Majid once again had a question with no answer, not because it was a difficult question, as much as a forgotten and untouchable one.

Majid now had learned much more about the community he was living in. He had learned about the freedom of expression without political correctness, the struggles of college students, the classes of people and their principles, the cultural values and language barriers, and most of all, the way of survival. So, Majid realized **it is in active engagement that people can learn from one another and break the rigid walls of prejudice separating them; for humanity has a much better chance of survival when it unites.**

The summer of 1983 came to an end and Majid began the second year of his graduate work, or actually the second semester in Statistics. At this point Majid was not paying much attention to the politics anywhere. Off and on, he would listen to the arguments of the Iranian students around the table at the Chuckery cafeteria, but he did not have the desire to participate in them. Iran was offered a great deal from Iraq to stop the war, but A. Khomeini had rejected it. The Iranian students were mostly against that war, but a few pro-Iranian government students felt that Iran should advance into Iraq as far it could. A. Khomeini through his Mahdi Army wanted to advance as far as Israel, as if the United States and other countries were going to sit still and watch it happen. Majid was concerned about **the sound**

principles that make a society function effectively, a place that would be desired by its population. With all the sadness caused by the war and the economy in shambles as a result of the war, Iran was becoming much less desirable to live in and a very difficult place to start a family.   I guess the main reason to separate from the place of your birth and conform to a new set of standards has to do with "the way of life" and the ability to deal with "the pain of change."   This is why one can say, **if the pain of change is less than the pain you currently endure, you will change.**

By Christmas of 1983, Majid was feeling much more comfortable with the American way of life.   He did not feel much different from the rest of the community and enjoyed how people were involved in a free election.   He enjoyed the straight talk more than tarrofing in which one does not know what was really in that person's mind.   To have a new beginning, it required more savings in the bank, so he started working additional hours at school to set aside as much money as possible.   Also Ozra wanted to see Majid passionately, but due to a high inflation in the cost of living in Iran, that was close to impossible.   So Majid also had to figure out a way to pay for his mom to come and visit him and this was no pocket change.   The rest of that school year went by uneventfully other than when Siamak was offered a job from a company in New Orleans.   After Siamak moved out, Fariburz who was in his last year in the mechanical engineering program moved in his place.   This was followed by another summer that was quite similar to the one before.

The summer of 1984 came to an end, and Majid began the last semester of his graduate work in statistics.   By then Majid was working out regularly in the gym.   He was very comfortable with his environment, and best of all, he had developed a personality that could crack a joke at any instant.   While the new year meant the loss of some of the old faces in the graduate office, it had delivered a few new ones.   Now the balance was five guys to four girls, four foreign born versus five Americans, and five new TA's versus four second year students.

Majid, David, Greg, and Tah were in their second year, while Lisa D., Michelle, Senjar, Dillip, and Lisa T. had just joined in.   Majid was tired of blind dates and he was looking for someone intelligent as a girlfriend, and Lisa D. was definitely matching that profile. She was a few inches shorter than him, slim, with dark brown hair and eyes. She was shy and kept to herself, and she normally spent a few hours at the office but was not much into small conversations. Her parents were of Italian ancestry, but born and raised in the United States.

Majid had an immediate crush on Lisa, but he was too shy to express his interest. What if she had a boyfriend and what if she was not interested in him. A couple weeks after school was in session, there was a cookout sponsored by the Math Department that Majid attended. There she was - Lisa sitting at the table with a plate of food in front of her. Majid decided to quickly get some food and sit right beside her. "So what are you taking?" Majid asked to break the ice. She responded, "I have just started my Masters degree in math." "How do you like it so far?" Majid continued. "Oh just fine," she said and the small talk continued. Lisa was much into sports and decided to play soccer with a group of guys, which to Majid who loved to play soccer and volleyball, was absolutely awesome. Lisa seemed to be the answer to Majid's prayers. She was a ball of fire under a bit of ash residue, and Majid was starting to feel that heat in his heart.

While Majid's eyes were chasing her in the office for another couple weeks, he did not have the guts to ask her out. I guess he was afraid of rejection since they both worked at the same office. It was about mid-semester when she had a question about one of her homework problems, and Majid seemed to have the solution. That was the perfect time to ask her if she wanted to go see a movie with him at the University. She had never gone out with someone who was not born in United States, so she responded "I don't know, maybe some other time." That answer was not a "yes" nor was it a "no." Majid popped the same question to Lisa after a couple weeks, but this time in front of Michelle. "I don't know," Lisa responded, but Michelle who was a newly wed asked Lisa "Why not? Majid seems like a fun guy to hang out with." Lisa then responded, "I guess a movie would be alright." Majid was quick to thank Michelle with his eyes and body language. Majid was not planning to ask her again, for his Persian pride would have held him back. It was his first time ever asking someone out and he was awfully happy with the outcome. Majid remembered the Popsicle that he gave to the four year old Michelle just a few months earlier and now someone by the name Michelle returned the favor, and perhaps initiated the most monumental change in Majid's life. Majid once again realized that **it is in giving that you receive; it is in surrounding yourself with goodness that happiness can find a path to you.**

Finally that Friday arrived and Majid was ready to take Lisa to the movie at the University. The bad thing was he did not know what the movie was about, so not too long into the movie, Majid and Lisa with much disappointment left "Scar Face" which was a very violent movie and not exactly what Majid had in mind. However they ended up at an ice cream shop which gave them the ability to connect intellectually.

The following Friday they set up a dinner engagement at a place called the Brown Derby which was relatively nice. However when they arrived, there was over an hour wait. Since they both were hungry, they decided to simply go to Wendy's. Hardly anyone was at Wendy's that Friday night since no one in their right mind takes their date to a fast food restaurant.

Majid, unlike previous situations, wanted to get to know Lisa and her set of principles. He also wanted Lisa to learn about him and his values. While he had a big crush on her, he did not want to be disappointed a number of weeks later. This is why he spoke for at least three hours about his philosophy in life, his cultural and religious background, and just about everything that meant something in his life. Lisa quietly listened to everything and asked many questions. With every word spoken, Majid was mentally and intellectually getting closer and closer to her. That night, after dropping her off at her house and departing from her with a little kiss on her cheek, Majid went back home while leaving part of his soul behind.

Majid could not wait until Monday morning to see Lisa at the graduate office. After seeing Majid at the Chuckery with Lisa, her brother John who was heavily into working out and body building had a couple of positive remarks about Majid. On the following date, Majid was invited in their house where there was a small stereo in the basement. Lisa asked if Majid cared to listen to a song from Neil Diamond with a big question on her face, since most young students at the time were into hard rock. Majid could not believe his ears for he had a number of Neil Diamonds' tapes at his apartment, and for him this was perhaps a sign from above. Majid was in high spirits that night for finding someone among many that was literally in tune with his feelings and emotions.

Within a short period of time, Majid and Lisa were bonding as if they had known each other for years.   Lisa had a strict upbringing in the Catholic faith, so the relationship was developed based on respect and high ethics.   For their next date, Majid, who was an excellent cook, invited her for some Persian delicacies at his apartment.   Dinner consisted of rice, broiled chicken and stewed vegetables.   He also had chilled red wine on ice. Everything was arranged nicely on a candle-lit table.   Majid's roommates were nowhere to be seen.   One of Majid's friends called him from the adjacent apartment overlooking the parking lot.   "Oh, Lisa is here with some flowers for you," he said, then paused and with a big laugh continued, "Boy, you guys have it backwards."   Actually, Majid and Lisa were open to new ways of thinking, rather than being chained to the old set of standards. **The problem with a large number of people is that they chain themselves to a set of old, "no value added" traditions and behaviors that at times may be harmful, and they do not understand why these behaviors are not beneficial and even destructive at times.**

Unlike many of his friends who were afraid of taking a risk to question many of their values and habits, Majid did not hesitate to experience new concepts in life.   **Many of the students and populace from the Middle East, who for the first time migrated to the United States, looked at this nation as the leader in advanced technology.   However, they still considered their own old cultures at a much higher level.**   Therefore, it was easy for them to stay here and advance in the work environment but it was difficult to mix with the rest of the society.   Iranian students however had an advantage since they were brought up during the pro-western period of time when the Shah of Iran was in power. Because of this, they had a much easier time blending in with the American life style, but due to a strong cultural heritage they were too proud to let go with their traditions.

The main original migration to the United States was by the Pilgrims, Puritans, Quakers, and Catholics centuries ago, looking

157

for religious freedom. Within the past half century, this was followed by those escaping religious persecution and the ones running away from communism while searching for political freedom. There were even some who were just looking for a better life. Most of these folks cut all the ropes connecting them to the past when they left their homelands, and immediately found home here when they left the boat behind.

In the modern times and the past number of decades however, most people have been one airplane ticket away from their place of birth or anywhere else on earth. **Therefore the main reasons for migration in modern societies were to obtain higher education, seek political refuge from injustice, and in many cases look for better job opportunities.** This meant during the past decades, no one really had to cut and leave any ropes behind when joining the new society, even after becoming a United States citizen. In particular, those in their fifties and beyond had a harder time to breakdown their paradigm of thinking, learn the new language, and find a way to mix with the new society. This was perhaps why the new immigrants had found more comfort among their own groups and barely had the need to unite with the rest of the society. **Diversity can only add value when people mix, and not when they have little interest to participate and find ways to separate themselves from all the factors that make the new country - home.**

On the other hand, people in most societies, always seek to find the easiest way out of the social problems - many times by oversimplifying them. **Closing our eyes to perceived problems in a community is not an answer. It is just the postponement of the solution, which sometimes can come at a detrimental cost to the population.** For instance the issue of race in our country remains the eight hundred pound Guerrilla in the room that many folks had avoided dealing with in the past, so it continues to surface at different times even to this date.

Lisa and Majid had similar interests and values, yet they were born over 9,000 miles apart from each other, with diverse religious and cultural backgrounds. They were fully aware of these differences, but both were open-minded about their dissimilarities and understood that diversity could be a great asset in their lives if it was looked at in a different way. **If we change**

the way we look at things in life, our lives find a new meaning and purpose. When Majid was invited to attend Lisa's Catholic Church, he accepted immediately, since he agreed with this philosophy. **It is in learning new ideas that one can find freedom of mind and not in clinging on to the ideas of the past that require no change. Learning about new concepts does not suggest accepting everything new. It only means improving our ability to look at things in a different way. Unfortunately, those who fear change always deny learning new things. Those who refuse change most commonly find any possible way to resist any action that can lead them to a common ground with others who are different. In the long-term this can create outlooks so strong yet so shallow which are completely based on feelings and not logic.** At times our perceived views, or shall I say **our perceptions can be very harmful to us and our society - if they are based on deeply rooted unchallenged assumptions!**

Majid attended the Catholic Church with Lisa on a number of occasions, not because he was running away from Islam, but to find out about the principles in common and the differences between the two religions. He was not trying to find something better, but to better define the role of religion in one's life. Majid read about the history of Christianity and tried to understand the significance of many rituals so passionately pursued by its followers. He also tried to compare different religions to find the similarities:

A) People of different religions ardently believe that their way to the holiness or God is the only way,

B) Believers, regardless of their faith wish to provide good will toward all those in pain, whether it is financial, physical, or mental,

C) Rituals play a very important role in comforting people and causing them to willingly return to their religious place of prayer, and

D) The level of wealth and faith in a lot of cases are inversely related; that is, one's faith is much stronger - when financially less secure.

As Majid's affection for Lisa was increasing, so was his interest about her immediate and extended family. Her father, Elder was a Mechanical Engineer who had worked for General Tire for over twenty years. When he was young, he had learned the brick laying trade in Pittsburgh, Pennsylvania, prior to serving in the Korean War. Through the GI Bill, his college tuition was completely paid for. Jean, her mother was a homemaker after she married Elder about thirty years earlier. She struck Majid as shy, respectful, fairly religious, and extremely orderly. She was highly valued by her husband and the three children, and very influential in the family decision making. Lisa's older brother, Ron, was a Mechanical Engineer who had graduated from West Point, while John, the younger brother was enrolled in the Mechanical Engineering program at Akron U. Lisa even began her college program in Mechanical Engineering at the University of Akron, but later changed and graduated with a Geophysics degree. Perhaps Elder was somewhat partial to having his children acquire a degree in Mechanical Engineering.

For the New Year celebration Majid and his roommates were invited by Siamak to his place in New Orleans. This was an inexpensive opportunity for four guys to visit New Orleans during that time frame. It was also a great opportunity to give up the snow and freezing temperature for the nice weather. The peer pressure from his roommates played a bigger role than Lisa's desire for Majid to stay home with her. It was a long trip to and from New Orleans, but the environment was far from what Majid was used to in Akron, Ohio. The French Quarter looked like a world of its own, the way people danced and stripped in Bourbon Street with the high level of alcohol consumption. The odd behavior of the young men and women as the result of being intoxicated was beyond Majid's comprehension. Majid and his friends entered one of the bars in the area and soon after, they were mostly on the dancing floor. Majid did not do the same for his heart was trapped somewhere else, and through all the madness he was comforted with his love for Lisa.

During the long trip back home, Majid began to think about different aspects of his life. It was becoming more apparent to him that it would be very difficult for him to move back to his homeland, especially being in love with someone who was born and raised in the United States. Even though Majid was not born in the United States, he had been residing there since he was almost seventeen years old. He was more at ease with the new environment in the United States than the one he left behind, especially after it was modified by a theocratic government.

Everything in Majid's life was changing and he had to find his way to paddle in the ocean of life. To aim for the future, he had to make sure he had a strong standing. He had to come to an understanding and a closure with his past, before he could build a platform to launch his future. So before Majid could begin the next chapter in his life, he had to let go with his past. With much sadness in his heart and tears in his eyes, he wrote the following poem in the early hours of the morning, and finished before the crack of dawn:

"The House Is Shaking"

It is windy, very windy,
    Trees are down and branches broken,
        The long winter storm is still around,
            Gloomy houses with white rooftops,
                Who knows when this blizzard stops!
Minds are frozen, hopeless thoughts,
    clustered on surface, masses in haze,
        Firewood stacked, in everyone's heart,
            There are no matches, but only desire,
                For someone else to build the fire!
Mother gazing through the window,
    Frightened she is, from the flurry,
        Father wearing the worn out cloak,
            Glaring at sky, and losing hope,
                Snow is falling in much scurry!
You could see it in his eyes,
    Bitterness toward the skies,
        Why is the supreme judge,
            So unwilling to put a stop,
                On the injustice, and the lies!

Innocent minds, trusting hearts,
    Blocking out the roaring sound,
        The children - are having a ball,
            With the water, dripping down, &
                The wind that, shakes the house!
It is windy, very windy,
    Trees are down, branches broken,
        The raving storm is shaking our home,
            Father is walking, he is in deep thinking,
                Mother is crying; the house is sinking!
Children playing, with the toys,
    Lost in a valley, full of noise,
        The game maker, knows his play,
            In his rule book, we are the pawns,
                All is for him, and none for all!

The house is shaking, no more waiting,
    Father is fuming, weary of darkness,
        Flames one of the logs, in the fireside,
            By the agonizing pain, burning inside,
                Glazing fire, from a volcanic stone!

Tired of silence with a crackling voice,
    "Hey kids, stop playing, with the toys",
        Paying no attention, he takes the dolls,
            Looking at the kids, with a loving voice,
                "How could you play in a sinking house?"
Our house is made, just on gravel,
    Bricks of culture, there is no mortar,
        Fireplace of faith, has no chimney,
            Coverlet of courage, losing its bed,
                Lantern of heritage is dripping oil!
The house is shaking, fireplace glazing,
    Bricks are braking, coverlet burning,
        Lantern is dimming, gravel is gone,
            His house was shaken, Cyrus awaken,
                Majid's lullaby was his last Goodbye!

"Goodbye my love" - The home of Cyrus,
      You freed the slaves - yet wordless to my pain,
"Goodbye my love" - The home of Khayam,
      You left me no wine - have you gone insane?
"Goodbye my love" - The religion I learned,
      Peace be with you - but with God I'll remain,
 "Goodbye my love" - The language of love,
      "Shaharzad" is lost - "Shahid" the new name!
"Goodbye my love" - The center of culture,
      7000-year history - washed by a - 7-year reign!
"Goodbye my love" - The land that I loved,
      Who stole it from me? - The blood in my vein!
"Goodbye my love" - For this heart is broken,
      This train is passing - cloud of tears full of rain!

Becoming Years

Majid began his graduate work in Electrical Engineering in the spring of 1985. Since he already had finished his supplemental graduate level math classes, he only had another year and half to complete his work. Because of this, Majid had to move into the Electrical Engineering graduate office, where he shared a very large room with Matt and Mike. Majid's only visitor during the lunch break, just about everyday, was the lovely Miss Lisa.

At this point in his life, Majid seemed very happy and full of confidence. Teaching the electronic laboratory classes was a breeze for him, and the money was even better than his earlier teaching assistantship. Majid spent a good bit of his time with Lisa going to the gym, hiking, canoeing, playing volleyball, and occasionally playing racquetball. In many ways Majid was beginning to reflect his present environment. While very active, Majid still had enough time to think about life and what he sought after. He was no longer obsessed with issues beyond his control and was only focused on what was within his reach.

After many days of thinking and much internal debating, **Majid concluded that his ultimate goal in life was - to be happy.** But how could someone be happy regardless of the outcomes in one's life - of course, other than losing a loved one? He decided one's happiness can be independent of the outcomes if one can find the person inside, and then find what can bring him happiness. In other words, first we have to know **who we are**, and then **what it is** - that we desperately need to complete us.

To objectively find the answers to "Who we are" and "What it is" one must be able to breakaway from the paradigm of thinking that has shaped the person throughout his or her life. After finding the answers, to the best of our abilities and logic, we should accept incremental changes in our life style. That in turn, would help us reach an intellectual capacity that makes us connected to the source within and as a result to the universe beyond.

This state of mind, which is receptive to change for a higher goal, and a common goal for all forms of life, is what Majid defined as the state of happiness for him.

The more Majid was willing to step out of his comfort zone, the more he was questioning his own set of beliefs. He had evaluated every step of his life and was feeling trapped by a set of rules that had defined him. He could no longer be imprisoned by the environments that had dictated their interest on him. Majid did not very well know who he was, nor did he realize what he wanted; but he was beginning to understand what he did not desire. He had come to believe that **one must be open-minded and have a comprehensive understanding of different socio-political environments in life, before choosing a pathway randomly, or simply following the path of the older generation.**

Majid had studied Aristotle in his Western Culture classes during the first four years of his education, and was extremely moved by the concept of "Being" and "Becoming." He did not see any difference among the members of the animal kingdom, human beings included, since the only thought process was developed by the environments we live in. He noticed, as animals, we all eat and defecate, look for a shelter to protect our existence, and reproduce to continue the cycle of life.

In addition, there was no difference in the basic needs anywhere in the world, apart from how our environments prepare us for those daily challenges. Our settings do play an important role, for instance, in some places cats and dogs easily get along with each other but in many places they are each other's worst enemy.

This is why Majid concluded that all the animals are born into a **"World of Being,"** in search of basic needs, and then enter a pre-defined world due to one's environment, which he called **"World of Existence."** In this world, since our surroundings are controlled by the matter within, it can be repackaged and called the material world. Since in the material world, everyone struggles for all the things they do not have - one has no control over the outcome, and no one can reach the absolute happiness.

During this period of time, Majid attended the Catholic Church a few more times with Lisa and noticed the emphasis on

165

the elements of social justice within the church and beyond. Majid who was trying to find out "Who he is" and "What it is" was able to find one piece of the puzzle while attending one of the church services. He realized **he was open-minded** since he was willing to attend a religious setting that was far different from the way he was programmed. He also recognized that it was a lot easier to figure out what things are, when there was **a point of reference**. This is why he looked at Catholicism through Lisa's faith and Shia Islam through Ozra's belief as he could remember. He felt when we intelligently and without bias compare the set of values, rituals and even spiritual behaviors we can find a clear path in our lives. I guess one can say Majid did not believe in blind faith, for he felt the faithful blindness can cause irrational behavior in modern societies with adverse effects. Here are some general observations by him about Catholicism compared to the Shia Islam:

a) Churches and Mosques were considered as holy and highly respected places for prayer,

b) People attended church on a weekly basis, but attending a mosque took place on special occasions and preferably for daily prayers if possible,

c) Churches operated at certain times with multiple services offered on Sundays, but people for the most part attended and departed the Mosque per convenience, yet they were required to pray five times a day,

d) Families attended church together, while men and women were separated at the mosque,

e) Both religions believed in helping the poor, and fasting – though having different methods,

f) People sat in a pew at church and followed the same rituals, but experienced different sermons on a weekly basis. Those attending the mosque took their shoes off and sat on the floor, but they did not follow the same rituals, and at best it was random.

At times there was a call for prayer, and many times a

number of ladies prayed in a group setting. Traditionally there has been a weekly Friday gathering, but nowadays most people ignore it since it has become a political propaganda machine rather than a religious platform by many observers,

g) The main messages given in the Catholic masses were how the life and teachings of Jesus should be incorporated into one's way of life, and the significance of the Trinity as the core of their faith. The main message during the Shia mosque setting had to do with the life of the prophet Mohammad and the 12 Imams, and the unjust treatment of them in most cases.

h) In churches, the priests did not intentionally tell stories to make people cry, however for the Shia clergy this was a technique to get the most tears out of the followers on special holy days. Crying was even encouraged and many clergy believed it would be rewarded by God. This perhaps played a role for the believers to be very emotional.

i) Because of government regulations and the tax exempt status, churches in the United States were prohibited from getting into political discussions. However, in an Islamic State, political discussion was encouraged. Since no one could blame anything on the local government, foreign powers were normally used as a scapegoat. This created a negative feeling toward such nations, very much like many of the so-called news media in the world.

j) Both religions lit candles in memory of the dead,

k) Jesus was the center of all celebrations in Catholicism, most importantly the Crucifixion and Easter. There was a lot more complexity in Shia involving the prophet Mohammad and the 12 Imams. Currently there are about eleven national holidays that are associated with religion. This indicates the enforcement of the religion by the government in the people's daily life,

l) Catholics did not have emotionally driven behavior as the result of the religion; however in Tasua and Ashura that are related to Imam Hossein, some people after walking and chanting for a long period of time, begin hitting themselves with a chain during the walk and a small number have even cracked their own sculls with a sword - not deep enough to result in death but large enough to bring about major bleeding, and finally,

m) Return of "the Savior," in which it is a reference to the return of Jesus to bring about peace to the earth and save the believers – is a fundamental Christian belief. The last Imam or Imam Mahdi for the Shia Moslems is also supposed to return to earth to deliver peace and justice. This concept is currently being utilized by Hezbollah's Mahdi Army - as if it is the "Army of the Imam Mahdi."

Looking at the two religions as a basis of learning, and avoiding a blind acceptance of the path with the least amount of resistance, Majid came up with the following conclusions:

a) There was a spiritual side to all the religions that is concerned about the welfare of humanity wherever it may be,

b) Through a life time of repetition, rituals have become stronger than the set of principles that have started those religions,

c) People of all different religions took pride in converting others to their type of religion, out of love for those individuals,

d) Christians were more concerned about being saved by believing in Jesus, while Moslems looked at fighting for social justice as the way to be saved,

e) Shia leaders and people were much more emotional than others,

f) Shia religion in Iran was being used as an ideology, therefore providing a platform to push any new agenda, in the name of Islam, versus, Catholicism which was purely focused on one's faith; hence, we see the following of the old rituals and close adherence to the main principles.

While many felt a sense of confusion about their beliefs and their practices, it was becoming clear to Majid that he had a choice to follow what he wanted.   Since his emotions had gotten him into trouble at many points in his life, he did not want anything emotional.   He also did not care for any rituals so strong that in the process he could have lost the principles they stood for. After reviewing the Persian poetry and reaching back to his old heritage, Majid came to believe that as a person of God one is only required to do good, be kind, and live a spiritual life.   He believed everyone has a custom-made religion that is personalized to their way of life, whether they recognize it or not.   **So, Majid defined his own religion, or his own ladder - to God - through the source of the spirit within and by following an easy set of moral values, common to all the religions, yet tailored to his spiritual life style.**   This way Majid did not have to discriminate between any of the religions, and he was able to treat them all the same.   This is why he called himself -a Majidist.   This way, he could only be measured based on his good deeds and not based on any affiliation to a known religion.   Here is Majid's simplistic view of his principles:

God is the Universe:	Respect everything in the nature,
God is the Creator:	Help build for all those in need,
God is the Source:	Do not value material things,
God is the Life:	Respect life in all its forms,
God is in Wisdom:	Learn and pass no judgment,
God is in Sharing:	Give from your need,
God is in Logic:	Apply it cleverly,
God is in You:	Find Yourself.

This was the beginning of the "**World of Becoming**" for Majid.   He did not want to live the rest of his life by other people's characterization of a religion; hence, he formulated and favored his own.   **As humanity, we are not aware that we carry a baggage full of useless stones, which stand for a set of principles that have never been challenged.   We blindly practice these customs, and adhere to all the rules, since it is extremely difficult for us to break away and leave the stones behind.**   This move was the beginning of a transformation from a "World of Existence" to a "World of Becoming," and to Majid it meant a sense of freedom from the past and the ability to welcome the future.

The summer of 1985 was approaching. Majid and Lisa were greatly anticipating the arrival of Ozra, who was coming to visit her son. Majid had visited his mom about six years earlier. Before Ozra's arrival that summer, Fariburz had moved out after his graduation and consequently there was an extra empty room available. Lisa and Majid spent approximately a week cleaning up the three bedroom apartment, especially her assigned room and the bathroom.

Considering the amount of respect Ozra had for her sister-in-law, Majid decided to go to the Cleveland Hopkins airport with his Aunt Sima. There she was – Ozra, pale as ghost leaving the airplane. The 24 hour long trip from Tehran to Frankfort, later to JFK, and eventually ending at Cleveland was not easy on a 59 year old woman with a heart condition. However, a mother's love holds no limits, and Ozra would have taken the flight to Mars if she had to. As exhausted as she was, with one look at Majid's face, life was pumped back into her body and tears of joy were covering her face. She then stretched her arms around Majid, laid her head on his shoulder, and cried for a few more minutes. Sima, with tears of joy, began rubbing Ozra's back to reduce the tension in her body.

On the way back, Majid briefly stopped at his uncle's house to drop Sima off, as well as enjoying a cup of tea and some pastries. On the way home, Majid who was still in shock to see his mother after so long, let Ozra do all the talking. There were many stories - the horror of the Iran-Iraq War and all the human casualties, the crazy rate of inflation, the story of the dead, and all those having a hard time making a living.

Finally Majid and Ozra arrived at his apartment, but there was a small problem that Majid had overlooked. The apartment was located on the third floor which was a major problem for Ozra who had a severe case of asthma. Going up the steps in a dusty environment is not exactly what the doctor ordered. It took her ten minutes to go up the two floors since she took her time. Majid loved to tease his mom, off and on, by asking her how many turtles passed her by on the way up to the apartment.

Abbas was excited to greet Majid's mom at the doorstep. When any of the parents visited, the circle of friends treated them as if they were their own parents. Majid quickly showed his mom to her room; she was impressed. He left to get some hot pita bread and cheese, and when he returned he saw his mom praying. But how did she know what way was Mecca, since the person has to pray in that direction? Abbas had shown her a random direction and it took her a few days to realize it was actually the wrong way, after she had asked another parent who also did the Namaz. This, of course, did not make her happy!

It was an early June afternoon when Majid drove his mom to his uncle's house. On the way to Uncle Massood's home, Majid drove in front of the girls' dormitory where a large number of girls were sun bathing. Looking at all the girls lying on their blankets with barely anything on, Ozra who was completely covered up, screamed in shock and disbelief. She felt as if it were the end of the world, but Majid comforted her and tried to explain that people in different parts of the world look at things in a different way. Ozra was not sold on that, but she let it go since there were many other hot issues on the table.

Ozra had brought a number of gifts for Majid. Among her gifts were a few items from one of the relatives that Majid knew very well. The gifts were by no means cheap and they were very elegant. During the ride back home from his uncle's house, Majid brought up the issue of the unexpected gifts with Ozra, and he wanted to know why they would do such a thing. Ozra explained that the family's oldest daughter had also obtained a degree in Electrical Engineering, and she was at an age that she would be looking for a good husband. The two families, without consulting their children, had come to a conclusion that this would be a great marriage for their two children. During the full discussion, Majid, who was mentally traveling in a world of his own, was at best confused. While marrying one's first cousin was an acceptable and common practice within certain regions of Iran, Majid believed it was not medically a good choice. He was also physically and mentally infatuated with Lisa, so his mom's proposal was dead on arrival. Majid without much hesitation expressed his feelings to his mother to her dismay.

This is when, as the second major element of happiness, Majid had to let go with some of the cultural values that were making his baggage too heavy. During his young life, he was programmed to respect the elders, accept their demand with no questioning, and tarrof whether the outcome would make him happy, or not. While Majid was committed to respect many features of his old culture, he did not believe anyone should follow a path without fully understanding and analyzing it.

The reason that many societies have a hard time pressing forward is not that they do not welcome the modern technological advancements, but, it is because it is very difficult for them to break from cultures that are very old and highly respected. Majid had to figure out how to resist the cultural ropes that tied him to a set of behaviors that could cripple him in his decision making, yet still be able to enjoy the poetry and the philosophy which was deeply rooted in him. He had to find a way to separate his new dynamic world that had elements of old philosophy from a static world that was entangled with the older way of thinking - a world that was afraid of change.

Because of the original generational and the later environmental changes, there was a huge gap between Ozra and her son. The way Ozra looked at things was in difference to the way Majid desired life, and this was causing emotional pain for him. As a result, he could feel the frozen air between him and his mother. She was feeling rejected by her own son and confused on how to break the news to her husband. On the other hand, consumed by a tremendous amount of guilt, Majid was fighting to remain on the side of his true feelings. **In becoming, one has to un-become; for it is in breaking of the ropes - from the safety of the shore - that one can travel in the ocean of life.** This is why Majid had to educate his mother about where he was in his journey, rather than allowing the differences in the environment create animosity in the family. He decided to explain all the reasons behind his decisions, one by one, and explain them to her from a cost-benefit point of view in his life, without allowing the old cultural standards to play a role.

In this process, Majid stumbled on a big factor that shaped his "World of Becoming". **It is in un-becoming that one becomes.** Suppose we learned 2+2 was equal to 6 and we faithfully believed that. It is close to impossible to learn that it is actually 4, if we do not understand why it is not 6. So, **change has no hope, when people do not understand that they have to stop the way they do things before learning how to do them in new ways.** This is why discontinuing a behavior is part of becoming, and logically understanding a new conduct would be the second phase of becoming.

"I am, therefore I exist," - was a statement that Majid had learned from one of his Western Culture classes. In his mind, that seemed to be a reference to the **"World of Existence,"** perhaps, not. On the contrary, Majid believed that, one has to let go, before entering the **"World of Becoming."** Therefore, he acknowledged and documented - **"I have become - for I only was."**

It was about a month after Ozra had arrived that Majid broke his ankle in a friendly soccer game. The pain was so severe that he fainted as he tried to stand up on his foot. His friends brought him to the Akron City Hospital immediately. While in pain Majid begged his friends not to tell anything to Ozra, for he could not afford his mom having a major asthma attack and end up in another hospital. After all Majid did not even have insurance to cover his own cost. This is why Majid pulled himself together and found a way to call Ozra. He told her that he was staying over one of his friend's house that night. Ozra accepted this and asked him to get back home as soon as possible the next day. Majid agreed but deceivingly added that first he would need to complete some work at the university which would take a few hours. People from Iran were okay with a "white lie" if it saved the day, and Majid had no problem saving his mother from ending up in a hospital.

After an operation that placed eight pins in Majid's ankle, it took about mid-day before Majid found consciousness in a waiting room with three other zombies. His eyes were open but he could not move any part of his body. His spirit was locked in his body and he had no key to open it. It was a scary feeling, and for a moment he felt he was dead since he could not even call the nurse. It took another half an hour for his body to start tingling all over the place. Before he could think of anything else, he started worrying about Ozra, and what if?

173

Finally the doctor arrived and Majid was able to bend over to see the big cast on his leg covering below his knee and all the way down including his foot but not over his toes. Majid was then strolled through the hallways into his room where Lisa's lovely face took the sweat off his brow. **The best way to measure love is if someone is there with you when are in pain and not only in the good times.** An hour later the door opened, it was Esi, his wife Fariba, and of all people - Ozra. Esi was very intelligent for he had stopped over Majid's apartment and asked Ozra if she wanted to go to the park with his family. On the way to the park they were first going to stop to visit one of their friends in the hospital, but they did not tell her it was her son. This way Ozra while shocked to see her son, realized he was okay and that it was a simple operation; so she had no room to panic. Wow!

The shocking news for Majid was the hospital and doctor bills over $3000. Before he was released he had to explain how he was going to pay for it. Majid barely had $1000 in his bank account – what was he to do? In place of money, he could only offer them the truth. Two hours later a lady from accounting came in with a proposal for Majid. She said, "The doctor that did the operation waived his fees, considering you are a graduate student, and in your life you will find a way to do the same for others. The anesthetic doctor is willing to be paid by payments, and the Catholic Church will pick up the $1800 hospital fees." Majid was speechless, for kindness can be without boundaries - beyond nationality, religion, dialogue, and any artificial man made label. While Majid already believed, that day it was once again proven to him that **God is Love and God can not be trapped in the small boundaries of human minds.**

Majid's Aunt Sima and her children were visiting her cousin in Canada at the time. All things considered, Uncle Massood asked Majid and Ozra to stay with him, so that Majid did not have to climb three floors for the first few days. Poor Lisa had to travel at least half an hour every day to take Majid and his mom to different places. This is the time Ozra felt the true love between Majid and Lisa. It was the first time that she realized their love had no boundaries, and their hearts were as one. This is when she saw in Lisa, her own love for Majid. Since she could not deny that pure love, after Lisa left that evening, she held her son's hand and blessed their love for one another.

That night, sleeping on one of the couches, Majid had a dream. It was an amazing dream that Majid would remember for the rest of his life. It was before dawn when Majid felt a source full of love and light penetrating his entire body. His body was shivering and his pajamas were covered with sweat. Majid opened his eyes, looked all around and focused on the door to the basement. There it was - a source of light from a fading bearded face, emitting rays of hope and love. While Majid did not feel his body was floating, he had an out of body experience of joy and absolute love. Majid immediately gave grace to the God, and surrendered himself to his will and his Holy Spirit.

While Majid always felt God's presence in his life, the sunrise that day was the start of a new beginning for him. That day, Majid realized, sometimes the Lord helps you climb from the rough side of the mountain to the peak.

When Majid broke his ankle, what little did he know that this was God's way of getting Ozra to feel affection toward Lisa as if she were her own daughter.

Through some of the tough times caused by the lack of money and some disagreements during her stay, Majid maintained his love and respect for his mom. He did not know how to solve many of the problems, caused by generational, cultural, and social dissimilarities. However, he felt there is no crisis in the world beyond solution, if people remain patient and try to solve their differences through mutual respect. He believed, the resolution to any monumental conflict is only possible, if we give it love, and stay away from any ill feelings - especially hatred. He felt, anyone who tries to find a solution through hate, will be disliked, and all those who find an answer, by means of love, would experience God's love. **One can never solve any problem by hating it, rather by owning it, respecting it, and applying love and patience to it.** Therefore, this is exactly what Majid did with

175

his mother, and as a result, God blessed him with a new lesson in his life. **It is in loving that one can find God, and it is in absolute love for all God's creation that one can feel his presence - spiritually.** Majid concluded that "**Unconditional love is the spirit of our God and our Creator, while evil lives within the demons of hatred and demise**".

During the six weeks that Majid's foot was in a cast, Lisa and Ozra became good friends. At the beginning of that summer, Lisa had changed her mind about finishing up her Master's degree in math, and she wanted to obtain a degree in the Secondary Education. She had to learn how to laminate, make creative objects for her classes, and many other things. This is when Majid and Lisa created a master piece for Ozra's birthday. Ozra had never celebrated her birthday and she was totally shocked with the little surprise. Her first gift was a personal poem from Majid and Lisa to show their love for her. It was laminated in a lovely setting with different color butterflies all around the poetry verses. The second one was a set of Corelle-ware dishes.

Not long after that night, Ozra and Majid were invited over Lisa's parents' house for some late afternoon cake and tea. Majid's mother, being a Muslim, had her own set of convictions in life, and Lisa's parents with a Christian faith had their own. Majid did not know how well everyone would get along, but he was not worried. **His faith in "God" was much stronger than any doubt - caused by a moment of weakness or "lack of God."**

Upon arrival Elder, who had traveled the world through his job requirement, gave a big Italian hug to Ozra. At the moment, she was still trying to make sure her veil was covering every string of hair in her head. Ozra, during the sixty years of her life, had never shook hands with another man, other than her husband and her own sons. As a result of this sudden episode, her face turned totally purple and she gently pulled back with a strange smile. As the result of that incident, Majid and Lisa were cracking up. However in one look, while neither Ozra, nor Elder felt any aggressive behavior toward one another, **they both sensed the difference between their environments, was the caliper, for the measurement of their behaviors.**

The night went well, considering neither side could effectively communicate with the other side. Majid had to play the role of the translator on both sides. This actually proved to be a challenging job since one can not just translate the words but also the gestures, the disguised cultural values, the slangs, the hidden religious views, etc. Majid even translated the wise remarks in a funny way to get the proper reaction from the opposite side. While many do not realize, **this is the biggest component missing in international communication, the inability to connect with others emotionally, though the translation of the language is flawless.**

Before the sun had vanished over the horizon or in actuality, the earth had further spun around, Majid on his crutches hopped into the two-door orange Ford Maverick right after Ozra took the backseat. Lisa then drove to Lake Anna in Barberton, Ohio, and strangely enough everyone walked around the lake - even Majid on his crutches. Though Ozra could not walk fast, she simply adored the lake with its two beautiful swans, and this was a simple way for Majid to make his mom happy. Simply put, **"What is the cost of making someone happy? Absolutely nothing,"** for love is not measured by any hard currency.

Ozra's return ticket to Iran was set for the middle part of September. While she purchased fairly cheap gifts for everyone, the number of presents was beyond Majid's savings. Majid's Aunt Sima showed her great kindness by generously taking Ozra shopping and even paying for some of the gifts. When people returned to Iran even after a short visit, the culture of tarrofing required a gift for everyone, even for those relatives that one could not remember their name. Majid did not support such behavior, but out of love and respect for Ozra, he borrowed another five hundred dollars from his roommate Abbas to help his mom and her **cultural addiction.** Majid believed that **it is in giving, that you receive**, and how could one find a better candidate than his own mother. It was also very important to Majid to have his mom bring back a number of gifts to the family that had sent him all those lovely presents, and that was not a cheap proposition for a person who was still in school.

After three months of pain and joy, questions and answers, social and cultural connections and gaps, once again – it was time to say, "Goodbye." **It was time to separate the mother from her son --- It was time to shed tears for the loved ones, yet**

having no power to change the outcome --- It was time to leave the questions for the years to come --- It was time to say Goodbye, to Ozra, his mother. Since the words were too timid to crawl out of their throats, their tears mingled in one, all the way to the airplane door. The stewardess did not have the heart to stop Majid from walking his mom to her seat, and then - **Majid watched the airplane with his mom -- disappear in the clouds. And in the cloud of his mind -- he wondered if he would see his mom -- once again!**

Ozra's visit in many strange ways had created the kind of heat for Majid and Lisa to melt together, and then with her love and being the center of attention, Ozra had molded the two souls together. While Ozra's original will was to separate the two, God's will for her, was to be a bridge between the two souls. These events that occurred led Majid to believe that **the Captain of any boat in the rocky waters of life is God - whether we have the intelligence to recognize it or not.**

After all the excitement, due to Ozra's visit, once again Majid and Lisa had to re-focus on their studies. Majid had a small refrigerator in his office, and to pay back Abbas for all the money he had borrowed, he decided it was time for a lot of peanut butter and jelly sandwiches. Lisa met Majid for lunch just about everyday at his office, and the two shared their food with one another.

Majid and Lisa's fondness for one another had grown many fold and they had come to respect each other for what each person had to offer. **Even though they had extraordinary types of stones from diverse trips in their lives, it seemed more exciting for them to share their experiences rather than finding a place to hide, or to quarrel over them.** Intelligent people find ways to learn from their differences, while fools look for any point of variance to separate themselves from others. **Ignorant people make colossal monuments from the fear of the unknown, and in a self-defeating process, they find comfort in hate, and in no time, they become the soldiers of demons in the vacuum of love, or – God.**

It was late October when Lisa and her family decided to visit her Grandma in Pittsburgh. Majid was curious about the rest of the family, so Lisa invited him along. Majid loved just about every member of Lisa's extended family. They were full of fun, family oriented, and they sure had many stories to tell. **While loving a person means a lot in a marriage, the person marries not only his partner but the spouses' family.** So, on the way back, Majid who had his last question answered was formulating a marriage proposal in the back of his mind.

After that trip, Majid consulted his uncle regarding his love for Lisa, and if there was anything he should consider. Uncle Massood, a psychiatrist, was perhaps the most knowledgeable person since some rich folks paid him handsome amounts of money to help them with their marital issues. Majid had a short yet valuable discussion with his uncle and took some mental notes. He wrote down all the issues in life that made him happy or sad then he put them in an orderly fashion based on their importance to him. He then identified which areas he was willing to change versus what items were off the list. Through this process Majid and Lisa found the answers to any possible known problems, so that their love would be built on mutual respect for each other from day one. At this point Majid and Lisa had much more work to do before he could propose to her.

It was January of 1986 and both Majid and Lisa had one more semester to finish up with their school work, unless Majid continued with his PhD in his area of expertise. This time the table was turned around and Lisa was in the hot seat. Jean, Lisa's mother was reading the writing on the wall, and she was concerned about her daughter marrying someone from a different country, and it was not just any other country, it was someone from - Iran. She was concerned about how the rest of the family would react to such an announcement. The information obtained from the news media at best, was very confusing to her about the foreign students who attended American universities, especially the ones from the Middle East. What if he marries her daughter and takes her away. There were many what ifs and there were no answers, and rightly so. On the other hand, Elder was not a bit concerned for he had seen the world. He was actually happy to see that his daughter was dating an engineer or someone in the technical field.

To many simple-minded people with static minds that had a hard time breaking from the past, Majid was - a man from the Middle East. That was the alpha and the omega in their half sentence, and - that was that. But, Majid with a dynamic mind was far from being a carbon copy of such mind sets - trapped in a cluttered mirror of assumptions and perceptions. While this type of behavior was expected in the third world countries, Majid expected a much more open-minded society in the United States. He wished for a society that could see beyond the issues of religion, gender, and race. It was Majid's dream to live in a society that was open to change and a culture that cultivated a breath of fresh air.

Luckily, Jean was not a closed-minded person, even though it was Majid's first feeling after Lisa had brought up the issue of marriage. Even though it took a few days of discussion, Lisa, just like Majid, was able to push forward with her hopes and dreams rather than the dreams of a generation behind her. **It is always the new generation that breaks the paradigm of the thinking of the past, and sometimes to the old generation's dismay.**

Now Majid had to figure out how to buy a wedding ring. At the same time, he wanted to make sure his father was also approving of his marriage. So, Majid sent a letter to his parents and asked them if they would approve of him marrying Lisa. If so, their approval would be in the form of the wedding ring for her. This was a very smart move by Majid since it was very hard for his parents to attend his wedding. This way they were part of it from the beginning, showed their consent, and most importantly it took care of a major spending at a time when Majid was saving his money to buy a used but reliable car. Majid's parents were happy with their son's decision and within a short period of time purchased the wedding ring to Majid's specifications. However such items were prohibited from being mailed out by the government in Iran, hence his aunt, who was visiting her son in another country, took the ring with her and mailed it to Majid from there.

It was the first week of April when Majid received the ring. It was breath taking to say the least. The ring had a creative arrangement of diamonds - the largest being a one-half carat tear-shaped diamond set in an 18 karat gold band. He immediately set a dinner reservation at Tangiers, an expensive and classy Middle Eastern restaurant. He asked for the table next to the water fountain in the center, which had a bit of distance to the main stage

180

with the belly dancers. Majid had called Jean in advance to make sure Lisa was dressed properly for the occasion without knowing the ring had finally arrived. While Majid looked handsome, Lisa was an absolute knock out that night, wearing a black-lace dress that hugged the curves of her graceful figure. After the first glass of wine, without getting on his knees, Majid pulled out a short poem from his pocket while hiding the ring beneath it, and gently recited:

> Love Is An Act Of Art,
>   It Is A Painting, On,
>   Two People's Heart,
>
> Love Is A Candle Light,
>   In A Dark, Or Shiny Day,
>   Brightening The Way,
>
> So, I Say, My Mona Lisa,
>   My Beautiful Painting,
>   My - Little Dove,
>
> Will You Marry Me,
>   And Be My Love!

There it was - the fireworks in her eyes, like the finale on a 4th of July, when she saw the ring that she had patiently waited for. "Yes, I Will", was the quick response after two and half years of dating.

A couple weeks after Majid proposed, the wedding date, was set for August 2, 1986. Lisa and Majid attended some classes held by the Catholic Church for the new couples. Those classes were very helpful on marital issues, and in solving any issue of concern before the wedding. Prior to their marriage and based on a mutual understanding, they decided to get married at her church and by her way of upbringing and traditions. Majid who was respectful of all religions, based on his view of God in his life, was at ease with all those arrangements.

Lisa was a committed, yet open-minded Catholic believing in the Father - the Son - and the Holy Spirit, as the core principle of her beliefs. Similarly, Majid believed in the embodiment of Love – Truth – and Patience as the core of his philosophy in a spiritual life, respectively. Could anyone argue the parallel understanding? **Majid did not believe any of the religions have a monopoly on God, but God through his Love, is the center of all events held in his name - that would bring love, peace and prosperity to all mankind!**

Majid and Lisa completed their second degrees in May of 1986. While that was wonderful, they still had much to be anxious about. While Lisa was worried about the wedding preparations with her mother, Majid was more concerned about finding employment.

During an earlier visit to the state of North Carolina, Majid and Lisa had decided to find employment there, and to relocate to one of the its major cities. Therefore, Majid rented a room in Raleigh, NC, for a couple of months, to identify and look for job opportunities, while Jean helped Lisa plan the wedding.

Lisa's parents had all the burdens on their back. They had to find a place for 150 guests, book that date, and then coordinate it with the actual wedding at the church. Jean let Lisa, her only daughter, use her wedding dress and had it altered to her size by a professional. Lisa and Majid also had to choose three bridesmaids and three groomsmen, respectively. Tuxedo's and matching dresses were to be rented and purchased. The wedding cards were to be mailed, food arrangements to be made, different type flowers to be chosen, music for the church to be selected, and many more tasks to be completed. But Majid was over 600 miles away and could only follow the activities by a phone call or a visit after two to three weeks.

After eight years of a continuous college life style, Majid was preparing for a number of changes in his life. He was anxiously waiting to get married, relocate to a different state, find a job, and become accustomed to a new environment. Like anyone else, Majid was nervous about all those changes, but very excited. As we say goodbye to our past, many times we look back to make sure we have not left anything of value behind. During his lonely nights in Raleigh, Majid had enough time to reflect on his past experiences, so he would be ready for the future. The following is a highlight of those guiding ethics he did not want to leave behind, as articulated below:

- What impacts one in life, is not only the changes he welcomes through learning, but also the stagnation that occurs by remaining ignorant.

- To be saved from judgment, do not caste any stone made of ignorance.

- Those that raise their voices to prove a point are either very emotional or stand on low ground.

- The solution to any problem can only come out of love and never out of anger.

- Politics of deception never stops by the truth; it stops at the pocket book.

- Refuse labels at all cost, religious or otherwise, it only limits you to one brand of thinking.

- Ignorance is a luxury item for all those who can afford it.

- Rich and poor can both stay ignorant, one because of arrogance, and the other for the reason of poverty.

- Ignorant people always work against their own interest.

- Failure does not stop success, it gives it more value.

- Money has no value, but if used wisely, it can be value added.

- To find your destiny, one should dig deep within.

- The hope to a bright future can only be delivered by the youth, in a diverse world.

Majid was not happy with the events happening in his homeland like many other Iranians of his generation. However, unlike many of the disgruntled Iranian students that had lost faith in God as a backlash to a heavy dosage of religion in their system of government, Majid's faith in God had greatly increased. By this time, he had learned from his own mistakes in life and the blunders of others and could not afford anymore oversights. He had a bag full of old cultural values, his philosophy in life, two masters' degrees, and residence in a country that could deliver him equality and freedom. Before marriage, Majid believed that he had to put a final touch to his viewpoints and thought processes about humanity, its existence, and its hope toward a bright future. This was important for him to do, since after marriage and full employment, it would be close to impossible to finish his philosophical outlooks on life.

Majid noted, **as we follow our material interest in life, it causes further demand on natural resources. This in turn, will create unintentional damage to the environment due to some known and many unidentified scientific facts.** The excessive desire in a materialistic world, will also lead to needless atrocities, battles, and wars that can not be avoided. He sensed the mental distractions by the media and socio-economic slavery caused by those in power in many different countries would ultimately create a clash among a variety of faiths and cultures. Also the increased demand for the goods that are beyond our needs will accelerate the damage to the environment by placing a higher requirement on the sources of energy.

This materialistic life style, if not challenged, will cause the environment to experience what is not natural to its existence. **Remaining in the "World of Existence,"** Majid noted, **human beings, unlike the rest of the animal kingdom, will find a way to self-destruct. The world in which matter is the center of decision making will only go so far before it would implode.** One perhaps can say humanity is much like an uncontrolled cancer cell spreading the disease to the entire body, or in this case, the entire earth. This is why, Majid stated, **"World of Existence" will end with the human's demise!**

For Majid, the big question remained to be the ability for change. He felt the older generation think and feel they have a better judgment of all the issues at hand. However, in most cases, elders are fearful of doing things in a different way, so the only natural response for them is to resist change. Since their experiences are in a different time frame, he argued, their practices become irrelevant to the concerns of fast changing and exuberant societies.

Majid believed that in the modern world, the advancement in technology would put a higher demand in the rate of change in our lives. This high rate of change in the social and cultural values, as the result of the technological spread, will create anxiety for all those who fear any major changes. Therefore, those who can not acclimatize the changes to their way of life will form movements to revert and fight back the modification in the people's behavior. This in turn, will give a rise to the fundamentalist pressure groups to lead the stagnant minds, and all those who are simply incapable or afraid of modernization.

Majid firmly believed **the solution to the problems in the "World of Existence" can only come from the youth of all the societies, if and only if, they could find a way to define themselves in a diverse world.** Through his understanding of life, he noted, **once people have an opportunity to learn about the other cultures and upbringings, all societies will find a way to self-correct, and converge to the same set of principles.** This to Majid was an essential must to the "World of Becoming", and the only solution to the problems generated by the "World of Existence". Majid concluded that "**There is no challenge greater to humanity than humanity, its rituals versus its spirituality, its past versus its future, and its greed versus its better judgment.**"

Majid may have completed his world views and his philosophy in life, but none of that helped him with employment in the research-triangle area. So three weeks before August 2nd, the wedding day, he drove back to Akron for more preparation. The excitement revolving around the wedding was enough to wipe the disappointment off his face, and Lisa's support was essential to breed hope back in his spirit. The worse case scenario would have been for Majid to complete his PhD in a short period of time considering all his graduate work credit hours, and Lisa to teach in a high school in Akron.

Majid one last time returned to Raleigh before the wedding to turn in the apartment he had rented for a couple of months. That was about ten days prior to the big day.   On the way to Raleigh, he had to pass UNC-Charlotte.   Two months earlier, he had called the university and was told they had no electrical engineering program.   This is because it was listed under a different name at the time.   As he was passing the university, the light in front of the university's main entrance turned yellow, and contrary to his normal response, Majid chose to stop.   While waiting at the light, he decided to drop a resume at the math department.   In doing so, he realized the university had both electrical, as well as electronics engineering programs.   So he left a resume at both departments.

A week later, by late Wednesday, Majid returned and stayed at his uncle's house.   The next day, there was a party at Uncle Massood's house right after the rehearsal for the wedding. Since none of Majid's immediate family were in the country, his uncle and aunt played the role of his parents.   Majid had done nothing to prepare for the wedding other than trying out the Tuxedo a couple times, so he decided to make 200 cutlets.   A cutlet was simply made of hamburger meat, grated baked potato, onion, and some spices, fried in vegetable oil in the form of an ellipse.

Finally the most gorgeous summer day, Saturday August 2nd, 1986, with the high of 72 degree Fahrenheit arrived.   Lisa's relatives mostly from the Pittsburg area and Majid's friends from seven different states were all there.   The wedding ceremony was celebrated at Saint Augustine Church where Ozra had visited during her stay and had lit a candle.   So, Majid felt his mother's presence when he said "I do".

Afterward, and after many professional pictures were taken, the married couple arrived at the party room for the wedding reception, in a well decorated BMW.

The couple received many gifts, mostly in cash, since neither one had a job. However the best gift was not the large sums of money from Lisa's parents, and even Majid's uncle and aunt. It was an interview set on early Monday morning, two days after their day of unity, from UNC-Charlotte. On the way to Disney, Majid met with a number of professors at the UNC-Charlotte. Within a week after the couple returned from their honeymoon, Majid and Lisa were offered jobs at the electrical engineering and math department, respectively.

Summary...

Throughout this book, it was very clear that Majid, like anyone else, was a byproduct of the environments that shaped his viewpoints on life. Majid was conceived to bring about change to the lives of his parents, and so seemed to be the case. His voyage in life was determined by an Este-khareh, an apparent message from God. From a young age, Majid always tried to paddle his boat in life with his perceived notion of the truth. This is why he constantly challenged and corrected his path.

Going against the flow, was one way for Majid to allow for the process of change to occur. He stood for the fall of a dictator and refused to stand for the rise of a theocracy. He declined to pray in a language he could not understand, while discovering a universal spiritual God by turning his back on a ritualistic theocracy. He stood for the change from the rituals we become so accustomed to because we lose the meaning of the principles they stand for.

Majid may have been a step or two ahead of his age group from the same country, but he was not the only one in the United States who was in touch with the technological advancement of one society going forward, and the mandatory ritualistic behavior of another society marching backward. The exposure to the two environments allowed Majid to observe the differences between the two societies. This in turn made it easy for him to know what stones he had to leave behind and which ones to bring along, even if it caused him pain at the time.

One can conclude that Majid did find happiness in God by looking within, in a spiritual way rather than a ritual one. The "It" he was looking for was the intelligence to know what rocks to leave behind and what to carry on!

Observation:

The biggest question in a global economy and merging cultures remains to be - how to respect one another and get along better. This can happen if we come in touch with other cultures and values and learn to respect them unconditionally. This writing was intended to show that when people with different backgrounds are exposed to a diverse setting, there can be a convergence in their values and life styles. In this book, it was rather obvious, that Majid was open to learning how to look at things in a different way. His young age removed the fear of unknowns, while his distance from his parents took away the reinforcement of old ritualistic behaviors.

It is very critical to always ask why and to be open-minded to the process of change but only after gaining knowledge about the issues at hand. If we embrace change rather than defying it, become acquainted with those with a different set of principles from us, and let go with the traditions and rituals of those before us, then and only then, can we hope for a converging world rather than a bitter one. This is why it is vital for the young generation to participate in global issues, whether it is related to our economy or our safety and security.

A comprehensive wisdom and good decision making does not come with age, it comes with exposure to different environments and life styles. The amount of change and advancement in societies is not only the function of all those who embrace them, but is impacted more by those who deny them in the name of religion, politics, experience, cultural traditions, and so forth. The reason that highly declared religious nations have limited technological advancements, is not due to the lack of doctors and scientists, it is because of lack of cooperation from those in power.

Those who find themselves at odds with my writing, possibly the older generation - are not ready to leave any of their bags of stones behind. Middle-age people may agree with the content but find themselves, too apprehensive to change. Perhaps, the ones that are young or young in heart would be the ones that may find these viewpoints in line with their way of thinking.

This is why I propose that the youth of all nations between the ages of 18 and 19 should participate in a global program, financed by the United Nations, to help build the under-developed nations. In this volunteer process, not only is the interest of poor nations served, but it also creates a single global voice of peace and harmony among the youth. This would help any affluent young adult to understand and respect all that he or she is given, and in turn, the ones that are less fortunate would learn the kind of skills that could help them be successful with their lives. This inter-connectivity among the youth would also help the future societies to work closer with one another. What do you think? Is anyone ready for change?

"Whose phone is ringing?"

Are we born, in a prison of mind,
At a place of birth, with no keychain?
Are we within the borders of ignorance,
Yet proud of all - the writing on the walls?
Are our cell numbers the date of our birth,
In the shadows of our past - **just walking**?

Why are these imaginary chains,
So hard to break - using no brain?
Who can master this maze of life,
And dares dusting the spider webs?
Why are the prison cells so narrow,
In the small minds - **like a ghost**?

Is anyone knocking, somebody calling?
What is your number - too late to reply?
Is the glass broken, your heart spoken?
Looking for a broom - may I ask why?
Is the room dirty - with bags of stones?
Whose phone is ringing - **Is that you?**

About the author

Majid Babaie was born and raised in Iran until age 17 when he came to the United States in March of 1978. It was Majid's intention to gain higher education and then return to his homeland. The United States government had been in good terms with the Shah of Iran for decades. While he was attending the University of Akron the 1979 Islamic Revolution occurred and caused a complete change over in the system of government in Iran. This in a large way had an impact on Majid's decision to divert his life plans.

Majid started his career as a university professor in the electrical engineering program at UNC-Charlotte in 1986. He worked in the automotive industry from 1992 to 1996 with emphasis on design and manufacturing of electronic modular units. Since 1996 he has been the co-founder and CEO of a sub-contract manufacturing company in the Charlotte, North Carolina vicinity. He still continues teaching at UNC-Charlotte and is a member of different advisory committees at the university.

Majid and his wife, Lisa, remain active in their church with different humanitarian projects such as the War on Hunger (Charlotte CROP Walk). The two are blessed with a twenty year old daughter, Michelle, and a seventeen-year old son, Jonathan.

Majid is also a "Paul Harris Fellow," serving over a decade at a local Rotary Club.